PENGUIN BOOKS
ROSES LOVE SUNSHINE

David M. Pierce was born in Montreal, Canada. He lived for some years in London, where, among other things, he wrote songs for the pop group *Meal Ticket* and acted in a Shakespearian theatre group. He co-authored a musical with fellow Canadian Rick Jones and has written songs with Jeremy Clyde. His other publications include three volumes of verse and a cookery book, written with singer Annie Ross. He has written two other books featuring private investigator Vic Daniel, *Hear the Wind Blow, Dear* and *Down in the Valley*, both published by Penguin.

D0789467

DAVID M. PIERCE

ROSES LOVE SUNSHINE

PENGUIN BOOKS

PENGUIN BOOKS

Published by the Penguin Group
27 Wrights Lane, London w8 5tz, England
Viking Penguin Inc., 40 West 23rd Street, New York, New York 10010, USA
Penguin Books Australia Ltd, Ringwood, Victoria, Australia
Penguin Books Canada Ltd, 2801 John Street, Markham, Ontario, Canada l3r 1b4
Penguin Books (NZ) Ltd, 182–190 Wairau Road, Auckland 10, New Zealand

Penguin Books Ltd, Registered Offices: Harmondsworth, Middlesex, England

First Published 1989
1 3 5 7 9 10 8 6 4 2

Made and printed in Great Britain by
Richard Clay Ltd, Bungay, Suffolk
Filmset in Monophoto Sabon

For Bonnie Lee

I invented many things herein including streets, people, bars and businesses, but someone with a more macabre imagination than mine is responsible for dreaming up Hollywood, West Hollywood, Studio City and the rest of the San Fernando Valley.

CHAPTER ONE

Promises are made to be broken, someone – probably a woman – once said.

I'd promised myself never to fly again, yet there I was stuffed to the gills with downers, a drink in each hand, God knows how many thousands of feet up in the air, my precious and unique life in the careless hands of some happy-go-lucky goofball who thought he was still piloting mail over the Andes.

The plane hit an air pocket; I hit the made-for-midgets washroom. Crouched there on the floor, I pondered anew the mysterious and deadly power one small blond person, attractively packaged, to be sure, can have over a massive hunk of macho maleness like V. Daniel, aging but you better believe still tough private investigator. And one bat of her deep blue eyes was all it had taken.

Fool, fool!

Our flight, Aero México 227 from sunny Mazatlán, finally arrived at LAX on time, if you count in Mexican time, forty-five minutes late if you don't. I was worn to the proverbial frazzle, sunburnt (nose and shoulders) and extremely thirsty. Evonne was tiresomely vivacious, beautifully tanned (all over) and so hungry she had even eaten the plane food, a kind of chipped burro on last week's rice.

After the usual holdups at Immigration, baggage retrieval and Customs, we caught the free hotel shuttle to the International, in whose parking lot I'd cleverly left my car for nothing at the start of our vacation ten days earlier, thus avoiding the airport's extortionate parking fees. Then we joined the traffic on the San Diego Freeway and headed north toward the San Fernando Valley. It was late on a Sunday afternoon in the middle of July in the Year of Our Lord 1986, and Los Angeles was swelteringly hot and sickeningly smoggy, and the cars were bumper to bumper. The rent-a-wreck in front of us sported a sticker that read 'Honk if you believe in Jesus. Or geese'.

In other words, welcome home.

Some thirty minutes later I dropped off my darling at her house. Naturally I helped her in with her luggage. She had surprisingly little, merely two large trunks, one medium-sized one and two smaller ones. Plus, of course, the enormous raffia basket in which she had packed her collection of souvenirs and gifts, of which I will only mention three rolled-up paintings on bark, one hand-dyed rug, a large wooden box that said 'wooden box' on it in Mexican, a varnished candle-holder made from a gnarled chunk of driftwood and a decorator lamp fashioned from a stuffed iguana. The lamp had been sprayed a bright lime green, and the bulb screwed into the unfortunate reptile's mouth – the perfect gift for the man who had nothing, including taste. I was terrified she was going to give it to me.

After a farewell smooch I drove east to my adobe hacienda over on Windsor Castle Terrace, which was needless to say neither adobe nor a hacienda; at that time my mom and I shared the top floor of a stuccoed duplex, one flight up from the building's owner and my mother's best pal, Phoebe (Feeb) Miner. Mom wasn't in; she'd been staying over at my brother's while I was away. When I was unloading the car Feeb leaned out of her front window to tell me Mom hadn't been too well and I should give her a call.

As soon as I'd aired out the apartment, I did so. My brother Tony answered. He was two years younger than me and looked about ten years younger. Thanks for the card, he said. Feeb was right, he said. Mom had suffered, well, not a relapse, but she had taken one more seemingly inexorable step inwards to wherever it is people with Alzheimer's disease go. His wife Gaye was finding it hard to cope, he said. Did I want to get together sometime soon and have a word about it? Sure, anytime, I said. Give her a kiss from me, and I'll see you soon.

I hung up, closed the windows, turned the air conditioner on, then unpacked my one piece of luggage in which, among other holiday items, were the tasteful and well-chosen gifts I had brought back – a double hammock for Tony and his family, a cotton blouse for Mom, and for Jim, a bartender friend of mine, a dirty bottle of something yellow and disgusting that had a dead worm in it. A thoughtful choice, I thought. In fact, after a shower I thought I'd take it over to him right then and have an American drink for a change. Not that I'm particularly chauvinistic, but I'd had enough pitchers of lethal margaritas and deadly daiquiris for one lifetime; the only problem with Mexico is that it's so relentlessly and insistently Mexican.

Jim was the night barman at the Two-Two-Two, a friendly, well-lived-in haven up on Dakota not far from me where I was wont to sit and muse and sip brandy and gingers and exchange witty repartee with Jim's stunning bar girl Lotus and play the occasional canny game of eight-ball.

When I walked in Jim was reading the paper and sipping a glass of red wine.

'Goodness gracious, a customer,' he said when he saw me. 'I'm agog with surprise and pleasure.' And, indeed, the place wasn't exactly hopping that Sunday evening; there were a couple of regulars at the bar playing some sort of game, two kids shooting noisy pool, and two young men in lookalike fawn jumpsuits sitting on one of the old leather sofas holding hands.

'Here's another surprise,' I said when he had served me up

my usual. I put the bottle on the bar with exaggerated care. 'This is a demijohn of extremely rare Yucatán nectar, goodness knows how many weeks old. I brought it back especially for you as I know you love fine things.'

Jim was so delighted with his gift that for a moment he was speechless.

'That is one of the nastiest-looking objects I've ever seen,' he said finally, peering at it closely, 'and I've been a bartender all my life.' Jim was a thin fellow, with a thin, lined, almost handsome face; he always wore long-sleeved white shirts with old-fashioned arm garters when he was working. He cleared a space on one of the shelves behind him and eased the grimy bottle into it, making sure it was lined up neatly.

'Reminds me of the temperance preacher,' he observed when he turned back.

'That right?' I said.

'He was preaching on the perils of the demon drink and to demonstrate he dropped a worm in a glass of cheap whisky. The worm took one sip and died. "Now brethern and cistern, what does that prove?" he asked. Voice from the back said, "Drink enough and you won't get worms."'

When I was done laughing, which wasn't all that long, he leaned over the bar toward me and said, 'Will you be receiving chez vous tomorrow?'

'Sure,' I said. 'Office hours nine thirty to one, two thirty to five, Monday to Friday. Saturdays by appointment.'

'Got time for me like at ten?' He looked around secretively.

'Sure. What's up, Jim?'

'Better I tell you tomorrow,' he said in a stage whisper, taking another look around.

'OK by me,' I said. I had another drink, then Jim stood me one, then I stood him and the two regulars, whom I knew slightly, one each, then they stood me one, then I had a quick one at the Corner Bar down the street, then I went home,

4

stopping at a 7-Eleven on the way for a few staples: baloney, bread, milk, butter, buttermilk, that sort of thing. I was tucked up in bed eating a baloney sandwich and reading the new John D. MacDonald I'd bought at the airport ten days ago but still hadn't finished when Evonne phoned. She was in bed too, she told me.

'I just called to say I had a lovely time, mi corazón, in case you hadn't deduced that for yourself by now,' she said.

'Me too,' I said. 'A lovely time. Sandy, but lovely.'

'Tomorrow I'm going to do nothing but sleep and eat and weed,' she said.

'All right for some,' I said. She worked at one of the local high schools so was, of course, on summer vacation. 'Oh. I got a client already.'

'Who's that?'

'Remember Jim from the Two-Two-Two? Jim.'

'What's he want?'

'God knows,' I said. 'But from the way he was acting it could be big. I'd like a big case, something I can get my teeth into, like a missing heiress or maybe some gorgeous young starlet who's being blackmailed because years ago she posed inadvertently for some nudie pictures.'

'Hmm,' Evonne said. 'Hanging around with younger women seems to be waking up your hormones.' She blew me a kiss and hung up. I thought for a moment, decided she had meant it as a compliment, and blew her one back.

'It's going pansy,' Jim said.

'What is?' I said.

'The bar, for Christ's sake,' he said. 'What else?'

'The world?'

I looked at him. He looked at me. Then we both gazed out the front window for a spell. I noticed it needed a wash again; hell, it had only been a month or two.

It was morning, just after ten o'clock. We were in my office on the corner of Victory and Orange, sitting on opposite sides of the desk. I'd been a little late getting in so I had hardly started working on the accumulated mail when Jim had pulled up in his five-year-old Toyota, parked right outside, then had entered my office as reluctantly as if some high-priced dentist with the shakes was waiting inside instead of a moderately priced (cheap) private investigator with the shakes.

'So?' I put to him after a while.

'So? What do you mean, so?'

'So what?' I said. 'You can always get a job somewhere else if you don't get along too well with our gay brotherhood.'

'Make that sisterhood,' he said glumly. 'Listen, Vic, I don't want it to get around, but I happen to own that cobwebbed estaminet.'

I raised my eyebrows, but I wasn't all that surprised. It was a common-enough practice for apartment owners and bar owners and suchlike to claim the real (mythical) owner was lurking in the background so they could pretend to pass on hassles without doing anything about them.

'I bought it over five years ago,' Jim said, tilting his chair back on two legs. 'My God, is it that long already? We had a house in Sherman Oaks almost all paid up, there was a fire, one of the kids died in it after God knows how many operations, my wife couldn't stand the blame or the guilt or me or whatever, so we split the insurance and she took the other kid and moved back East to Mater and I in a fit of folly purchased the Two-Two-Two. I've an apartment right above it, and I don't want that to get around either, it makes me too easy for the thirsty and the indigent to find. And now I'm going queer, Jesus, at my age.' He managed a wan smile and waved one hand at me in an effeminate fashion.

'Tsk, tsk,' I said.

The phone rang. I excused myself and picked it up.

'Vic? Oh, good, you're back. It's me, Cissy.'

'Hi, honey, how is everybody? How's Maria?' Maria was her pet tarantula; she kept it in a glass case in her kitchen, over the stove where it was warm.

'O K, I guess,' Cissy said. 'Her appetite seems to be better.'

'Glad to hear it,' I said insincerely. 'So what's up?'

'It's Wade,' she said, referring to her brother-in-law. 'Someone broke into the garage the night before last and trashed the place some, but he won't even talk about it. We're worried it might happen again. And something else happened, too, which was worse. Maybe you can get something out of the dope.'

'I can but try,' I said. 'Around noon suit you?'

'Anytime,' she said. 'Thanks, Vic.'

We both hung up.

'Trouble?' Jim wanted to know.

'Sounds like it. Guy I know runs a film-processing business out of his brother's garage, or he used to until someone broke in and tore up the place. Anyway. Back to you. I saw those two guys on the sofa last night at your joint, but I'd hardly call that going gay.'

'You should have been in there Saturday,' Jim said. 'The bar was loaded with them. My regulars come in, have one round, then make some weak excuse and take off. I don't know what the hell to do about it. I was working bar down in Manhattan Beach one time when the same thing happened; a couple of lavenders waltzed in, then a few more couples, and in a month the whole place was wall-to-wall limp wrists.'

'Why did they pick your place?'

He shrugged.

'Who knows, it's just another bar.'

It wasn't really just another bar, Jim was being modest. He and Lotus and an English bartender now long gone had over the years created a special feel to the place, almost a literary atmosphere built around competitions, most of them word games of one kind or another that Jim stole from puzzle magazines, blew up on to cardboard sheets with magic marker and then tacked up along one wall and all behind the bar. There were anagram competitions with weekly winners and letter-square puzzles and monthly competitions to see who could make the most words out of a given set of letters. Jim also ran regular football pools and pools on potential Oscar winners and movie quizzes; at one end of the bar was a whole shelf of well-thumbed reference books. It seemed there were always a couple of guys somewhere in the place arguing bitterly over whether or not, say, the word 'demi-tasse' was still foreign or could it now be considered American by usage.

So the Two-Two-Two wasn't just another bar, and even if it was, a man tends to love what is his, even if it is just another gin joint on another dirty street and not Le Bar Ritz. Or is it estaminet?

'That place make you any money?' I asked him after another while.

He made a face. 'The short answer is no. And so is the long one. I was pulling down more tending bar for someone else. You know what the action is like, a lot of beer, a few shorts, a little lunch business. But, Goddamn it, I like it the way it is. I don't want a war, but I was hoping maybe you could come up with something that might make your gay crowd uncomfortable so they'd get the message and go somewhere else, say San Francisco.'

'How about that cute sign you already got over the bar?' I said. The sign I was referring to read 'No toggafs (anagram!)' 'What do they think of that?'

'They smile,' he said.

'You could put one in the window,' I said. 'A bigger one. In neon. And maybe spell it right this time.'

'Very funny,' he said.

'A scream,' I said. 'Also, you must know, being an educated man and all, that there are such things as customers' rights, I mean legal ones, never mind the moral ones.'

'I know, I know! But what am I supposed to do? I'm going crazy serving all those banana daiquiris and tequila-fucking-sunrises; they make me nervous, I can't relax in my own place.'

'How does Lotus feel about it?'

'She's cool,' Jim said. 'I think she likes the action, in fact, because it means she doesn't get hit on all the time.'

'Let me have a think about it,' I said, 'but I don't see any easy answer. I have a feeling something's got to give.'

'Well, it's not going to be me,' Jim said. 'I'll close up first.'

'Maybe I'll get inspired,' I said. 'Who knows? Anyway, leave it with me for a couple of days.'

'With pleasure,' said Jim, getting to his feet. 'Got over those Mexican trots yet?'

'Any day now,' I said.

'Where were you exactly?'

'A tourist trap called Mazatlán,' I said. 'I should have gone to ye olde Yucatán where the Mayans once lived and built those huge pyramids so they could chuck screaming pop fans off the top of them. You should visit it sometime.'

'Are you joking?' Jim said. 'I can't even remember the last time I took a holiday. You know what a replacement barman costs these days?'

'A fortune,' I said, 'and that's not counting what he steals.'

Jim grinned, gave me a wave, and took himself out. My computer was already set up on the desk, so I switched it on and went back to the mail. Into the wastebasket went an important communication beginning 'The end of loneliness is but one short telephone call away'. Call me a cynic if you like, but I had my doubts. Following closely went an offer to buy at a special subscription price a complete set of hand-painted ceramic thimbles with their own natural-wood display shelf. Not even Evonne, I thought. Then I wrote checks to various utility companies and entered the amounts in the computer. There were three checks for me, I was pleased to discover, a large one, a useful one, and one for peanuts, all for past services professionally rendered; I entered them as well and asked for my new balance which turned out to be almost healthy despite my recent madcap and spendthrift days down south. I was on the move at last.

The phone interrupted my dreams.

'Victor Daniel here,' I said.

'Oh, good,' a lady's voice said. 'I've been trying to get you.'

'I've been away,' I said. 'South of the border. I flew, of course. Who is this?'

'My name is Sylvia Summers,' the lady said. 'We sort of know each other. Dear, don't.'

'I'm not doing anything,' I said.

Sylvia Summers laughed. She had a nice laugh.

'Not you, my daughter Deborah,' she said. 'She's making faces at me through the glass. I thought your answering machine was on the blink.'

'I don't have one,' I said. I hate them as much as I hate electronic bug catchers and fake log fires. 'What can I do for you, Miss Summers, or is it Mrs, and where do we sort of know each other from?'

'It's Mrs,' she said, 'and you drink brandy and ginger ale, don't you?'

'Often,' I said. 'But you can't be my favorite barman Jim because he just left.'

She laughed again, then I placed her. She was a pretty, not so young anymore – but who was? – actress who moonlighted tending bar for a local catering firm; I'd seen her three or four times over the years, the most recent being when she was pouring me generous doubles at Lubinski, Lubinski and Levi's (Family Jewelers for over Twenty Years) re-opening party.

'Ah ha,' I said. 'Comes the dawn. The catering lady.'

'Right on,' she said. 'Listen, here it is. I've been separated from my husband for almost two years. Last month I finally got him to think about a divorce. Now I think someone is having me followed, and it has to be him – I mean, who else?'

'You think someone is following you, you don't know for sure, you haven't spotted anyone?'

'Almost,' she said. 'If you know what I mean. And I know my charming husband and I know when he's up to something. And if he calls me up and says I should get out more and have a good time and have a fling or two while I'm still young and feel free and all that jazz, believe me he's up to something.'

'Do you think he might be after custody rights to Deborah and any other children there might be by trying to get evidence, for example that you're a loose and fallen woman?'

'There's just Deborah,' Mrs Summers said, 'and, no, I don't. I don't think he really wants her, isn't that terrible? I think he's trying to scare me, that's what he wants, so to avoid all the hassle I'll agree to his divorce terms. And as far as being loose and fallen, I freely admit I have been known to take a drink or three. I've even been known, since he left, to get lonely and once in a while to actually spend time with a member of the opposite sex.'

'Ah, you actresses,' I said. 'You're all alike.'

'So, OK, I thought, you want hardball, pal, you got hardball. Let's see how he's been spending his nights, and knowing him as well as I unfortunately do, he's been spending them anywhere but alone with a good book. Care to climb aboard, or is this sort of sickening domestic garbage beneath you?'

'I wouldn't go that far,' I said. 'A job is a job is a job, as someone once remarked. I think it was Harry James. Now.' I got a notepad out of the top left desk drawer. 'Details. Is the glass Deborah is making faces through the glass of a phone booth?'

'Yes.'

'Are you phoning from a booth because you think your own phone might be tapped or bugged or whatever?'

'Melodramatic as it sounds, the thought did cross my feeble mind,' she said. 'Why take a chance on letting that jerk know what I'm up to?'

'Why, indeed.' I thought for a moment. 'We'll have to meet somewhere cleverly and invisibly because I need some things from you.' I checked my diary – because of the holiday, aside from one babysitting job on Tuesday and the regular monthly reminders for me to check out the security arrangements at places like the Valley Bowl, Arnie's New 'n' Used Cars, and the Star Family Grocery, it was as blank as a Giants' scorecard. We set up an appointment for that afternoon; I told her what to bring and how to cleverly and invisibly meet me. Then I hung up and went back to the mail.

Another client – all right. Maybe she wasn't exactly the starlet I'd been hoping for, but at least she was a thespian. Maybe her daughter Deborah was a starlet. Maybe her daughter Deborah was Sandra Dee, thirty years ago. Maybe I was finally going loco.

CHAPTER TWO

Wade's garage was some miles east of me right near the turn-off for the Burbank airport. I pulled in to the driveway and parked behind a tarted-up Volks which was parked behind an old Ford which was parked behind a partially restored old Buick which was parked behind what looked like the chassis of a Jeep, most of which belonged to Wade's older brother Willy, car freak and mad inventor. I checked out the hammock where Wade was usually to be found, but it was empty except for a tortoiseshell cat, so I tried the garage door, which was locked, then went up the path to the kitchen door and rapped on it.

After a minute Cissy came and unlocked it for me. Earth-mother and then some was what you thought of when you saw Cissy: ample of breast, placid of brow, normally dressed in a caftan of some kind, often with a headband, always barefoot until she pulled on her old, beloved biker's boots and took off on her brand-new Honda 750 on some errand of mercy – a massage, a back stretch, a healing potion, a Tarot reading or perhaps just telling someone what phase of the moon was best to plant their home grown. Cissy looked down, down in the depths of the dumps, which was highly unusual for her.

She let me in, gave me a matronly hug, then sat me down at the kitchen table and poured out a tall glass of fresh lemonade she took from the icebox.

'Here's looking at you, Black Eyes,' I said, toasting Maria the tarantula, who was hiding under some foliage in her case. 'Glad to hear you're better. So where is Wade, that dope?'

13

'In bed, where else?' Cissy said crossly. 'Go on in and see if you can get any sense out of him; I don't even want to talk about it. Want some carrot-cake first?'

'Later, maybe,' I said.

I went down the hall and into Wade's bedroom. He was sitting up reading. There was a half-empty bottle of Almaden red on his bedside table, also a large package of corn Fritos, also his dope box, also a pack of miniature Mars Bars.

'Hi, Wade,' I said brightly.

'I'm reading,' he said without looking up.

'What are you reading?'

'A book.'

'Where's Suze?' Suze was his girlfriend, a stocky, bow-legged black mama with the world's most beautiful mouth; I knew she was somewhere around because they never seemed to be separated by more than a few yards.

'In the living room,' he said. 'Reading.'

'What happened the other night, Wade?'

He stroked his skimpy goatee and pretended he hadn't heard me.

'Not talking, are we?' I said. 'The old silent treatment, eh?'

He took a sip of the wine and kept reading.

I sighed and got out of there. I found Suze, like he said, next door in the living room, reading. She was also munching on something raw and crispy; everyone in that house, day and night, ate nonstop.

'Hi, Suze,' I said brightly.

'Hi, Vic,' she said. 'How're you doin'?'

'I'm glad someone's talking around here,' I said, 'and I'm doing fine, thanks. So what gives with him?'

'Shit, man,' she said. 'Who knows? He's being an asshole is all.' One of the family dogs, Rags, wandered in from Cis and Willy's room and came over to try and scrounge a pat. I obliged. I didn't see my pet, my darling, Shusha the golden-haired labrador who invariably took over the hammock when Wade wasn't in it.

'What happened the other night?'

'All I know is someone got into the darkroom and busted it up some.'

'How'd they get in?'

'Willy says they cut through the chain with some kind of long-handled metal cutters like shears only smaller and longer.'

'Hmm,' I said. I looked over her shoulder to see what she was reading; it was something called *The Secret Life of Plants*. 'Good book?'

'Far out, man,' she said. 'Did you know plants miss their mothers?'

'Who doesn't?' I said. 'Anyway. I'm wondering if the perpetrator just happened to have metal cutters along with him or did he know in advance what he had to deal with?'

'Good question,' said Suze. 'But who's to answer?' She got up, stretched, and headed for the back door. 'Wanna see what else that prick did with those shears?'

'Not much,' I said, but I followed her anyway. She led me down to the end of the back garden, past the vegetable plot and the two walnut trees. There was a fresh mound of earth on one side of the plot and above it a wind chime in the form of a cross made from colored glass tinkled in the occasional breeze.

'Shusha,' I said. 'Goddamn it.'

Suze nodded. 'Beaten, I dunno, twenty, thirty times. Wade and I buried him, it was too much for Cissy; then Willy made the cross.'

Shusha. Of all the harmless mutts. A marshmallow could have taken him two falls out of three. Once I saw a mouse run two inches in front of his nose; all he did was wag his tail. Shusha even liked Maria. I'd taken him to the beach and to the country a million times in pre-Suze days and once dog-sat him for a week when the whole household went back East for some relative's funeral. That dog was so smart he knew he was going for a walk before I knew I was going to take him. Goddamn it anyway.

We went back into the cool of the house.

'So what do we do?' she asked me. 'Cissy's doin' her nut, she won't even let Rags out off the leash, everything's locked up, come on, man!'

'No wonder she's scared,' I said. I wandered over to the fake fireplace above which was hung a moth-eaten deer head with Willy's extensive collection of caps hooked over the antlers. 'Although it's not likely he's coming back.'

'Oh, no?' said Suze. 'He already did. You wanna celery stick from the garden?'

'No,' I said. 'I do not. Tell me about it.'

'At least Cissy and me thought it might be the same guy; he came around the day after, askin' for Wade. He was a mean-looking dude, too. Wade was in bed, natch, and we didn't know what to do, so I said he'd gone to Mexico because the card you sent us was right there on the table and it gave me the idea. So the guy says somethin' like, "Oh, yeah?" and he splits.'

'What did he look like aside from mean?'

'Black as Toby's ass,' said Suze. 'I mean black. In a white suit. Little mustache like some hot-shit Romeo. Some kind of leather cap. Shades. Cool, baby, cool, if that's what turns you on.'

'What was he driving?'

'I didn't see.'

I sighed, then looked over her plate of munchies and settled for a slice of raw zucchini, the best of the pitiful lot.

'Wade's going to have to make a move sooner or later,' I said. 'Not even he can stay in bed for ever.'

'Wanna bet?' said Suze. 'He did it for two weeks once, only came out to take a leak.'

'Gang up on him,' I said, manfully finishing the last of my zucchini. 'You and Cissy and Willy. Set Rags on him. Set Maria on him. Starve him out. Cut off his sex life. When he's got something to say, get him to give me a call, O K?'

'I hear ya,' she said. 'I know what I'll do, I'll hide his stash, that'll make him talk, that'll make him beg for mercy.'

She gave me a small grin. I gave her a wave, had a word with Cissy in the kitchen, telling her not to worry, and got out of there before she got out the carrot-cake. I like cake, but I'd just as soon not have it made from vegetables.

Well, it was getting on to that time, so I took the Ventura West back to my part of town, parked in an alley a couple of blocks away from Dewey's Coffee House, dropped into a used bookstore on the corner, invested two bucks in four paperbacks – three mysteries and one Philip K. Dick I'd only read a dozen times – then walked across to the coffee house. I went in and took a stool at the far end of the counter as close to the rest rooms as I could get. I was a few minutes early, so I ordered some waffles with Canadian maple syrup, which was about as Canadian as Pancho Villa, then downed a cup of so-called coffee. I'd just gotten my change back from the counter waitress when Sylvia Summers and her daughter Deborah came in. As per instructions they took a booth near the front of the restaurant so if there was someone watching them he could do it from outside, thus reducing the risk of me being spotted. I did wait a moment just in case to see if anyone looking remotely like he was in my line of endeavor did come in after them, but when no one did, I hied it back down to the corridor where the rest rooms and telephones were; it had a dog leg in it so the last section of the corridor was out of sight of the main room.

After a moment or so Mrs Summers turned the corner and

came towards me; I was at one of the phones pretending to make a call. She had left Deborah, also per instructions, in the booth; if anyone was watching, he or she or them or it wouldn't get the idea Mom was up to anything but a visit to the ladies', in other words, she wasn't about to pop out the back way.

We smiled at each other and shook hands quickly. As I mentioned, she was a pretty woman, Mrs Summers, with a sweet mouth and retroussé nose. She was wearing a pair of extremely tight-fitting white jeans, white sneakers with no laces and a man's white sweat top, out of which she dug a large envelope which she passed over to me. She also slipped me a key to her front door, patted my cheek, then disappeared into the ladies' room. I disappeared into the men's, where I wasted some time washing my hands and making faces at myself in the mirror, then I ambled back out through the restaurant and into Ventura Boulevard, not bothering to stare fixedly at the Summers girls as I passed their booth. I did notice that Deborah, who was dressed exactly like her mother, was only about eight, if that, far too young to be a starlet even in Hollywood. Oh well. What are dreams but the frailest of bubbles?

I didn't linger in the neighborhood outside as it seemed more important at that time to remain inconspicuous, if possible, rather than try and get a fix on whoever it was, if there was anyone, showing unwonted interest in Mrs Summers.

When I got back to my office I opened up, turned on the air conditioning, which made its habitual noises of complaint, then plunked myself down at the desk and opened up the envelope she had given me. Inside were all the items I'd asked her to bring: a photo of her hubby, some particulars about him and his new home, his business address and so on – plus five items I hadn't asked her to bring: five twenty-dollar bills. A thoughtful woman, Mrs Summers, I decided.

The photo showed a pleasant-looking fellow in tennis whites holding a tennis racket upraised threateningly – I presumed in jest. As I also presumed it had been Mrs Summers who took the picture, I wondered if there wasn't something vaguely Freudian about it all. He looked his height, which Mrs Summers had given as an even six foot, and his weight, 180 pounds, but he didn't look his age, thirty-eight. Who, you may query, in Southern California does look his age? V. Daniel for one. Mr Summers' business address was listed as Suite 2202, 100 Century City West, his new home address a street I'd never heard of in Sherman Oaks, where in happier days my friend Jim had lived with his family. He drove a new navy Seville, but Mrs Summers didn't know the license number. She had enclosed one of his business cards; apart from the name, William J. Summers, the address and the telephone number, it said simply 'By Appointment Only'. I said, well, shut ma mouf.

I didn't feel like starting on William J. Summers that day, that Monday afternoon in July, I don't know why, I just didn't feel like it. I have whims, too, you know. I had no premonition of trouble, although such a commodity is not unexpected in domestic messes, nor did I feel the comparative bliss Evonne and I had enjoyed south of the border might somehow be tarnished by getting a close-up of other people's marital shambles; the very idea. I just didn't feel like it.

So instead I called my three main security clients to let them know I was still on the job. Big John over at Valley Bowl said all was copacetic and when was I dropping by to get my ass wiped.

'I'm just back from Mexico,' I said, 'so please find some other figure of speech.'

Mabel, wife of Arnie, of Arnie's New 'n' Used Cars, said business was terrible but all my gadgets seemed to still be working when that dumbbell she married remembered to switch them on. However, Mrs Benoni of the Star Family Grocery, after pumping me vainly about who my companion had been on my holiday, as she had been trying for two years to fix me up with her sister's daughter Evalina, a Junoesque Tuscan beauty who had a mad pash for me because I was the only man she knew who outweighed her, Mrs Benoni said they had fuse trouble or something and would I please drop by.

So I locked up again and headed out into the heat and the hell and the haze of Victory Avenue in the late afternoon. Nat King Cole used to croon something about an orange-colored sky. If you've ever lived in or visited the San Fernando Valley you'd know he wasn't being poetic, romantic or fanciful, merely accurate.

When I got to the grocery Mrs Benoni and her niece moved in on me like I was relieving Mafeking. Thank God the place was busy so they had to let up on me after a while to check out the customers; love may be love, but so is money.

I took me and my toolbox out back through the storerooms and had a look at the fuse box, which needed a special key to open it, one of the extra bits and pieces I'd been responsible for. It turned out none of my equipment was involved with the fault; one of the inputs from the refrigeration unit was loose and sparking if you wobbled it, so I tightened it up, put the cover back on and locked it, then ran the gauntlet again past the ladies. I stopped long enough to say, 'Mrs Benoni. What is it we do each night before we lock up, switch on and go home?'

'We search the place,' she said. 'For the bad man who stays behind to open the door for the other bad man.'

'That's my girl,' I said. Evalina moved towards me purposefully. A minute later I emerged alive but shaken, drove home, cleaned up, had a baloney and relish sandwich just to hold me, then drove to my brother's to deliver the hammock and say hello to Mom.

The hammock was received with suitable gasps of admiration from the kids, Martin and Martine, who wanted me to hang it up for them right away, but I said not a chance, it wouldn't be fair to deprive my dear brother of that great pleasure so they would have to wait for Daddy to get home. Knowing Daddy as I did and well knowing the mood he was in when he finally fought his way home after a day downtown at LAPD Records, I suspected he'd be far from delighted with the chore. My brother's wife Gaye was not overpleased with my modest jest.

Mom was not well; I could see or thought I could see the regression even in the ten days I'd been away. She seemed to take longer to do things, longer to say things. When I bent over the lounger she was sitting in to give her a kiss, she caught hold of my hand and held on to it until she dozed off some twenty minutes later, something I couldn't ever remember her doing before. Tony still wasn't back yet, so I took the opportunity to sneak out, giving Gaye a sort of awkward hug on the way, and headed rapidly for happier climes, namely to Dave's Corner Bar and a large bowl of his infamous chili. He was so harassed because his latest bar girl had just walked out on him that I had to ask him twice for extra crackers.

Tuesday morning I was apprehended by the boys in blue, always somewhat of a humiliation but particularly galling in my case, given my line of work. It happened like this. There exists a gadget that tells you if a room is bugged. It looks something like a portable radio with a microphone attached to it by a cord. It also looks something like a Geiger counter, take your choice. If you've ever been at a live music concert when the roadies are still setting up, something I'd done a lot of earlier in my brilliant career when I'd been companion/chauffeur/drinking buddy/bodyguard/fixer/gofer for a rising pop star back East, you know what happens if a live mike is placed too close to a live speaker – you get a loud, unearthly electronic wail called feedback. Well, said gadget works on roughly the same principle, although in the trade we call it spectrum analysis.

I didn't have one but I knew who did so that morning after a late breakfast of toasted English muffins with cream cheese at Fred's Deli on Ventura I drove east to Glendale and the retail outfit of J & M's Home Security Ltd, which was, and still is, to be found on a small side street just off Brand Boulevard. There used to be a tacky joke and magic store right next to it that sold kids' perennials like stink bombs (Warning! Not To Be Used Indoors!) and Nail Through Thumb and Bloody Finger In Box – you opened up this little cardboard box and inside was a gory finger which suddenly moved because it was your own finger sticking up through a hole in the bottom. But the store was gone now; on the boarded-up window was a brave, hand-lettered sign saying 'Martha's Woolery – Opening Soon'.

Phil the Freak was behind the counter in J & M's as usual, soldering something to something else. When he was done he willingly rented me the gadget I wanted for one day for thirty bucks plus a hundred-dollar deposit, wrote me out a receipt, showed me one or two of his latest items, including a nifty parasitic transmitter that you planted in a power line and it used the electricity in that line to send signals over that line to far-away places. He gave me a copy of the company's latest catalogue, then finally let me go. And where I was going of course was to Mrs Sylvia Summers' apartment, the only tiny problem being that in all the data I'd asked her for I'd neglected to ask for her address. Listen, I could tell you about some of Mahatma Gandhi's little oversights that would frankly appall you.

So, as it was on the way, more or less, I stopped at Moe's

hotdog and hamburger shack and sweet-talked Son of Moe into letting me use his private phone, not for the first time. Naturally, Mrs Summers wasn't in the phone book, what member of the Profession was, even the owner of a seal act who hadn't worked since the demise of Orpheum time wouldn't be caught dead with his name in the phone book.

I could not recall the name of the catering outfit she worked for so I called my old pal Mr Lubinski who of course wasn't in but his lugubrious cousin Nate Lubinski was and he knew the name and I finally convinced some woman at Jollies' Catering Service that I wasn't Vic the Ripper and she came up with the address. As I did have a phone number for Mrs Summers, why, you may ask, did I not phone it and by some simple ruse to foil any potential eavesdropper, such as pretending to be a department store with a package to deliver, get the address that way? Because no one was home at the Summers' apartment is why, as I had told her to take her and Deborah off the premises that morning, which would draw away from the place her theoretical tail. Brains – some got 'em, some don't.

Mrs Summers and her daughter lived in a modest, self-contained apartment over a garage off Wilcox in festive West Hollywood. I knew the area well as once I'd helped set up a neighborhood watch scheme a couple of streets away. I turned into her driveway and parked in front of the garage. A path led around the side and then a flight of stairs led up to the small front porch. Inside, all was white and all was tidy except for one corner of the girl's room which she was obviously allowed to use as a refuse heap.

I plugged in the gadget and gave the small front room a sweep – nothing. Nothing in Sylvia's tiny bedroom, nor the kid's room, nor the kitchenette, nor the bathroom, nor the phone. The advantage of using the gadget instead of having a careful look around is fairly obvious. Some bugging devices are so tiny these days, literally the size of a pin head, they can be hidden almost anywhere, and often are, by unscrupulous characters, as I must to my deep shame confess. Thus, a proper search can take for ever and be futile to start with. With the gadget I was all through in ten minutes or so and could safely assume the place was clean; the really undetectable bugging systems such as the laser beam that picks up speech vibrations from outside a window and then is passed through a computerized decoder were still far too expensive for commercial customers.

It was after I'd locked up and was going down the stairs that I was apprehended by two sheriff's deputies, one of whom was standing at the bottom of the steps holding a gun in both hands in the approved manner and pointing it right at my sternum while the other did the same thing from behind an orange tree in the garden.

'Freeze, mister,' said the one at the bottom of the steps.

'I'm froze,' I said. 'But is it all right if I put my hands slowly and carefully straight up over my head first?'

CHAPTER THREE

The deputy who had been crouching behind the tree holstered his weapon, advanced warily, staying well out of his partner's line of fire, had me assume the position, gave me a quick frisk, then said to his buddy, 'He's clean, Frank.'

'Gentlemen, I can explain everything,' I said, staring at the wall in front of me against which I was leaning, legs well back and spread wide apart.

'I bet,' said Frank.

'I happen to be a private investigator. My license is in my wallet. Also in my wallet is a piece of paper from the owner of this dwelling, one Mrs Sylvia Summers, allowing me access. Also, I have a key to the premises that she gave me. Also, I parked in front of the house openly, went up the stairs openly, and came back down them openly. I rest my case.'

'Give, please,' said Frank's partner, holding out his hand. 'Slowly, please.'

I slowly dug my wallet out of my back pocket and slowly passed it over. After a minute he said, 'It checks out, Frank.'

'Also,' I said, 'if you perchance work out of South Station, maybe you know a Lieutenant Ronald Isaacs, nicknamed Abie. I hope so, because he knows me.'

Frank laughed. So did his partner.

'OK, relax,' Frank said. 'We know him all right, we got the call to investigate from him.'

Then I laughed heartily.

'Well, well, what a coincidence.' I didn't bother telling the boys how I knew Abie or they'd split their sides. When I'd set up the neighborhood watch I mentioned I'd been given his name as the local cop to use as a contact. What happens in a neighborhood watch is one local resident who for whatever reason is usually at home is selected as go-between for the locals and the cops, and whenever any member of the scheme sees anything suspicious he calls that go-between, who immediately calls the contact at the local station, in this case, Abie. So there I was, hoist by my own, or almost my own, neighborhood watch.

'You boys got here quickly,' I said as I was putting my wallet away. I didn't bother doing the old gag of counting my money to see if it was still all there; I haven't amassed that much wisdom in my life, but I have learned not to be too funny with certain types of people – Customs men, policemen and bank loan officers.

'No faster than usual,' Frank said mendaciously, because one of the problems with a watch scheme was that it usually took twenty minutes or so for a free patrol car to get to the right area on a quiet day, let alone a busy one. I figured they must have already been in the vicinity for some reason. I won't speculate on what that reason might be, but one of the world's best and most famous hotdog stands was but two minutes away, and Frank's partner still had his toothpick in his mouth.

'What did you say that thing was?' Frank asked casually as I was retrieving the gadget which I had left on the steps.

'That? My ghetto blaster,' I said. 'I got to have sounds wherever I go.'

'Sure you do,' said Frank. 'Come on, Claude.'

'I'm coming,' said Claude. 'See you around, Mr Victor Daniel, height six foot seven, age forty-three, weight two hundred and thirty-two, hair, brown, eyes, brown.' All of which details he had obviously got from my license.

'Stop showing off,' said Frank, leading the way down the path to the front of the house.

'I keep meaning to have it changed,' I told Claude. 'The hair bit. My hairdresser calls it pepper and salt these days.'

They had my pink and blue Nash hemmed in so I had to wait til they left before I could get out of there. They took their time about it; Claude had to call in first, then he said something to Frank, then he got out again and went up the path and came back a moment later with two oranges from the tree in the back.

'You're under citizen's arrest,' I said. 'For theft, trespassing and leaving the gate open.'

He laughed, went back and closed the gate, then they finally drove off slowly. If there was a best of the bunch, the Sheriff's Department was it – best trained, best educated, best physical condition, most honest. Some were almost human occasionally.

Now what?

It was going on noon.

It was hot. Actually, it was hotter than hot. I couldn't do anything about Wade yet, but I could make a start on Mrs Summers' spouse. I could also return the gadget. I could also have a word with someone about Jim's problem – like maybe a shrink. I could also go around the corner and then straight ahead for three blocks and then turn left for one and have two hotdogs, no onions but heavy on the chili, and a root beer while I thought things over, so, being no fool, I did. The root beer was some unheard-of local brand, but it was still root beer, and the chili dogs were as usual greasy, scorching hot and sensational.

Then, as it had to be done sometime, I trekked out to Glendale, dropped off the gadget, picked up my deposit, then drove back into town and zig-zagged my way down to Santa Monica Boulevard in glamorous West Hollywood.

Glamorous West Hollywood, which is logically situated just west of Hollywood, has three main types of citizens: the elderly, most of whom have been in their small apartment buildings for decades, if not centuries; the youthful, many of whom are or would love to be connected with show business, who stay for a year or two and then move on, up or down, to the hills or the Valley or back home to Winnebaga Falls; and the gays. Many of the youthful are also gay, naturally, or unnaturally, however you view it. In any case, West Hollywood had become, like the Castro in San Francisco, one of the few areas in the Western world where gays of both sexes could exist comparatively safely and in comparative freedom and with a considerable amount of openness. When West Hollywood incorporated itself as a separate city, its first mayor was gay.

I wanted a men-only bar called the Green Flamingo, and I found it because I went where it was, on the corner of Santa Monica and South Tangerine, opposite the large Rexall drugstore and right next to a boutique called Heavy that sold gentlemen's leather wear and the latest in contrasting accessories such as chains, dog leashes, studded belts and spiked bracelets. I parked in the back lot of the bar, then walked around front and went in.

It was cool inside, a welcomely cool, and a modest but lively lunch-hour trade had already gathered. The place itself was mostly black and chrome with the occasional potted plant. There was a beautiful old nickelodeon in one corner and an equally gorgeous girl behind the bar whom I knew slightly more than slightly – his name was really Richard Delacroix, but when he was all dolled up he preferred to be called Miss Peggy.

We made our hellos and how are yous and have you seen so-and-so latelys, then he brought me an icy bottle of Lowenbrau and asked me what on earth I was doing in the Flamingo in the middle of the day or at any time, come to that. I hadn't – here he paused to look coquettishly away – I hadn't taken the plunge!

'I've got enough problems already,' I said. He gave me a wide smile, opened a bottle of non-alcoholic wine for a customer, called out 'Behave yourselves, you two' to a couple across the room who weren't doing anything at all as far as I could see, then he gave me his attention again.

'One of the problems I do have,' I said, 'I thought you might be able to help me with. Any chance we could sit a minute and have a quick word?'

'Matt!' he called out immediately. 'Take the bar, will you?'

'Where?' a short, portly fellow called back. He was wearing a tight skin-colored shirt that had all the muscles in the upper part of the body drawn on it.

'Come on, Babes,' Richard said. 'Walk this way.' He led me out back past the rest rooms, both of which were marked 'Hers', and into a small office/storeroom. There was only one chair in the room; he gestured to me to take it while he perched on the edge of the cluttered desk. Enough light was coming in through the rear window so he didn't bother turning the desk lamp on.

Richard took off his wig, a black page boy, then sighed with relief. Underneath it he was completely bald, shaven-head bald, not bald bald. He still looked cute enough to eat.

'Remember the first night we met?' he said after a minute.

'Do I not,' I said somewhat ruefully. He'd saved my butt, if not my life, once in a parking lot downtown; I'd been jumped, beat up, mugged and cut and was about to be cut up some more when five-foot nothing in stilettos and mini skirt steamed out of a nearby red Mustang with a Little League baseball bat in her hands, and, as I lay watching, she cold-cocked both my assailants with two ferocious swings to the head, picked their pockets and stripped them of their watches and rings, then was kind enough to drop me off at County Hospital down the road.

'I was a blond then,' he said. 'Going through my trashy phase.'

'Still don't know why you bothered,' I said.

'Call it idle fancy,' he said. 'Or else the speed I was on that made me think I was Wonder Woman.'

'Listen, Wonder Woman,' I said, 'I got a pal, Jim, he owns an estaminet in the Valley called the Two-Two-Two.'

'What's an estaminet?'

'Where have you been?' I said. 'It's a bar.'

'Oh, yeah,' he said. 'I heard two of the girls talking about it. Quiet. Like a library. Sounds nice.' He took a compact off the desk and began putting on fresh lipstick.

'I wish you wouldn't do that,' I said. 'It makes me nervous as hell.'

'That's your problem, sweetie,' he said, batting his eyes at me.

'Cut it out, will you? Anyway, Jim wants to know if, one, his joint is going to go all gay, and two, is there anything he can do about it?'

'Maybe to the first, sit back and enjoy it to the second,' Richard said. 'Jesus, I look like an old bag today. Lots of the girls would like a quiet place near home for nights they don't want to do a big scene, and why should they have to schlep all the way down here if they don't want to? I don't think there is a gay bar in that part of town yet, is there?'

'As one who has made a detailed investigation into such things, i.e. bars in my neighborhood, no.'

'So your pal Jim either likes it, lumps it, or leaves the sinking ship,' Richard said, starting on his eyelashes.

'That's about what I figured,' I said. 'I don't mean to pry, but do you have a piece of the action here?'

'I'm just a wage slave, dear, like millions of other poor girls,' he said.

'How'd you like to run the place out there?' I asked him. 'As manager, in full charge, with a slice off the top and whatever else you think would be correct for a man of your talent, beauty and ability.'

'Well!' Richard said, arching his eyebrows. 'Now that is a thought.'

A car outside in the parking lot pulled up with a screech of brakes. Richard looked out the window.

'Oh merde,' he said. 'Farmers.'

I got up and looked out. A beat-up old convertible with a bumper sticker that said 'Defend Our Right To Bear Arms!' was canted up on some sand and gravel beside the back door, and six rednecks, all in T-shirts and jeans, were piling out of it.

'Not again,' Richard said, pulling on his wig.

'Got a gun handy?' I looked around for something to use as a weapon.

'Do you mind?' he said. 'As someone remarked not long ago, I got enough problems already.' He headed for the door with me close behind.

'OK then, I'll just have to out-think them, which shouldn't be hard,' I said. 'Leave it to me.'

We waited until the sound of their boots had passed us in the hall outside, then we went out. I had an idea and told him about it. He went out the back way fast. I walked into the estaminet proper. The hicks were all lined up along the bar, being funny. I saw a pipe wrench in the back pocket of one of them, the one who looked to be their leader. All the customers had frozen into watchful attention, but they didn't seem particularly worried for some reason.

I put on a big smile, a totally disarming real-estate agent's shit-eating grin. I already had my wallet out, so I strolled up to their leader, flashed my license quickly, and put out my big paw.

'Howdy, boys, Vic Daniel, Sheriff's Department, here, good to see you all.' The kid put out his hand automatically, and I gave it a hearty shake, putting plenty of muscle in it. 'Gonna be in town long? Matt, where's your manners, how about a drink on the house for these good old boys, as they're guests in town and all. Beer, boys? Or how about a little shot of something?'

The boys allowed that a beer would be fine, and Matt had six Millers, the cheapest beer in the house, lined up and opened in less time than it takes to tell about it. Then Richard came back in, or rather, Miss Peggy sashayed in, giving it all she'd got, which was plenty. A couple of the boys almost popped their cornpone eyeballs because Miss Peggy was no rough-chinned cheap drag trade; Miss Peggy had great legs and a peekaboo décolletage, and she wiggled when she walked.

'Miss Peggy!' I exclaimed. 'I told you you'd get a different class of customers with a gorgeous gal like you here to serve. Oh, do us a favor, will ya, honey bun, pop your pretty head out the door and tell my back-up man and the sarge I'll be out in a minute as soon as I pop one with these good old boys here.'

Miss Peggy obliged. You could feel the tension drain away. Someone near the jukebox even had the sense to put a record on and even more sense to play 'Peggy Sue' and not 'My Way'.

Miss Peggy came back. Miss Peggy flirted outrageously. I thought she was also flirting with death when she persuaded one of the boys to jitterbug with her, but, what the hell, live it up I always say.

Finally the boys left. I waved them goodbye from the back door with a cheery 'Now you all come back, you hear?' I wondered how far they would get before the sand I'd told Richard to put in their gas tank would start to work. A fair distance, I hoped; the middle of the Mojave Desert would be fine.

'That takes care of that,' I said, feeling rather pleased with myself. 'You get that sort of thing often?'

'First time today,' Richard said. 'Poor sickies. Imagine being so retarded your idea of good clean fun is to beat up fags. Actually, we don't get hardly any of it anymore; not like the old days in Venice.'

'How come, got the cops on your side finally, or you just outnumbered them around here?'

'The cops are better,' Matt said, 'especially as now it's us paying their wages. But it's just not worth the dime to call them, those rubes would be more than likely gone by the time anyone got here, and even if they weren't, would you like to try and sue some cracker who lives in the dustbowl somewhere for a few hundred bucks' worth of broken glass that's covered by insurance anyway?'

'Not much,' I said, finishing the last of my beer. Matt produced another one without being asked and carefully poured it out for me.

'So what do you do then, just let them have their fun and then pick up the pieces?'

Richard laughed long and loud.

'We usually beat the merde out of them and throw what's left out the back door for the coyotes,' he said. 'Little Matt here teaches karate.'

Matt made a karate-like sound in his throat.

'Simon over there in the corner doesn't wear that terribly macho motorcycle chain around his waist just to keep his skirts up. And his friend Tommy could have destroyed at least three of them without getting his nose shiny. Times have changed, my dear, but ta very much all the same.'

'Who was it said, "The bigger they are, the harder they fall"?' I wondered out loud. Matt thought it was Rocky Marciano. Richard suggested Napoleon. I plumped for David in the bible.

After a bit I took a seat in the corner next to Simon and Tommy's table and had a little ponder, which is a habit of mine – once in a while I find a bar that will let me in, seat myself in some dim, secluded corner, and ponder. I was pondering principally about William J. Summers, age thirty-eight, height six foot even, weight one hundred and eighty pounds, hair streaked blond, complete with forelock, owner of a new navy Seville. Claude isn't the only man with a memory stalking the grim streets.

I admit I also pondered briefly from time to time about other assorted subjects, like the wisdom or lack thereof in having a fourth beer and a certain blond that I found myself missing when I wasn't with her even when I was sober; usually I only thought of girls when I was somewhere between feeling no pain and completely out of it.

Anyway, what I decided to do about William J. Summers was to try for a Mexican standoff, a situation wherein it is to both parties' advantage to call the whole thing off. To come up with evidence admissible in a court of law against him – photos, written depositions and the like – would involve a lot of my time and a lot of Mrs Summers' unemployment insurance. Also, I wouldn't be able to do all the work myself, so there would be others on the payroll – one man does not a successful shadow make. Well, he does but he doesn't, if you follow me.

About then Richard came over and joined me. He had changed into his civvies, if that is the correct way to phrase it – blue slacks and a pale blue cashmere sweater, blue socks and highly polished moccasins. He sat down heavily in the booth next to me and called out to Matt to please bring him a double Chivas up. When Matt brought it over Richard downed it in one go, looked at the empty glass for a moment, then had Matt repeat the process.

'What's up?' I asked him. 'Not those hicks.'

'Are you jesting?' he said. 'I have to go somewhere I do not want to go. Not at all at all at all.'

'Want someone to hold your hand?'

'I wouldn't mind,' he said. 'But I wouldn't ask it either; you don't know what you're getting into.'

'How bad could it be?' I said. 'A mother-in-law convention? Your nephew's bar mitzvah? A funeral?'

'You're getting warm, my dear,' said Richard, looking down at his feet. 'I'm sick to my stomach already.'

'Well, let's get at it then,' I said, getting up. 'It won't get any easier sitting here, whatever it is.'

We walked toward the back door.

'Say hello from me,' Simon said as we left.

'Me, too,' his friend Tommy said.

'Sure,' Richard said.

'Mine or yours, dear?' I said when we got outside.

'Yours,' he said. 'I'm not up to it.' So we climbed into my highly valued Nash Metropolitan and headed slowly over the ruts out of the lot.

'Where to, Richard?' I said when we hit the street. When he didn't answer, I looked over at him. He had his head turned away from me, but I could see he was crying.

'Fuck me,' I said. 'What is it, pal?' I pulled over to the curb, and we sat there, the motor idling.

'It's my friend,' he said after a moment, around a hiccup. 'Friend. What a word. You remember Phillip?'

'Sure,' I said.

'Well, guess what Phillip's got.'

'Yeah,' I said.

'And guess what Phillip's going to be a week or ten days' from now.'

'Yeah,' I said.

'And guess what I've got, too, and have like a fifty-fifty chance of dying from in the next few years, not that I care.'

'Yeah,' I said.

After a few more moments Richard got himself together sufficiently to give me directions to the hospice down on Third where Phillip was dying. I found the place without any trouble. The building had been a sort of doctors' and dentists' co-op, Richard told me, then the local gay community had leased it and turned it into a home for the terminally ill. We parked in the back of the one-story building, then Richard took a few deep breaths, then we got out and slowly walked around to the front. The only indication of what was going on inside was a neat sign beside the door saying 'The Hospice' and beside that an address where contributions could be sent.

We went in. A wimpy-looking type in casual clothes behind the reception desk looked up and said, 'Hello, Richard,' then got up and came over to shake both our hands. The room was clean and simply furnished, just the receptionist's desk and chair, a few other straight-backed chairs for visitors, and a small table with some flowers and a pile or two of pamphlets on it. Richard gave me a little wave and disappeared through one of the doors at the back. I took a seat and waited.

The receptionist lit up a cigarette and sat back in his chair. I picked up one of the pamphlets. It told me a lot of things I didn't want to know. It told me the hospice had twelve rooms at present and in each one a man lay dying. The average length of stay was forty-five days. It told me that in San Francisco 1600 people had already died out of a case-load of roughly twice that figure. It told me Aids was now the third most frequent cause of death there, after heart attacks and cancer. It told me most predictions suggested there would be over a quarter of a million cases in the States by 1991 with roughly 170,000 deaths. It told me how the disease wastes the body and turns the sufferer prematurely old. It also told me the receptionist, like all the hospice workers, was a volunteer. I took the 'wimpy-looking' back, fast.

Some Muzak began in the distance; it didn't exactly cheer the place up. I put back the pamphlet, got out my wallet and put a couple of bills in the contributions box on the desk, then looked at the wall for a while.

It was almost an hour before Richard came back out. Nothing much had happened in the meantime; the receptionist had answered a few calls from people requesting information and one from some crackpot who screamed at him. Someone from the drugstore up the street came in to deliver what looked like a box of candy. I finished looking at the wall and looked out the window instead.

Richard came out walking slowly, his face ashen. He said, 'See you, Chuck,' to the receptionist, and we got out of there. I didn't say anything, there wasn't a lot to say, you don't ask how someone is when they're dying. So I shut up for once in my life; if Richard wanted to talk, he'd talk.

Richard didn't want to. When I dropped him back at the bar he still hadn't said anything. I watched him go into the Flamingo then decided it was time to move my ass, to go west, old man, west where one William J. Summers had his office or offices or business premises or work space or mailing address or working environment or whatever the hell it was.

I didn't bother phoning for an appointment.

CHAPTER FOUR

As Beverly Hills is *the* place to reside in town, Century City is the place to have a business or at least a business address. It is a collection of attractive, if you like that sort of thing, high-rise office buildings off Santa Monica Boulevard some twenty minutes west of the Green Flamingo. In between the buildings are a grid of clean streets and a considerable amount of well-tended greenery. Century City is where you will find your high-priced medicine men, specialists in all fields of the healing arts, including, it is perhaps unnecessary to mention, the field of psychoanalysis. Or is it swamp? It is also where you will find anyone else who wants expensive and prestigious premises and is able to pay for them: film and TV production companies, money men, personal managers, realtors, and dentists specializing in gum surgery.

I found 100 Century City West without a lot of trouble and eased my car down the ramp that led to the parking floors under the building, stopping at the movable barrier at the entrance. A sign informed me that there was no parking except for authorized visitors or tenants. After a short minute an attendant came sprinting up from a lower floor. He was a young man in clean white overalls and a matching white house-painter's cap. He came over to me with a polite smile; his ID tag complete with photo that was pinned over his breast pocket said his name was George something. I got a pair of wraparound sunglasses from the glove compartment, put them on, then rolled down the car window and looked furtive.

He bent down to look in the window.

'Help you?'

'Could be, kid,' I said out of the side of my mouth. I passed him over a folded-up ten spot, then gave him a flash of my license, keeping one big thumb over my name. 'Know a William Summers, regular tenant, drives a navy Seville?'

'Sure,' the kid said. 'Suite 2202, isn't he?' He unfolded the bill long enough to see whose picture was on it, then folded it up again, but that's all he did with it; he didn't tuck it away.

'So what do you know about him?'

The kid shrugged. 'Nothing much. I park his car for him sometimes and he gives me a buck. At Christmas I get a bottle of scotch. I don't like scotch, so I give it to my uncle; he'll drink anything.'

'Put that away before it catches cold,' I said, referring to the banknote. 'You must know something else about him, does he pay his bills on time, does he take his secretary to lunch, does he go home at night with the office boy?'

'Well fuck you, mister,' the kid said. He tossed the bill through the window on to my lap. 'Now beat it or I'll call a cop. A real one.'

'Kids today,' I said sadly. 'You just don't know who's on the take anymore.'

I reversed up the ramp as speedily as possible just in case he was quickwitted enough to jot down the car license number. I knew he wasn't dumb. The only reason a car hop making shit a week would turn down an easy ten dollars was if he thought he could make even more telling William all about me. Which, I say modestly, was exactly my plan.

I had some phone calls to make but I had to go home anyway to change clothes so I did so, then got myself a glass of buttermilk and then went to work. Mrs Summers was in and relieved to hear her phone and apartment were clean. I thanked her effusively but with dignity for the money, told her to plead total ignorance if her husband got on to her, asked her to be a good girl for a few days, if possible, just in case, and reassured her that things were proceeding smoothly. Then I called her husband's office to proceed things some more.

'Barbra Lorrimer for William Summers,' a lady's voice said crisply. 'Can I help you with something?'

'I'd sure like a word with the boss if he's available.'

'I'm afraid he isn't,' she said regretfully. 'I can perhaps reach him at the Beverly Hilton if it's vital; he's closeted with some oil types all afternoon.'

A likely story, I thought.

'Well, that is too bad, Barbra honey. I'm Big Jim, an old stompin' pal of Bill's, or Slick Willy as we used to call him when we were kids.'

'Oh really,' she said frostily.

'God, it's been years,' I said. 'So how's he doin'? Makin' a buck? That's some joint you work in, I was by there the other day. Is he still married to that pretty little thing, what was her name, Sally, Sylvia?'

'I believe it's Sylvia,' Barbra said. 'Now, if you'll excuse me, I have a call on another line.'

'Wait a minute, honey,' I said, taking a loud slurp of the buttermilk. 'Don't run away. When's the best time to get him? Does he get in early? Where's he go for lunch? How late does he work? Come to that, how late do you work, Babs? Don't suppose you'd like to have a couple of bourbons and branch with an old cattleman like Big Jim some evening?'

'I'm terribly sorry,' said Barbra, not really sounding all that sorry, 'I must take that other call. I'll tell Mr Summers you inquired about him. Big Jim, wasn't it?'

'You got it, honey,' I said. 'Big Jim Jackson of the Florida Jacksons, in fact it was an uncle of my great-granddaddy who give his name to Jacksonville.'

'How interesting,' said Barbra. 'Goodbye.' She hung up. I

hung up, then called William's home number. As soon as the answering machine clicked in, I gave it a few minutes of silence then rang off. I planned to do that a few times a day for a while, if I remembered. I had an assortment of other annoying tricks up my sleeve as well; William J. Summers, the heat is on.

The last call I made was to my employer for the evening, Mrs Rose Lewellen, it was her husband Lew I was supposed to babysit. Lew was your bona fide genuine real-life film producer. I don't know how good a producer he was, not knowing how you measure such things, but he was a terrible nuisance when drunk because when he was in his cups he firmly believed that all men were born to be brothers. He also had a penchant for the gutter.

I'd literally found him in one the first time we met; he'd just been tossed out of a dump down on Little Santa Monica called the Shamrock when I chanced by. It wasn't quite by chance; I was supposed to be working. I'd been in my car watching the darkened windows of a second-story flat across the street for what seemed like for ever. As it was one thirty by then and the lights inside had been turned off over two hours ago I didn't figure the bail-skipper I was keeping an eye on was going anywhere that night, and anyway, I could see the front door of his building from the Shamrock, and there was no back way out, as I'd checked. The service door was padlocked, and the fire escape long ago had rusted into uselessness.

All of which led me to believe I could safely duck into the Shamrock before it closed for a couple of quick ones to prepare myself for the long dry night ahead, which very thing I was about to do when Lew Lewellen landed on the sidewalk in front of me, rolled twice, and wound up as I said, neatly lying in the long of the gutter. With the luck of the truly drunk he wasn't hurt, however, merely somewhat bemused at his predicament.

'Whither bound, sailor?' he called to me as I tried to sneak by.

'Inward bound,' I said, pointing one thumb at the door of the Shamrock.

'See if they do curb service,' he said. 'There's a good chap. What a good chap you are. I could use a libation.'

The upshot was that I persuaded the harridan behind the bar to call me a cab, as I suggested it was bad for the joint's image to leave drunks cluttering up the gutter right in front; it might scare off the carriage trade. I wheedled Lew's address out of him, and as he hadn't a penny left on him, I had to give the cabbie fifty bucks of my own before he'd take him. Even though I'd had the foresight to tuck one of my business cards in Lew's jacket pocket, I figured it was lost dinero, but miracles do happen; the following day I had a call from Rose Lewellen thanking me and a couple of days later she sent me a check for an even hundred. I sent her back a thank-you note and suggested that the next time her hubby hit the tiles he should take along a keeper, preferably a large one. And that's how my babysitting sideline started. I suppose I got a call from her once every couple of months, saying she'd seen the signs and the cat was getting restless and ready to prowl again.

One of the minor problems involved in babysitting Lew was what to wear. I had to be able to pass muster in such diverse social stratas as the Polo Lounge and the Brown Derby as well as East Side pool halls, downtown beaneries, Glendale cowboy taverns and, once, the go-cart racing in Encino. I settled on a tan corduroy suit worn over a lightweight cotton rust-colored turtleneck, got the word from my boss that the job was still on, made sure I had some cash and my plastic with me, also a homemade cosh a girl I knew once had given me as a valentine's present – a tube of soft leather filled with ball bearings and then sewn up at both ends. She claimed at the time she'd arrived at the choice of gift after consulting the I-Ching. I sometimes wondered what she would have given me for Christmas if we had still been seeing each other then.

The Lewellens lived, of course, in Beverly Hills, right next to the house where Jack Benny used to reside. Their place was modest by local standards, only one Olympic-size pool, a tiny four-car garage, and the projection room couldn't have seated more than twenty or so.

A pretty Mexican señorita opened the door for me after I'd identified myself over the intercom at the front gate and been buzzed in. Lew was in his den warming up with a pitcher of bloody marys, Mrs Lewellen told me. She was a quiet, unassuming lady in her forties; I'd gotten to know her a bit over the years and I liked her because she was completely untheatrical and seemingly unaffected by her husband's antics. She told me once she'd met him the first time at Warner's where she was a researcher and he was one of several associate producers for some witless afternoon game show. She also told me the first words he had ever spoken to her were something on the lines of 'You have the kind of restrained beauty that waters innocence and could revive a corpse.' She told me she had answered, 'Put a sock in it, Flash.' They had been happily married for twenty-three years and had one child, a boy of fifteen who was not only polite to visitors but was even polite to his parents. I don't know . . . what's Beverly Hills coming to these days?

Mrs Lewellen accompanied me out of the living room and down the carpeted hall to the den, where she left me with the words, 'He's all yours, and you're welcome to him. Try and bring him back in not too many pieces.'

I went in. Lew had on his horn-rimmed specs and was flipping through a script. 'Be right with you, my man,' he said. 'Pour us one, will you?'

I poured us one, large ones. There was a plate of celery

sticks to be used as stirrers, but when I went to put one in his glass he shouted, 'How many times have I got to tell you, Martha, if I wanted celery I would have ordered the Waldorf salad!'

I grinned at him; he glared back at me in mock fury then went back to the script.

'Rubbish!' he said after a minute. 'Rubbish, rubbish, bull-shit rubbish. Why does the world send me naught but rubbish, my man?'

I didn't know, so I didn't say anything. I took a sip of my excellent bloody mary and had a look around the room; it was a museum of Hollywood mementos and souvenirs, of signed stills of stars and cartoons of same. There was a Muppet puppet hanging from strings that was Lew to the life in front of a large bookcase that held all the well-known books on films and film-making and a lot of obscure ones including several in French.

'You read French?' I asked him.

'Pu-leeze,' he said. 'From childhood already.'

'Très bien,' I said.

Lew skipped to the last page of the script, muttered, 'What else, baby,' wrote the date and the word NEVER on a piece of scrap paper, stapled it to the cover of the script, then tossed it up on a shelf alongside a pile of others.

'All right!' he said. 'And another foreskin bites the dusk! Ready to move it, my main man?'

'Ready when you are, L.L.,' I said. He leaped to his feet, stretched his five-foot-five frame, rubbed his hands, scratched his bald head, exchanged his horn-rims for a set of round granny glasses, patted his wallet, tried on several caps until he found a plaid one he liked, grabbed his safari jacket, and we moved it.

We continued moving it until five the next morning, criss-crossing the city like demented hop-heads in search of some elusive fix. Famous bars, nameless bars, a Mexican dancehall in Silver Lake, a deserted Ethiopian restaurant on Sunset. He shot craps with some Latino kids who must have been all of six downtown near the flower market, and lost. He shot pool with a one-armed cowboy in a bar called Funtime down near the Forum, and lost. He fell briefly but deeply in love with a tiny hooker in the Stagecoach.

Sometime during the evening we found ourselves at the roller derby at the old Olympic boxing arena, surrounded by screaming ethnic housewives; it seemed we had the good fortune to be witnessing a grudge match between the LA Queens and the hated New York Amazons. I informed him I had once read that both teams, in fact all of the teams in the league, came from LA but were given names of other detested cities just to stir up the shit. He pointed down to the infield and said to me, 'Look at that, Vic, that is the most tragic thing I've ever seen in my tragic life.' I looked where he was pointing and saw the LA team mascot, a midget who was wearing the team colors. Like the others, he had a number on his back, only his was 1/3.

And sometime during the early morning we found ourselves back at the Shamrock, all past sins forgotten, the same rough lady behind the bar, the same peeling leprechauns adorning the walls. Lew wanted to buy the place and have it moved, exactly as it was, clientele included, to the bottom of his garden in Beverly Hills so that it would always be there waiting for him, his own private time machine. When he heard it wasn't for sale, he cried bitterly. The state I was in by then, I might have shed a few tears also. But at least I didn't have to worry about driving; it had long been established (by Mrs Lewellen) that when Little Lew and Large Vic went on the town it was done in cabs. As I recall, the total fares I paid out that night, including generous tips, was just under three hundred dollars, which either tells you something about the price of taxis in Los Angeles or the distance we covered or both.

At three a.m. we were in an all-night, non-gay Turkish bath just off Santa Monica. At ten minutes after three we were politely requested to depart, then five minutes later not so politely. It appeared Lew's all-embracing love of mankind, which often took the form of wanting to hug and kiss total strangers, although strictly platonic, had been misunderstood by a huge tattooed individual in the cold tub. So we moved on, ever on, to an after-hours disco some cabbie knew about down on Fourth; there we lasted one drink before we got the heave.

'You infidels don't understand!' Lew kept shouting. 'We must love one another or perish!' It crossed my sluggish mind that Lew's tremendous thirst for love might have some tenuous connection with his line of work, but what do I know about such things, and anyway, don't knock my thirsts and I won't knock yours.

What kind of day had it been, I mused, when I was finally tucked into my lonely bed? A day like many others, of bits and pieces, unconnected fragments of some greater story in which I was but a poor, strolling player, an extra at the back of the crowd craning my neck to see what everybody was looking at.

It had long been my intention to someday write a few words on the subject of bits and pieces, to try and show, with some sympathy perhaps and maybe a trace of humor, that the existence of a small-time problem-solver like myself had few similarities with the feverish actions of those so-called TV sleuths. You know the kind, they usually work in pairs, and in one hour, minus commercials, previews and credits, solve baffling mysteries, put Colombia out of the drug business once and for all, wreck half a dozen cars, the newer the better, fall in love, visit their partner in hospital – who, unfortunately, never dies – save a good kid from going bad and do it all despite their irate superior's warning to stay off the case or else.

But why be content with merely an essay or a slim monograph?

Why not put it in story form, hire some hack to whip it up into a script; then Lew would shout 'Eureka!' instead of 'Rubbish!' and buy the rights, and I would buy Jack Benny's old manse and in the gentle evenings stand on the terrace with my violin saying things like, 'Stradivarius? It had better be a Stradivarius, I paid forty-nine ninety-five for it.'

That's all, folks – then I fell asleep.

CHAPTER FIVE

My first chore Wednesday morning after the tedious, painful and time-consuming business of getting myself together was to try and make someone else in the world feel as lousy as I did. In other words, to step up my harassment of William Summers. Of course I know harassment is a crime, but if he ever called me on it, I'd simply say, O K, sue me, take me to court, and that would be one more harassment for him.

My idea was to trail him from his home on San Clemente out there in Sherman Oaks to his office in Century City. I knew approximately what time he left for work in the mornings as it was one of the tidbits of information I'd asked Sylvia for. It is possible he was a touch hungover that morning as well because I finally had to sit on his rear bumper for ten minutes before it dawned on him what I was up to.

When he started to make clever moves to try and lose me and I was sure he'd gotten the message, I turned off myself suddenly and by keeping my foot down and cutting through an alley or two managed to get to 100 Century City West just ahead of him. Thus it was that when he drove up and turned in to park I was across the street from him and down a bit but still in full view.

As soon as he disappeared into the depths of his chi-chi black glass and aluminum place of work, I took off and headed back toward my stucco and cinderblock place of work where I opened up, selected a few business cards belonging to other people from my comprehensive collection of same and drove out again to Sherman Oaks.

I began with Mr Summers' immediate neighbor; he was on

a corner so he only had one. Although the two houses were obviously side by side, they were centuries apart architecturally, as is customary, if not obligatory, in that part of the world. What advantage there is in having mock-Tudor, French provincial, Spanish villa, modern cubist, Rhode Island gingerbread and fairytale castle all in a row is beyond me; maybe it has something to do with the climate. Mr Summers' was the cubist affair. I was knocking on the door of the mock-Tudor, which was complete with leaded glass panels, a huge brass doorknocker shaped like a lion's head and a protective canopy overhead made of wooden shingles. Oh, I say, dear boy.

After a minute a face appeared behind the glass, then the door was opened the couple of inches the door chain allowed, which let me see part of a woman's face. Part was enough. She took a good look at me. Something must have reassured her, perhaps the conservative suit and tie, perhaps the (fake) glasses, for she said, 'Yes?'

I handed her one of my cards, the one that said 'Mr R. T. Parson, Credit Controller, San Diego Savings and Loan Ass.' I told her how sorry I was to disturb her but I was running a quick credit check on one of her neighbors and if she would answer one or two short questions, through the door would be fine, I would be deeply grateful.

'Oh?' she said, brightening considerably. 'On who?'

I told her on who, got out a pad and pen, and put to her several questions I made up as I went along. I repeated the performance at seven of the nearby residences, finding three people at home who were willing to answer me. Two of them seemed to know William J. fairly well, and I hoped at least one of them would be thoughtful enough or malicious enough to tell Mr Summers someone from his bank had been around asking questions, especially as it was odds on San Diego Savings wasn't his bank in the first place.

By the time I got back to my side of town it was getting on to noon, late enough to give my pal Benny a ring, so I did, after yet another call with no message to Mr Summers' answering machine. Benny was up, he told me, but just. He was still on his first cup of coffee, he said, so keep it simple.

'You work for the IRS,' I said simply. I shuffled through the stack of calling cards I'd retrieved from the desk drawer where they were kept.

'Does that account for my unpopularity with the girls?' Benny asked.

'No,' I said. 'Got a pencil? Your name is Arthur Eck,' I read off one of the cards. 'You are a real person, or at least you were a few months ago when you came to see me. You toil in the claims department. Your phone number is 650-0640, your address is the Bairns Building at 1100 Santa Monica Boulevard. The number on your work sheets is 222/b/2, and you have a high voice and a slightly southern accent. OK?'

'I heah ya, sugah,' he said.

'You are calling one William J. Summers, at 444-6600, politely requesting a rendezvous at his office two weeks, say, from today. You can provide no further details at this time. OK?'

'What happens if the mark calls the real Arthur Eck?'

'The same thing, I hope, that happened when I did,' I said. 'He'll get some brainless secretary saying she's sorry but all she can do is confirm or reschedule the appointment.'

'OK, Magnolia,' Benny said. 'Considah it done.'

He hung up. I hung up. Now that's the kind of friend I like, instant, unquestioning obedience without even a mild query about any modest fee that might be involved. Or might not.

All right. You want hardball, you got hardball, pal, as Sylvia had said. I pondered on my next move while looking out the front window at the passing parade which consisted mainly of starving teenagers heading for the Taco-Burger three doors down from me. Then I came up with a really nasty one for Mr Summers; it wasn't strictly hardball, more like a spitter.

In the small bathroom at the rear of my office, in fact, taking up most of it, was a huge Bowman & Larens safe I'd picked up for nothing a few years back, and I mean that literally. I discovered it one morning lying on its side outside my back door in the alley. I'd borrowed a dolly from another of my neighbors, the Vietnamese two down who ran a video rental and also sold all manner of home entertainment complexes, and with the help of everyone in sight we'd managed to wrestle the safe through the back door, but then the dolly collapsed, so we manhandled it into the washroom and there it remained. I kept almost everything of any value inside it when I was out of the office: my Apple 2, electric typewriter, the phone, a .38 Police Positive with spare cartridges, all my files, of course, some mad money, and amongst other bits and pieces, an ever-growing assortment of legal papers, writs, torts, will forms, invitations to appear in court, real-estate deeds, you name it, I had it. Some of them I snitched from my brother's office downtown, some had been served on old law-abiding me, some I got from friends who no longer needed them. If they were already blank, fine; if not, I'd white out the personal details, then make copies, so, presto, they were ready to use again.

I found the one I was looking for, a summons to appear in a paternity hearing at one of the courtrooms at the top of the old Sheriff's Department headquarters downtown. Where it said, 'plaintiff' I carefully wrote in the name, address and phone number of Miss Sara Silvetti, then I looked through the phone book for a law firm with a suitably impressive name and entered it as her legal advisor. It but remained to stamp and address the envelope to William J. Summers and then to call Sara.

Sara was in. Sara was twenty years old, going on eighty. Sara was total punk. Not cheap hoodlum punk or that stuff you used to light fireworks with, but the other punk, the kind that has day-glo hair, ripped T-shirts, safety-pin earrings, gloves with no fingers and shredded tights. She was also a would-be poet, and one of the worst things about using her to help out, as I occasionally did, apart from her mercenary nature and lack of respect for her elders and betters, was the free-verse report she insisted on turning in after each job.

'Yeah?' she said loudly in my ear.

'Is that any way to answer the phone?' I said. 'Yeah. How about, the Silvetti residence, Miss Sara Silvetti here?'

'Rock on, Pops,' she said. 'Whad'ya want, I'm workin'.'

'"Coon,"' I said. 'That rhymes with "June". That help you out?'

'Nothing would help you out but a double lobotomy,' she said. 'If that.'

'Listen, Junior,' I said. 'If you get a call from a William Summers, middle initial J., as you likely will, do us a favor, don't say anything but "I have nothing to say. My lawyers are Batesby, Batesby, Clark and Burroughs. Got it?'

'I have nothing to say,' she said. 'My lawyers are Batesby, Batesby, who and Burroughs?'

'Clark,' I said. 'Clark and Burroughs.'

'O K, Pops,' she said. 'But it'll cost ya.'

'The check is in the mail,' I said and hung up speedily. The phone rang immediately, too quickly for it to have been Sara calling back. It turned out to be Wade.

'Decided to come clean, eh?' I said to him. 'What did they do, starve you out? Did Suze threaten to go home to Mother?'

'Worse,' Wade said mournfully. 'She threatened to bring

her mother here. So, all right, come on by whenever you like, I'll be here.'

'It'll be an hour or so,' I said. 'Tell Suze I love her.'

'That makes one of us,' Wade said.

I put things away, switched off the air conditioner, locked up, posted the summons to Mr Summers in the box on the corner and made my way to Wade's via Moe's – three hot-dogs, no onions, and a root beer, then a slice of yesterday's lemon pie. Wade and at least two cats were lazing in the hammock that was strung up beside the garage; he bestirred himself enough to give me a languid wave with one skinny arm as I drove up.

I parked, got out, stretched, leaned against the fender, then said, 'O K, Wade, tell Big Daddy all.'

'What's to tell?' he said after thinking it over. 'Is it the singer or the song?'

'It's going to be your ass in a minute,' I said. 'Come on, stonehead, get it together. Guilt is guilt, but let's move it. You got Cissy upset, Willy upset, Suze upset, you don't want to get me upset, too.'

'You're right,' he said. 'Off, you guys.' When the cats didn't budge, he dumped them on the ground, struggled to his feet, went over to the garage door, fumbled for his keys, then opened the new padlock. 'Bolted right through this time,' he said, pointing to the two half-rounds the padlock went through, the one on the door and the other on the jamb.

'What was on there before?'

'Piece of chain,' he said. 'With a lock, like you use on a bicycle. I got it inside if you want to see it.'

'When did it happen exactly?'

He told me it was the night of Saturday the 14th, the day before Evonne and I got back to town. We went inside the garage, and he switched on the overhead lights. Wade had a lot of money invested in that garage. Most of it had gone for a new automatic color developer, but he had all of the other usual stuff as well: an overhead rack for prints, various filing cabinets, steel developing tank, print washer, dryer, white enamel trays, and stores of developer, hypo and enlarging paper. And, as Wade was, not surprisingly, himself a photographer, he had one wall shelf full of cameras and assorted lenses and one below it piled with film.

The place didn't look all that trashed, and I told him so.

'It wasn't actually that bad,' he said. 'And me and Suze did some tidying up before you came. What got broken was my new Polaroid, one of those that takes two pictures at a time, passport size, which is a drag as they come expensive, and a couple more cameras. We figure he got pissed off about something and just swept them all off the shelf on to the floor.'

'Well,' I said, 'come on, Wade, what was taken? Out with it. He didn't break in here just to develop some holiday snaps of his kids at the sea shore.'

Wade smiled and stroked his attempt at a goatee.

'That's good,' he said. 'I like that one. What was taken? Nothing, man. Nada. Not a thing.'

'Nothing at all?'

'Not that I can figure out.'

'Why would somebody break in here and take nothing when the place is loaded with all kinds of stuff worth good money? Unless he was looking for something he didn't find.'

'That's what me and Suze thought,' he said. 'Because one of the drawers in that cabinet over there where I keep my own work was dumped out on the floor.' I looked at the cabinet in question and noticed that all the drawers were labeled alphabetically: A B C, D E F, G H I, and so on.

'Which one was dumped?'

'The second one,' he said. 'D, E, F. But, shoot, it's only my own stuff, going back years.' He looked up at me innocently.

'Wade,' I said, 'in a minute you're going to get me very

angry. Have you ever seen me angry? It's not a pleasant sight.'

He sighed and said, 'Don't tell Suze, OK? Or Willy or Cissy?'

I said I wouldn't if I didn't have to, provided he got on with it.

'I've been doing some porno,' he admitted finally, fiddling with some junk on a workbench at the back. 'For this guy.'

'Which guy?'

'Some guy I don't know.'

'How do you get paid?'

'I get a certified check sent me after I deliver the prints.'

'To where?'

'A place downtown,' he said, '4420 Davenport.'

'And what's 4420 Davenport, Wade?' I said. 'A house, a shop, a news stand? Jesus, it's like pulling teeth.'

'An office building,' he said. He turned around with a small camera in his hands and took a snap of me, only instead of the camera taking a picture a fake snake jumped out at me.

'Cute,' I said. 'Real cute.' I picked up the snake and threw it back to him. 'So who do you deliver the prints to down at 4420 Davenport?'

'No one,' he said. 'I leave them at the front desk in an envelope marked "Hold For Pick-Up".'

'What kind of porno?' I asked him then.

'You know, porno,' he said. 'Guys getting it on. Long Dong Silver. Muff divers. Porno.'

'Kids?'

'No kids.'

'Animals?'

'No animals.'

'Promise?'

'Promise. Just porno, man. Eight by tens. Glossies. They look like movie stills to me.'

I thought for a moment, then said, 'Wade, let me ask you this. Do you ever make extra copies of the film you develop, for whatever reason, to keep as a record or in case the originals got lost in the mail when you sent them back, say?'

'Course not,' he said. 'Why should I? No one does. Prints cost money, man. You print what the customer asks for, and that's what he gets, plus his negatives back.'

'Wade, old friend,' I said, 'I do not want to hurt your feelings, but that would go for pornography as well, I assume. I mean, there is no way you'd be tempted to start a little collection yourself or run off a few extras to maybe sell?'

'With Suze around, are you kidding?' he said. 'First of all, she'd kill me, and second of all, who needs it, and third of all, you can get stuff as good all over town for a few lousy bucks, and I wouldn't know who to sell it to anyway.'

'Hmm,' I said. 'Will you allow me this, then. Will you allow me that it is possible that there might be in your line of work some unscrupulous types unlike yourself who would make copies of anything they thought they might make an extra buck from?'

'I guess it's conceivable,' he said. 'It's more conceivable some paranoid type who doesn't know anything about the business might think that sort of thing goes on. But hell, Vic, most of the time I don't even notice what I'm working on. I'm too busy; all I care about is the quality.'

'When was the last time you did some work for the porno king of 4420 Davenport?'

'The day before I got broke in,' he said. 'Like that Friday. Want something to eat? I'm starving.'

We went out into the sun, he locked up, then we strolled up the path to the kitchen door. Wade produced another key and let us in. His brother Willy was sitting at the kitchen table reading a letter and looking highly pleased about something.

We made our hellos, then Wade dug out a carton of milk and some oatmeal cookies, which we all shared, including Rags, who came in to see what there was to mooch. I figured Cissy and Suze were both out or no doubt they'd have been in, too.

Willy wanted to know how it was going with me. I told him O K and asked him the same thing.

'Terrific,' he said, 'except for all the craziness about Shusha.' He shook his round, heavily bearded head disgustedly. Willy was a mild and gentle soul, a flower-power man, if there is such a phrase, a total pot-head like Wade, but also the inventor of peculiar objects that he made a considerable amount of money from in royalties. He had invented a perpetual non-motion machine, also a bad-vibes detector, also a pill that both put you to sleep and woke you up after a desired span of time.

Not all his inventions were money-spinners, however. He phoned me up early one a.m. to tell me of one of his brainwaves. It was a T V ad for dog food, see, and in it these two scruffy mutts were sitting around after supper, picking their teeth and burping, and one says to the other, 'Man, what a terrific repast. What was in that dog food anyway?' And the other one says, 'One hundred per cent cat. And not only that, it's called "Woof" so we can go to the supermarket and get it ourselves.'

It turned out Willy was finding life terrific, aside from Shusha, because he had just sold another one of his improbable inventions to an adult game company. This one was called the Tower of Benares, or something like that, and it involved three upright poles and sixty-four disks, and you had to move the disks from one pole to another according to some rules I've forgotten, and if you made one move a second, it would only take you 48,000,000,000 years to do it all the way through. If you made a mistake, unfortunately, you had to start all over again.

I didn't believe a word of it, but he showed me the letter and there it was in black and white, quoting percentages and everything. Sometimes I wish I could make my living by brains instead of brawn, but I'm not ready for the breadline yet.

I beat Wade to the last cookie, then he walked me out to my car. I asked him how the porno king had gotten in touch with him in the first place.

'I got a letter one day asking for my rates.'

'So you've never talked to him even on the phone?'

'Nope. Weird, isn't it?'

'What's weird is there's nothing illegal in porno these days, at least not in the kind you've been handling, so what's all the fuss about?'

'There's gotta be something,' Wade said, closing the car door for me. 'Thanks for coming anyway. I feel better.'

Indeed, there had to be something, I thought to myself as I drove away. Could it be that my dreams of a big case involving a starlet in a nudie-pix scandal were about to come true after all?

Read on, amigos.

CHAPTER SIX

After I left Willy and Wade I pulled over for a minute, got my trusty Rand McNally street map from the glove compartment, looked up Davenport, then took the Golden State Freeway downtown. I got off at the right exit for a change, Main, found the street and even found a place to park. After loading the meter I walked back to 4420. My thinking was, porno kings being what they are, it was likely mine was thick as blackstrap molasses in November and as suspicious of mankind as an ex-Nazi hiding in Argentina, so it would be normal for him to think a small-time hustler like Wade might have made copies of something that was none of his business; it was worth checking out, anyway. Also, I had nowhere else to start and nothing else to do.

Like Wade said, 4420 was an office building. I had a large manila envelope in one hand to give me a spot of cover, and holding it officiously I went up the steps and inside where it was blessedly cooler. I stopped in the lobby by the board that listed the tenants. There were some sixty of them but none had anything to do with photography or films in their trade names, nor were any of the tenants called anything obviously helpful like Dork Brothers or Climax or Goddess Monique – The Supreme Mistress. There was a middle-aged security type sitting at a booth next to the elevators; he didn't even look up as I walked briskly by, tapping the envelope in a distracted fashion against one palm.

There were eight stories in the building. I got off at the top floor and walked the length of the hall looking and listening for clues. I didn't find any, although what exactly I was hoping to find I didn't really know – a wisp of lace caught in one of the doors, a voice shouting through a megaphone, '*Rear Widow*, take six, roll 'em!'

So I poked my head into a couple of the offices and waved my envelope and said something about a delivery for some film company but I'd forgotten the office number and could anyone help me out. No one could.

I tried a couple more offices on the seventh floor and got nowhere, then three on the sixth, ditto. On the fifth floor I got some action; a pretty girl who was typing away furiously but silently on a beautiful new IBM looked up long enough to tell me to try straight across the hall.

I thanked her and went straight across the hall. On the door it said AIRGEOL, whatever that meant. I knocked politely and went in. There was a young, studious-looking individual at one desk examining something through a slide viewer and another studious-looking individual, this one a female, doing the same thing at another desk. I went into my spiel again, to which they both listened attentively, then the man said he didn't think it was them as they weren't expecting any deliveries, but what precisely did I have in the envelope?

Rand McNally is what I had, but I lied and said I hadn't looked too closely, I was just doing a favor for a friend but they were certainly pictures.

'What kind of pictures?' the lady asked me.

'Pictures of people without any clothes on, I believe,' I said.

They both laughed.

'Boy, have you got the wrong place,' the man said. 'We do aerial surveys.'

I blushed deeply, made my apologies and withdrew with dignity. There was nothing to do but try, try again, so I tried again, without luck, all the way down to the ground floor. I took a quick peek at the security man as I got out of the elevator and decided as a last resort I would have to employ one of the oldest, most useful and most failproof tactics ever invented – bribery.

I walked over to him confidently. He was a mild-looking gent, in gray uniform complete with cap. A small sign on his desk informed the world that his name was Stanley Evans. He was filling in worksheets on a clipboard, but after I coughed discreetly he looked up and said,

'Help you?'

I slowly eased a ten-spot out of my wallet.

'I was wondering if you would like to buy something nice for the kiddies, Mr Evans,' I said.

'Love to,' he said promptly. 'But have you seen the price of toys these days? It's outrageous.' He shook his head sadly. I extracted a second bill to keep the first one company and passed them over. He promptly tucked them away in his shirt pocket, then looked up at me inquiringly.

'It's somewhat delicate,' I said, leaning in closer. 'But as you're a family man too, I can tell you it's about my daughter Liz. Eighteen last month.'

'Tempus does fugit,' said Mr Evans wistfully.

'Does it not,' I said. 'To be honest, we haven't been getting on all that well, the old generation gap and that sort of thing, and I haven't heard from her for a couple of weeks, but I know she works occasionally for one of your tenants, so I thought I'd stop by.'

'Which tenant is that?' Mr Evans asked.

'Ah,' I said. 'Therein lies the rub. I forget its name, but I know it's a film company and I hoped you could tell me which one of your tenants is in that line of work.'

'Your sad tale, which I don't believe for a minute, brings tears to my eyes,' said Mr Evans. 'How I wish I could help you.'

'But you can't?'

'Alas, no,' Mr Evans said politely but firmly.

There was a pregnant pause.

'How about a little something for the missus, too?' I suggested after a bit.

He smiled and shook his head.

'Then how about a refund, you crook?' I said.

'Look who's talking,' he said. 'See you around. Don't slam the door. And don't come back without a gilt-edged invitation.'

'Bet you're not even married,' I said bitterly, 'let alone have kids, because who'd marry a skinflint like you?' I turned to take my leave.

'Her name's Concepción,' he called after me. 'Mexican. A living doll. And you should taste her ceviche.'

I was not a happy man when I got outside. Outwitted by a thieving, glorified doorman with less hair than me, even. Now what? I wondered as I coughed my way through the filthy smog back to my car. I climbed in and sat there for a few minutes running over my unappealing choices. I could stake out the joint and keep my eye open for such porno stars as Moby Dick and Long Dong, but they might be hard to recognize with their clothes on. Which wouldn't be the case with Candy Samples, reputedly the possessor of a 48–EE chest; she'd be recognizable wearing a two-man pup tent. But it was more than likely 4420 Davenport was where my mysterious porno king ran the business end of his naughty business; the studios, such as they were, would be somewhere else.

I couldn't go back and try Stanley again, that cheat, even as, say, an FBI man because he wouldn't believe that either. Nor could I disguise myself well enough to fool him. It is not easy to convincingly disguise six foot seven and a quarter inches of rippling gristle. My brother Tony could find the right office for me, he was a cop after all although he drove a desk, not a patrol car, but who wants to ask their brother for anything, let alone help? All it did was give him an even bigger edge on me than he already had by being the youngest and the cutest and the smartest and the nicest to Mummy and Daddy. And the most spoiled, needless to add.

I could try Stanley's replacement, if he ever had one, if he ever did get sick from Concepción's cooking or take a summer holiday or take an hour off to go to the wig store, but who knew when that would be? And I'd noticed a lunch pail on the floor by his feet, which meant he probably didn't even leave his desk to eat.

I could get Wade to deliver another envelope marked 'Hold For Pick-Up' and see who picked it up, but to do so I would have to spend a considerable amount of time in the vicinity, and if I was close enough to watch Stanley's desk I was close enough for Mr Smarty-Pants to see me.

I sighed. It looked grim. It looked like all that was left was Plan B – call in Punk Power.

I spied a phone booth down the block and rang her up. After the usual moans and complaints she agreed to meet me at my office in half an hour.

The freeway traffic was building up, so I was a few minutes late getting back. Sara was sitting on the bench in front of Mr Amoyan's shoe repair establishment that was at the far end of the row of small businesses that had me at the opposite end. She was stuffing her face with something that looked as unlikely as she did – it was either a corn-dog on a stick or something even worse.

I opened up and then in her own good time she came meandering in without knocking, as per usual. She perched herself on the corner of my desk, also as per usual, then leaned over to give me a nasty knuckler in the arm, also as per unnecessary usual. Maybe it was her way of showing affection. I must say she did look radiant that July afternoon, if you like red leather jackets with sleeves torn off, purple gauchos and green hair. And Minnie Mouse shoes. And handbags made of transparent plastic.

'What's up, Pops?' she said, shaking her head like she was a dog who just came out of the bath.

'Cut that out,' I said. 'I don't need a fallout of green dandruff all over my clean desk. And what's up is, want a little job, a simple task that shouldn't take you more than a few minutes?'

'Doing what?'

'Doing what you're told, for a change,' I said.

She rummaged through her bag, produced one of those long, thin, fake cigars that some women think are chic these days, and lit up with a wooden match that was about a foot long, the kind you're supposed to light log fires with.

'One of the tenants in an office building downtown has something to do with films or film stills, and I want to find out which one. A nothing task, really.'

'If it's so nothing why don't you do it?' the twerp wanted to know.

'Don't throw that wooden stick on the floor, please,' I said. 'The wastepaper basket is under the desk. And I don't have the time, is why. It's work, work, work for me these days.'

'Yeah, I'll bet,' she said, flicking her ash in the general direction of the ashtray. 'I bet you tried and struck out already and now you're calling in the reinforcements.'

'I did have a brief word with the security type there,' I admitted. 'A cheapskate named Stanley Evans who wasn't too helpful.'

'Whad'ya want me to do, try and seduce him?' she said, batting her eyes in a grotesque mockery of flirtatiousness.

I shuddered at the very idea.

'That'll be the day,' I said. 'Anyway, he happens to be

happily married to a living doll called Concepción. No, I have a far, far better plan and one with a much higher probability of success.'

I told it to her. She had to agree there was a smidgen of brilliance in it. I handed over yet another ten-dollar bill to seal the deal, plus ten new fivers for expenses, then she hobbled out on her silly heels, leaving the door open again as per usual in some futile attempt to rile me. Some people never learn.

Sometime later that evening or that night she must have stopped by the office because I found her 'report' lying on the office floor under the mail slot when I got in to work the following morning. The 'report' read as follows:

18 July, 1986.

Report No. 11

From: Agent S.S.

To: V.D. (Ha Ha)

'I cried for madder music and for stronger wine,
But when the feast is finished and the lamps expire,
Then falls thy shadow, V. Daniel! the night is thine,
And I am desolate and sick of an old passion,
Yeah, hungry for the lips of my desire:
I have been faithful to thee, V. Daniel, in my fashion.'

As instructed I made my way
By tedious bus this summer day   Expenses: $1.50
Followed by even more tedious bus
Downtown, a song on my lips,
A secret in my swaying hips –
Once again Agent S.S. was out in the field,
If the despond of downtown LA can be called a field –
A mine field?
Arrived. De-bussed. Wasted

30 mins at 'Rico's Tacos' as was   Expenses: $2.45
30 mins too early according to V.D.'s Master Plan.
Accordingly, accordingly
It was four forty-five precisely, my dear, when, again,
Following Master Plan (hereinafter writ simply as 'MP'), I
Entered 4420 Davenport alongside unknown female also enter-
    ing –
Mousy secretary slave bearing cardboard carton of coffees
No doubt for her whip-wielding, penny-pinching boss –
(Ain't they all the same, dear!)
Small-talked to give Mr Security le impression
We were together. (MP strikes again; credit where credit is
    due)
Up, up, up we went, in middle one of three (3) elevators.
Elevator contained mirror, buttons and alarm telephone.
What if the phone rang and it was for me?
Mouse de-elevatored halfway up.
I continued to top.
According to MP, cleaning women/cleaning firm start work
    at 5 p.m.
(Information obtained by V.D. reading upside-down work-
    sheets on
Clipboard on Mr Security's desk) starting with top floor.
Lingered in hall on top floor.
Found ladies' room.
Primped, powdered, combed and piddled.
5.05 p.m., enter cleaning woman.
Cleaning woman small, dark, foreign.
Beautiful lustrous black hair. White overalls.
Usual ring of office keys.
Usual mop-pail combo.
Waxer left against door to hold it open.
Spun my yarn, spun my sad tale
Of sister wronged, of innocence on sale;

Of mourning father, of ailing mother,
Of failing farm and wailing dog . . .
She believed not one palabra of my age-old story.
Her obsidian eyes mocked my every word.
I withdrew three fins from my reticule.   Expenses: $15.00
And said obsidian orbs brightened, nay gleamed
Like searchlights in the yellowing fog.
Seventh floor, one floor below, second office to the left
Of the elevators on the same side of the hallway
Dwells your man, my boy.
Dwells your boy, my man.
Evidence for same – photos, shredded into confetti, but
    photos nonetheless,
In the wastepaper baskets. Regularly. Daily.
QED (Quite Easy, Dear).
Surprised you never thought of a little folding money
Changing hands, but then you always were a niggardly tight-
    wad.
Bus plus bus home.   Expenses: $1.50
See yez,   Total Expenses: $20.45

                       ————

Sara. S.   (From $60.00, leaves $39.55)

                       ————

XXXXXXXX   My Fee: $39.55

                       ————

                Balance: $00.00

  Wasn't it Alexander Fleming who said 'Pills are OK, but
laughter is the best medicine after all'?

CHAPTER SEVEN

Thursday morning, at the office.

After reading, inwardly digesting and then throwing out Sara's 'report', I went through the mail, of which the most interesting item was an offer of membership in a Fruit of the Month Club that operated out of Oregon, so you can imagine what the rest of the mail was like. Then I strolled over to the deli for a late breakfast and to lay down a modest wager on the Dodgers, who were playing the Giants that night up in that wind tunnel they call a ball park in San Francisco. Then I idled away another half an hour until it was late enough to safely ring Benny.

I gave him until eleven thirty; he was awake, he said, but still in bed. After the usual small talk I told him the favor I wanted.

'No problem,' he said, 'give me five minutes to get myself together, then I've got an errand to run, so I'll meet you down there around the corner in about an hour, OK with you?'

'OK with me,' I said. I gave him directions, then hung up. Five minutes to get himself together? It takes me a good hour in the morning; but then I have more to put together than he does, and the pieces don't fit as well.

Then I gave William J. Summers' answering machine another call. This time I breathed heavily, which comes easy for me. I was rummaging through a desk drawer looking for some usefully headed notepaper with which to drop him a billet-doux, when by coincidence or serendipity, call it what you will, Mrs Sylvia Summers called me.

She told me her husband had phoned her three times yesterday wanting to know what the hell was going on.

'And what was your response?'

'Like you said,' she said. 'I pleaded the Fifth.'

'Good,' I said.

'Now what happens?'

'Now you get ready for a few more calls,' I said, 'starting in a day or two. I won't bother you with the gaudy details, but your husband is going to be one angry man because I am going to harass him into total rage.'

'Be my guest,' she said. 'Pour it on him, he deserves it. You think he deserves it, don't you?'

'Absolutely,' I said. Any doubts I might have had, because who knows what really goes on in someone else's marriage, let alone your own, I kept to myself.

'Listen, Victor,' she said. 'Old chum. I want to go out tomorrow night, and I'd just as soon not have any company, at least not until I get where I'm going, capisce?'

I said I capisced.

'Can you work out something?'

'Can I not,' I said. 'Leave it to Uncle Vic, the housewife's friend.'

She told me approximately when she planned to leave her house, and I said I'd be skulking in the background somewhere to take care of any tail and would get back to her just beforehand to finalize the details. She blew me a kiss and hung up. What a nice person.

I resumed my search for a suitable sheet of paper, found one that was headed Department of Labor, and decided it would do. I got the typewriter from the safe, lugged it back, plugged it in, thought for a minute, then wrote:

'Dear Mr W. J. Summers. It has come to our attention that one of your employees, Ms B. Lorrimer, is in contravention of Federal Law 1448/B, Section 3, which pertains to Obligatory Social Security Contributions by Employer, Unpaid, and the subsequent penalties involved. Would you please present yourself Mon. – From 2.00–4.00 p.m. with all the relevant documents from Jan. 1981 up to the present, at the address listed above. Yours sincerely, Ralph J. Jensen, District Supervisor's Office, California Division, Dept of Labor.'

Not my most brilliant effort perhaps, but it was still early in the day, and it would suffice to keep William J.'s blood pressure cooking.

Then darned if my phone didn't ring again.

Maybe it was my new aftershave Evonne had bought me because she liked the name: Eau Sauvage Extreme, made by one C. Dior. But perhaps it wasn't; perhaps it was my stars, my bio-rhythm, my spreading reputation, my ship coming in at last. Perhaps also it was a wrong number or someone trying to sell me tickets to the Policeman's Ball, if they still had such things.

But no, the caller was a Bill Jessop, and he wanted to hire my services. He had a small packaging plant right next to Arnie's New 'n' Used Cars, and Arnie's tough little wife Mabel had touted me to him.

Bill Jessop's problem was he was changing his insurers and he suspected the new company might have different security requirements than the old one and he was too busy to go into it all himself and would I do it for him?

I sure would, I told him. I told him I'd drop by later that afternoon if I had time, if not, Friday morning, when we'd go over it all, and if there were some changes or upgrading to be done, give him an estimate on them.

'Whenever,' said Mr Jessop. 'Take your time. It's not important. It can wait. It's just if I don't do it soon, my wife will never talk to me again.' He said goodbye and rang off.

I wondered briefly what his wife had to do with it and figured I'd soon find out; perhaps she was one of those wives who had something to do with everything. However, it was time to go, so after stowing things away and locking up, I did, and headed downtown again via the Golden State Freeway to 4420 Davenport.

I parked around the corner right on time, and there was Benjamin sitting on a bench waiting patiently for me. He was attired that hot and getting steadily hotter July day in the sort of garb any rising young California businessman might wear – lemon slacks, lemon shirt open at the neck, gold medallion on a chain around said neck, lightweight Madras blazer, black tasseled loafers and lemon socks. Tinted glasses. Briefcase. Right on, bro.

We embraced affectionately, as we hadn't seen each other for a spell. Some friendships undoubtedly suffer if you don't see the other party regularly, with others it doesn't seem to matter, the closeness is always there for some mysterious reason. And, aside from blonds, if there is anything more mysterious than friendships and the reasons thereof, God knows what it is. Superficially, me and Benny had nothing at all in common. I was basically honest; he had been born with chicanery in his soul. I was a 48-XL, he was a 36-Regular. I had the sort of bashed-in, broken-nosed stitched-up face of interest only to plastic surgeons and taxidermists; Benny's apple-cheeked and unlined visage could have come from any high-school yearbook above the caption 'Most Likely to Succeed'. He'd been involved in criminal or near-criminal activities since he was about five and had never even seen a jail; I, Honest Vic, had seen many, including several from the inside, and I don't mean on visiting day.

I filled him in on the rest of the details, then told him if a certain Nosey Parker, i.e. one Stanley Evans, a crook who had not only warned me off the premises but swindled me out of twenty bucks, if he wanted to know Benny's business, to tell him it was with AIRGEOL, fifth floor, suite 515, got it?

He had it.

We walked to the front of 4420, and in he went with the bouncy stride of the upcoming young executive. I gave him one minute to get to the elevators, of which I knew there were three because the nerd had told me so in her 'report'. I gave him another minute or so to go up three floors, wedge the door open, then to call down to Stanley, using the emergency phone, also mentioned by Sara, my punk Mata Hari. I allowed another minute for Stanley to take the second elevator up to investigate. Then I poked my head in the front door, saw the coast was clear, nipped over to the third and last elevator and took it up to the seventh floor.

I de-elevatored, went down the hall to the second office on the left on the same side of the hall as the elevator, following the obsidian-orbed cleaning lady's directions, and found myself in front of a door on which was a neat sign that read, 'D. M. Co., Knock and Enter'. I listened for a moment at the door, but all was quiet inside.

So I knocked and entered, hoping against hope I wouldn't be embarrassed by seeing any nude, nubile nymphets doing naughty things to each other. I needn't have worried. I found myself in a surprisingly large, discreetly furnished office. An attractive lady of some sixty-plus summers was sitting at an expensive teak-topped desk with stacks of closed folders and envelopes in front of her. On one end of the desk was an electric typewriter, on the other end what I presumed was the automatic shredder. Behind the lady was a very pricey copier, also a ten-cup coffee maker. On the walls, framed photographs of birds, animals, fossils and flowers.

Was this really the notorious headquarters of the porno

king of 4420 Davenport? Or had V. Daniel, man of a thousand goofs, goofed again?

The lady gave me a sweet, motherly smile, touched her already perfectly groomed hair, and said,

'Well, hello there.'

'Hello, yourself,' I said.

'And what can I do for you this fine day?'

'I'm not so sure anymore,' I said, giving her my version of a bashful grin. 'You're not quite what I expected.'

'I will take that as a compliment, sir,' she said pertly. 'Why don't you take the weight off those long legs of yours for a moment, I don't get many gentlemen callers these days.'

'I can't believe that,' I offered gallantly, sitting down opposite her in a remarkably comfortable chrome and leather affair. She gave me another smile and arched her eyebrows expectantly.

'You don't do aerial surveys, by any chance?' I asked her.

'Heavens, no,' she said.

There was a pause.

I couldn't think of anything else to say, so I said, trying to summon up a blush, 'I know it's a silly question, but you don't have anything to do with dirty pictures, do you?'

She laughed. 'Do I look the type?'

I scoffed at the mere idea.

She stopped laughing. 'Perhaps it's time you told me who you are and what exactly it is you want.'

I got out my investigator's license and handed it over.

'I have a friend,' I said, 'who I believe does some of your developing and printing. Someone broke into his workroom last week and broke the place up some. Someone also bashed a beautiful labrador to death while he was doing it. We think whoever it was was looking for copies of photos that don't exist; anyway, my friend was badly frightened, and so were the other members of his family, and he asked me to try and

73

find out why it happened and to try and prevent it happening again.'

'That's terrible about the dog,' she said. 'Really terrible. But how did you come to knock on my lonely door?'

'Skillful detective work,' I said modestly. 'Let's leave it at that.'

She thought for a moment, then looked over at me somewhat quizzically. Then she looked at my license again, and passed it back to me.

Then she said, 'Somehow, I can't imagine how, you found the right place, but you've got the wrong gal, dear.'

'Not for the first time,' I said with a sigh.

'I do use your friend – Wade, isn't it? – and see no reason not to continue to use him, all being well,' she said. 'He's competitive and reliable and knows what he's doing and he does it on time.'

All of which told me something about Wade I never suspected; although he did small jobs for me from time to time, I always had to dump him out of the hammock to get him started and bully him to keep at it. It just goes to show you, although I don't quite know what.

'And I can assure you absolutely I had nothing whatsoever to do with burglarizing his darkroom; why should I?'

'That's what we can't figure out,' I said. 'You don't happen to have in your employ a black gentleman, tall, nasty dresser, small mustache?'

'Dear,' she said, 'D.M. Company consists entirely of one, hard-working elderly lady.'

'Just you?' I said. 'You're the infamous porno king of 4420 Davenport?'

She laughed again. 'I'm afraid so, dear.'

I had to believe her. 'I know it's none of my business, ma'am, but what do you do with all those, uh, nature studies?'

'Why not call them what they are?' she said. 'I don't care. They're good, clean dirty pictures. I will not have anything to do with the other kind – in fact, if there's one thing I loathe and despise it is dirty dirty pictures and those who deal in them: pedophiles, bestiophiles, even necrophiles – I cannot for the life of me understand people like that.'

'Me neither,' I said.

She opened up one of the folders on her desk and gave me a look at her line. This time I did blush, almost. Then she leaned forward conspiratorially. 'Can you keep a secret, dear?'

'Until death,' I promised, leaning forward too.

'They're all out-takes from films; I buy them cheaply by the yard, get them printed up, select the best and send them off to my list of clients in the ubiquitous plain envelope. It sure beats selling mobile homes, which is what I used to do. Quite successfully, I might add.'

'Well, I'll be darned, ma'am,' I said. 'Sort of like a Fruit of the Month Club, but less perishable.'

'And it is all one hundred percent legal, I don't need to remind you,' she said. 'I even pay taxes. However, it does get tiresome watching people's reactions when they find out what I do, and also so many of my dear neighbors in this building would find some excuse to drop in, so as far as anyone knows, what I do distribute are these.'

She opened up another folder and passed it over.

'Don't tell me,' I said, taking in the photos on the walls. 'Let me guess. Animals. Birds. The lesser spotted grebe. Pelicans at sunset winging their way homeward for a good stiff drink and some fishy little canapés. In other words, nature studies.' I shook my head reprovingly.

'What's in a word?' she said, with another guileless smile. '"A rose by any other name would smell as sweet as that which has no name to set it off."'

'Ah, yes,' I said, getting up to go. '*Richard the Fourth*, Part Three. Or was it the other way round?'

I thanked the kind lady for her help and for her honesty, swore my lips were sealed and would remain so, then said I hoped my inquiry wouldn't interrupt her business dealings with my friend Wade.

'I don't see why it should, do you, dear?'

'That's good news, anyway,' I said. 'But where all this leaves me I'll be damned if I know.'

'Well, dear,' the lady said, 'it seems simple to me. If it wasn't my non-existent pictures the burglar was after, whose non-existent pictures was it? In other words, are you barking up the wrong nature trail?'

'You are not only beautiful but you have uncommon perception as well,' I said looking down at her.

'Oh, go on,' she said. 'I'll bet you say that to all the old porno kings.'

'I'll bet I don't,' I said. 'Have you ever seen Russ Myers?'

'Want a souvenir?' she said. 'Take your choice.'

I looked at the two folders that were facing my way, the one full of auks and gophers at twilight and the other full of young, naked luscious females having all sorts of things done to them all over. I hardly hesitated at all.

'Call that a choice?' I said. I selected a glossy of a mother horse nuzzling her baby horse in a bright green field in the rain somewhere. 'Boy, won't this look great on my office wall.' I noticed the back of the photo had been stamped with her business logo. I thanked her again and departed.

I took the elevator down to the basement, prowled around for a bit, then found the service entrance at the rear of the building, next to the boiler room. It was locked with pushbars so it could only be opened from the inside, but that's where I was, so it was but a moment before I was safely out on the street again.

Benny was long gone, of course, so I opened up my car to let it cool off for a bit, then headed back to my side of the Hollywood Hills, the San Fernando Valley, unfabled in song, unfabled in story, but often fabled in pulp magazines like *True Detective* and *Real Life Crime*. The picture of the horses I gave to a zonked-out panhandler who hit on me when I stopped for a red light. He was so overcome that when he gave me the 'peace' sign, he had his two fingers turned around the wrong way.

CHAPTER EIGHT

It seemed clear in the light of my new-found knowledge that all roads led back to Wade's garage, so when I got over the Hollywood Hills, I turned right instead of left and shortly thereafter parked once again in the driveway in front of Suze's yellow Volkswagen. Wade and Rags were both asleep in the hammock, Wade with a can of Coors held against his bare tummy. Both opened their eyes as I got out of the car but otherwise didn't move.

'Wouldn't say no to one of those,' I said, referring to the beer.

Wade reached down with his right hand, opened the cooler, dug me out one and held it up. I went over, took it from him and popped it open.

'News,' I said after a long swig. 'Hot off the presses. Good news and bad news. Which do you want first?'

'You choose, man,' said Wade. 'The last time I played that game the good news turned out to be the bad news and the bad news turned out to be the worst news I ever had in my life since the day I got my draft notice saying I was 1-A.'

'You lying worm,' I said. 'You've never been healthier than 4-F in your whole miserable existence.'

'I'm telling ya,' Wade said. 'I was 1-A. You should have seen me in those days; I was just outa school, I had muscles, I had skin tone, I had spring in my steps, I had clear eyes and exceptional peripheral vision, and then one fateful night I discovered . . .'

'Sex and drugs and rock and roll,' I said. 'Didn't we all?'

'Wrong,' he said dreamily. 'I discovered Jesus and went

and joined a commune in New Mexico. *Then* I discovered sex and drugs and country and western.'

'Fascinating,' I said. 'Anyway, the good news is the porno king of 4420 Davenport wants to continue doing business with you. The bad news, which can be deduced from the good news, is that it wasn't the porno king of 4420 who broke into the garage and killed old Shusha, and it probably wasn't the tall dark stranger with the little stash either.'

'Shee-it,' Wade said. 'Did you hear that, Rags?'

Rags wagged his tail briefly.

'So who the hell was it then?'

'Let's look at it this way for a minute, Wade,' I said, finishing up the beer. 'Let's try a little lateral thinking here.'

'How about some horizontal thinking?' he said sleepily.

'What else that didn't exist could someone have been looking for? I don't know, it's just an idea that came to me. For instance, what wasn't in the drawer that was gone through, the D E F one as I recall, the only drawer in the place that was disturbed?' I chucked the beer can into a nearby carton which was half full of other empties. 'Think, Lord Snowdon, speak to me, baby. And what about your invoices, where do you keep them?'

'The ones I keep I keep in an old bread tin in the kitchen,' he said, ''cause that's where me and Suze do the paperwork.'

'That may be good news, too,' I said, giving the hammock a swing. 'Because if someone was looking for prints that weren't there maybe he was also looking for a work order that was there that might have his name on it or his boss's name or someone's name. Perhaps you wouldn't mind terribly getting them for me, then we can go through them and see which ones start with the letters D, E, or F. There can't be that many of them.'

Wade emitted a long-suffering sigh. Rags wagged his tail again. I said, a mite impatiently, 'Come on, Wade, will you move your ass; I am doing this partly for you, you know, and I'm not getting rich doing it, not that I want to because dogs is one thing and money another. Still, I wouldn't mind a little spirited assistance.'

'I'm sorry, man,' he said. He pushed the dog out and climbed out himself. 'The whole thing's got me all shook up. Hang on, I'll get them. And even though I don't look it, I am grateful for what you're doing. So is everyone.'

'OK, OK, don't overdo it,' I said.

He went up to the house, went inside, and came back with the bread tin which he set down on the grass near the hammock. We both hunkered down beside it, took out a handful of assorted papers and began looking for work orders from people or companies whose names began with the letters in question, recent ones only, because it made sense that whatever was going on had started in the last couple of weeks or so. After ten minutes we both had a small stack of orders, maybe two dozen in all.

'You've been busy,' I remarked.

'Could be worse,' he said.

Of the twenty-four orders, half were from one particular photographic outfit that sub-contracted a lot of its smaller orders to independents like Wade. He told me that as far as he could remember they were all either industrial or architectural subjects. Six of the others were from D.M. Co., aka the porno king of 4420 Davenport, one every two weeks or so going back to the beginning of June. Two more were from a guy Wade knew who did weddings, bar mitzvahs, and baby pictures. One invoice was from a local kid Wade knew well who wanted to grow up to be a professional photog some day and who kept coming around and bugging him: it was for the developing and printing of twelve rolls of Fujicolor.

That left three invoices, and they were all for processing what looked like harmless rolls of holiday snaps. I went back to the car, got a notebook and pen and jotted down the names and addresses of the three private clients, plus that of the local kid. None of them meant anything to me or rang any kind of bell. Then I thought, what the hell, I might as well do it properly, so I borrowed the whole stack, drove three blocks to the nearest post office, made copies of them all, then dropped the originals back at Wade's.

He wasn't in the hammock for once but actually doing some work in the garage; the red light over the door – which meant stay out, he was printing – was on, so I left him to it, waved to Cissy who had waved to me through the kitchen window, declined with pretended reluctance her shouted offer to come in for a quick slice of turnip pie, and made a sedate getaway. I stopped at Moe's for some proper food – two hotdogs, mustard and relish only, and an orange crush – on the way back to the office.

Once there, I spread the two dozen invoices out on the desk and looked them over. I was just settling into it when in strolled Sara, a large paper flower pinned on to the top of her lime-green hair. Come to think of it, her hair was exactly the same shade of green as Evonne's stuffed iguana lamp, only on the lizard it looked better. Sara was colorfully attired in a yellow T-shirt five sizes too big, on which was printed 'Fat Jack's. Best Meat In Town. If You Can't Eat It, Beat It'. Charming. If she was my daughter, I'd run away from home.

'Wanna eat, Fats?' she said, giving my cheek a pinch.

'Just did,' I said. 'And close the door behind you.'

'C'mon,' she said. 'It's on me, if that's what you're worried about, and it probably is.'

'Go away,' I said. 'Far away. Don't you have a drug orgy or something to go to? Does the Foreign Legion take girls? Can't you see I'm busy?'

'What's so busy about all that?' she said, looking over my shoulder. She did smell nice; I guess she must have borrowed some of her mother's perfume for a change, she was usually redolent of passé flower-power aromas like patchouli or musk or old sneakers.

'Somewhere in here there might be a lead to a perp,' I said. 'Perp. Short for perpetrator. Perpetrator – another word for a guilty party. It pays to increase your word power, someone once told me. I think it was Jimmy Durante.'

'Who's he?' the twerp said. 'And what did the perp you're looking for perpetrate?' She leaned in even closer.

'A break-in at Wade's,' I said. 'Wade's is where I got you that trick camera that time, remember?'

'Sure, Pops,' she said. 'I ain't gone soft in the head yet, like some. So, go on.'

'It appears that someone with the initial D, E, or F was looking to see if Wade had by any chance made unauthorized copies of some photos he'd processed for them. The pieces of paper on this desk, which you can stop disturbing any time now, are all the recent work orders from Ds, Es, and Fs. All right so far, not too complicated?'

'Spare me,' she said. 'For once.'

'We can eliminate these,' I said, referring to the ones from D.M. Co., 'for reasons I am unable to disclose at this time, but suffice it to say, good, hard, intelligent detective work was involved.'

'Oh, yeah?' the twerp said. 'Who'd ya get to do it for you?'

I didn't answer her, why bother? I did give her a pitying look, however. She gave me a wide grin in return. I will say this about her, she had quite regular teeth.

'Hey, I know that address,' she said, reaching down and grabbing one of the sheets. 'That's where I was.'

'So you were, so you were,' I said. 'Now these twelve are all from another lab, and we think we can eliminate them for some more reasons I won't go into. And we think these two are weddings and babies.'

'Yeech,' she said.

'So that leaves us with these four.'

I lined them up neatly.

'Hmm,' she said, messing them up again.

'Any one of them say anything to you?' There wasn't much of a chance, frankly, as none of them said anything to me, and I was the brains of the outfit, the professional, the well-read one.

'Isn't she the news lady?' she said, reaching down and tapping one of the invoices with a two-toned red and black fingernail. 'On channel whatever it is? Forbes? Maryanne Forbes?'

'Oh, sure,' I said. 'I meant aside from that one.'

'Twelve Fuji,' she said, tapping her nail on the next one in line. 'What's that mean?'

'Twelve rolls of a color film called Fujicolor,' I said patiently.

'Sounds gross,' she said. 'What's left? M. Esher, something, address blah blah blah, something something, fourteen dollars and forty cents. L. S. Fritz, blah blah blah, six rolls of something for pick-up on Wednesday. All in all I like Maryanne Forbes. Well, I don't mean I like her; have you seen the way she does her hair? Doris Day lives again. But at least she's someone. I'd start with her.'

'Oh, no, you wouldn't,' I said firmly. 'You'll start with twelve Fuji and like it; he's a kid who lives in Burbank near Wade, there's his address, write it down. He wants to grow up to be a hot-shot shutterbug so it's just possible in his wanderings, pretending he was a war correspondent or something, he was snooping around and took a picture of something or someone he shouldn't have.'

'Like what?'

'How do I know?' I said. 'Maybe someone sneaking out of someone else's house with lipstick on his collar. Or some innocent-looking citizen walking away from a store that's just been robbed.'

'All the way out to Burbank?' she said. 'Jesus. Can I eat first? I'm starved.'

'Oh, all right,' I said. 'If you must.'

I locked up and took her down the line to Mrs Morales' Taco-Burger franchise where I watched her wolf down three tacos and a plate of chili rellenos. It had only been an hour since I'd eaten, so all I had was the combination plate with extra beans and a side of guacamole. The handsome Mrs Morales wasn't there, but her fresh daughter was; for some reason she kept throwing me amused glances and knowing looks and saying things like 'More hot sauce, Veec?'

Outside the restaurant after the meal, which I paid for, by the way, I dug out a five-dollar bill and five ones and gave them to the noodlehead and told her to push off and I'd see her when.

'How'd you like my last report?' she asked me when she was done tucking the money away down in one boot.

'Loved it,' I said. 'A model of its kind.'

She looked pleased. 'What do I say to the kid?'

'Be inventive,' I said. 'Isn't that what poets are supposed to be? Tell him you work for *Punkopolitan* and you're thinking of taking on new staff. Tell him anything, but try and get a look at those photos of his.'

'No sweat, Pops,' she said. She put on a pair of red shades and off she went toward the bus stop across the street. I strolled the few yards back to the office, put away all the invoices but those belonging to M. Forbes, M. Esher, and L. S. Fritz, then reached for the phone. For reasons of stubbornness I tried M. Esher first. I was connected to a lady who informed me in a pleasant voice that she was Mrs Esher.

'Mrs Esher, I'm one of the owners of Wade's Pictorial Services, the people who develop photos for you sometimes, and we unfortunately had a break-in here the other day, and some of our records and negatives were destroyed.'

'I'm sorry to hear that,' Mrs Esher said.

'Thank you,' I said. 'We were worried that we might not have filled your recent order, so I thought I'd just call and check.'

'Goodness,' she said. 'Aren't you nice to be so thoughtful.'

I cleared my throat deprecatingly.

'You certainly did fill our order,' Mrs Esher said. 'Martin picked them up last week. As a matter of fact, I've just now sent the ones of his mother on to her.'

'A family reunion, was it, if I may inquire?'

'It was Mother's seventy-fifth,' Mrs Esher said. 'We had a wonderful time. Family came from all over. Martin's brother and his wife Emily even came all the way from Alaska.'

'Fancy that!' I said. I thanked her for her time and her courtesy and hung up before she started on the grand-children.

I did the same number on L. S. Fritz, who turned out to be an elderly gent who knew Wade's brother Willy, which is how come Wade had gotten his business, and Mr Fritz let it slip that all his six rolls were of flower arrangements he'd taken for his wife's sister Lulu in the wife's sister's front room in Altamont.

That, whether I liked it or not, left M. Forbes, news lady, or was it anchor person or news woman or news person? Whatever it was, it left her. I didn't know what news people's working hours were, but I tried the phone number listed on the invoice just in case, expecting to get either a service or a machine. In fact, I got a real person, a female, but it wasn't M. Forbes.

'Maryanne's working,' this female told me. 'She won't be home until about nine thirty. Can I take a message?'

'If you're a friend of hers, perhaps you could help,' I said, using my lower, my most persuasive, might I say, sexy, tone.

'I'm her sister,' the female said. 'Connie Forbes. I suppose that makes us friends. What can I do for you, sir, as long as it doesn't take for ever because I'm off and running in a few minutes.'

'Won't take but a sec, Miss Forbes,' I said. I went into my story about the break-in for the third time. When I was finished, Connie Forbes said,

'Well, there's a coincidence for you.'

My antennae perked up.

'In what way, Miss Forbes?'

'We had a break-in here, too, a few days ago.'

Bingo, I thought. 'Really?' I said. 'Have the police come up with anything yet?'

'Ha, ha,' said Miss Forbes. 'Very funny, sir. Are you a professional comedian by any chance?'

'Merely a highly gifted amateur,' I said. 'Listen, I don't want to detain you, so could you please ask your sister to call me? There's a remote chance I might be able to help.'

'Why not?' said Connie Forbes. 'What could hurt?' I gave her my name, my office and home numbers, thanked her, then hung up.

A kid of Deborah's age more or less went by my window and stopped to press his grimy hands against it and peer in. I ignored the urchin, who finally went away. Happily, I leaned back in my chair. Happy is he who happy is. Happy is he who can see a bit of daylight, a trace, an inkling, at the end of the tunnel. It now looked like the same pictures had twice been purloined, or would have been if the second set had existed, and although I had no actual proof yet, I'd have bet my last Canadian two-dollar bill on it. Happily. And M. Forbes, news hound, would certainly know what was in those pictures. And I couldn't see any reason why M. Forbes wouldn't share that information with me.

Happily I put things away, whistling a merry tune the

while. Happily I locked up and skipped to my car. Less happily I drove through the fierce and ill-mannered afternoon traffic toward Bill Jessop's packaging plant, right next to Arnie's New 'n' Used Cars. Unhappily I got stuck for a good half hour in a traffic jam on Sepulveda. Angrily I shook my fist and honked with all the others. Hot and bad-tempered I finally pulled up and parked in front of the Vitabrite Distributing Company. Moods are strange, short-lived creatures sometimes.

CHAPTER NINE

Bill Jessop soon cooled me down again.

He was a calm and charming man in his fifties, with a neat brown and gray beard and the remnants of a Boston accent. By following signs, I found him in his office on the first floor of the building gazing judiciously at a bright orange and green bottle label he was holding up and turning this way and that. When he saw me looming in the door, clipboard – which I'd luckily remembered to bring – in hand, he put the label down and waved me in.

'Vic Daniel,' I said. 'Reporting for duty.'

'Bill Jessop,' he said, standing up to shake my hand. 'Who is deeply grateful for any excuse to stop working for a while. Sit, sit.'

I sat. He sat.

'Nice place,' I said. The office was cream and dark brown, the walls and the carpeting cream, all the shelves and furniture brown. Some of the shelves held examples of his wares, and on the walls were several framed ads for same. There was a spare desk opposite Mr Jessop's by the picture window.

'We like it,' he said.

'What's that for?' I said, referring to the label.

'My latest problem,' he said. 'Would you believe artichoke extract?'

'Why not?' I said.

'Would you believe artichoke extract for the Japanese?'

'That's one I'd have to think about,' I said.

'The problem is not the extract itself,' he said. 'Nor is it the bottling. Or the shipping.'

'The mix?' I suggested.

He laughed and scratched his beard vigorously.

'The problem is do we get the labels printed here or over there in the land of the rising sun? Strange what grown men preoccupy themselves with.' Then he said on his intercom to some invisible person,

'Milly, if you're finished with your nails, bring me in the insurance file, please.'

'In a minute, boss,' said the invisible Milly. 'I've got two fingers still to do.'

Mr Jessop laughed again, then said, 'C'mon, I'll show you around first.'

We hadn't gotten to the door yet when Milly appeared from the adjoining office with a bulky file in one hand. She was a middle-aged lady in harlequin glasses and the sort of trouser suit my mother often wears.

'Oh, God, not the guided tour bit,' she groaned when she saw us on the way out. Mr Jessop looked at her sternly and told her to put the file on his desk without any more backtalk, what kind of impression did she think she was giving his guest?

'Help today,' he said loudly enough for Milly to hear as we went down the hall. I nodded sympathetically.

He led me downstairs and did indeed give me the guided tour bit. We started in the shipping room where three youths in jeans were busily packaging, addressing and stacking orders to go. Then he introduced me to a Mr Lerner who was inserting a pile of blank labels in a new-looking rotary offset press ready for printing. Then we passed a lady in white who was running a stream of already labeled bottles through a machine that sealed them in airtight cellophane. Then we passed the lady who was doing the labeling. Then we continued on to the back room where four more ladies in spotless whites were bottling various products.

To the hairiest of the three youths in jeans Mr Jessop said, 'This is Vic, he's a detective, so hide your stash.' To the cute lady sealing the bottles he said, 'This is Vic, he's a detective and he wants you in the staff room in ten minutes for a body search.'

'Anytime,' she said, giving me a wink.

To the four ladies running bottling machines he said, 'This is Vic, he's a detective. Someone's been stealing artichoke extract, and he wants a urine sample from each of you.' No one seemed unduly worried about these threats, I noticed, and I also noticed no one either suddenly began working harder when the boss appeared or stopped working when he was talking to them. Then Mr Jessop took me into the staff room, got us both a cup of truly awful coffee from the dispenser, and gave me a brief run-down on his operation, which was not without interest to a layman such as myself.

What, basically, he did was to buy from all over the world products in bulk which he then rebottled, relabeled with his own company logo and then sold to retail outlets such as health-food stores, supermarkets and supermarket chains. Some of his products were expensive but none was a scam, unless you were one of those mistrustful infidels who thought yeast extract, odorless garlic and carrot juice were a scam to start with. Then Mr Jessop disappeared back into the shipping room for a moment and came back with a sample of one of his products which he presented to me with a flourish.

'Ginseng,' he said. 'Sprinkle some of this on your cornflakes in the morning, then look out.'

'Thank you,' I said. 'Does it come in a family size?'

After a bit we went back upstairs, and I looked through the insurance file at one desk while he got on with whatever he was getting on with at the other. Once I interrupted him to ask why exactly he was changing his insurance company.

'You ever been married?'

'Almost,' I said. Once I'd almost married Benny's Aunt Jessica. Sometimes I wondered what had or hadn't happened to her. Sometimes, not as often, I wondered what had or hadn't happened to me.

'Almost doesn't count,' said Mr Jessop. 'My wife's brother has just moved over to Sky Life. Do you know how much commercial property insurance my wife's brother, her only brother, her beloved only kid brother has to write in a year to make the Millionaire's Club?'

'Give me a hint,' I said.

'That is why,' he said.

I spent the next hour at the desk comparing the old policy which was with Cal Home and was still in effect, with the new one. Then I spent an hour having a closer look around the premises, especially at everything that had to do with security, every door, every window, the sprinkler system, the sliding metal doors at the loading bay, the skylight in the bottling room and the high-wattage security lights. I saved the burglar alarm system for last.

All systems, no matter how seemingly complicated, have only three elements: an electrical circuit, which is attached to a box, which is in turn attached to something that gives a signal. Break the circuit, and somewhere, something, maybe a bell on the outside of the building or a light on a switch-board at the nearest police station, or both, goes off. Obviously, all three elements need to be protected. The control box uses a special key. All wiring should not only be inside the walls but of the combination type, which means it is a combination of open-circuit and closed-circuit wiring.

As the terms indicate, open-circuit means there is a gap in the system somewhere which is closed by any window or door being opened, so the bell goes off. The only problem with this is it's comparatively easy to foil; if you make a break in the system anywhere with even a pair of scissors, let alone pliers, obviously you've broken the circuit for good, so no bell can ring. With closed-circuit the opposite happens. Electricity runs permanently through all the doors and windows; any interruption in that flow and off goes the bell again.

So the combination system is therefore and plainly a combination of both, so any burglar would have a bigger problem on his hands. To get to the wires he's got to go into a wall somewhere, into the plaster, then cut open the metal sheathing around the wires, then figure out which of the four wires inside is which, because the open-circuit ones can be simply cut, but the others have to be by-passed somehow. Make a mistake, and off goes the bell again.

Easiest of all systems to foil are the ones that use a telephone line to convey the dread message to either a police station or some private security company; telephone lines are usually highly accessible where they enter a building, so one snip and adios.

Anyway, fascinating though all this undoubtedly is . . .

Milly, when asked, promptly got me an exact-until-five-o'clock yesterday inventory of every bottle, vial, tube, carton, vat, cauldron, butt and firkin of muck in the place, plus the amortization picture of every machine, including office equipment, the two company cars, the two company trucks, and the building itself. Then she kindly lent me her own, her very own, pocket calculator.

Another hour went by, bringing the time up to four forty-five or so. I neatly wrote down my conclusions, then crossed over to Mr Jessop's desk where I coughed politely for his attention.

'Ahem,' I said. I handed him my final list of figures. He gave it a quick scan.

'Jesus, it's even worse than I thought,' he said.

'I could be wrong,' I said. 'I'm not really an expert on

anything but the hardware side of it, but I'm not off by much.'

'What price marital happiness?' Mr Jessop wondered. 'And can a price be put on it?'

'It sure can,' I said, pointing to the bottom line of my list. 'It's just under seven grand per year extra to go with your beloved brother-in-law.'

'John,' said Mr Jessop. 'My wife calls him Johnny-o.' He stood up, stretched lengthily, then said to Milly over the intercom,

'Darling, dearest, it's your adorable boss speaking. Would you have the kindness to try and get my brother-in-law over at Sky, if the little rascal isn't out playing golf somewhere?'

'Comin' up, boss,' said Milly.

'And, Milly,' Mr Jessop said, 'don't listen in for once. I wouldn't want you to learn any new naughty words.'

'I'm sure you mean that for me, too,' I said. I retrieved my clipboard, tidied up the desk I'd been using, handed over the calculator, then Mr Jessop walked me to the door.

'Many thanks,' he said. 'Mabel was right, you do know your stuff, despite appearances. Your outrageous bill will be paid immediately, if not sooner.' He gave me a slap on the back, and I left. On the way down the stairs I overheard the beginnings of Mr Jessop's conversation with Johnny-o. There were some naughty words in it but frankly none I hadn't heard before.

As I was so close, I popped next door to say hello and thanks for the recommendation to Mabel, but she was out of the office and so was Arnie. I was making my way back to the car, which I'd left in front of Vitabrite, when one of the kids I'd seen in the shipping room, the hairiest one, passed me going the other way, obviously just coming off work. Then he ran back to me.

'Excuse me, sir, but are you really some kind of detective?'

'Some kind is right,' I said.

'Listen, you don't happen to have a minute, do you?' the kid said.

Well, he was a nice-looking kid and he did call me 'sir', so I said, 'Sure, what's it about?'

'Ah, just something silly but it's getting to me, and I don't know who else to ask about it.'

'Tell you what,' I said. 'If you happen to know a spot near here where they sell alcoholic refreshment I'll graciously let you buy me something cooling, and you can lay it on me.'

'How about right there?' the kid said, pointing straight across the street to a modest, wooden-fronted estaminet whose sign proclaimed it to be Billy's Western Bar-B-Cue.

We introduced ourselves as we crossed over. Don, his name was; he'd been at Vitabrite over two years and liked it well enough; his boss was cool, and he, Don, helped with the deliveries so he got out and about once in a while. And he also got any of the products they sold at cost, which his girlfriend Linda liked because she was into that sort of thing.

Don said hi to the stringbean behind the bar at Billy's, ordered a draft for himself and a brandy and ginger for me, paid for them, then, after we'd moved to the privacy of a wooden booth at the back near the deserted bandstand, told me somewhat shamefacedly what it was that was getting to him.

'It's Linda,' he said, 'she's a rotten little cheat, and I can't catch her at it.'

'What's she cheating at?' I took a handful of free peanuts that were in a bowl on the table along with the line-up of mustard, catsup, relish, diced onions, hot sauce and toothpicks.

'Don't laugh,' the kid said. 'Gin rummy.'

I didn't laugh but I did wonder briefly if Mike Hammer or Magnum ever got involved with anything as petty as a gin rummy cheat.

'We play it a lot at her place,' Don said. 'It's not the money, because we don't play for any, just for silly things like who'll do the dishes or go out for some ice cream, you know, but it's the principle of the thing.'

I took a long, welcome swig of my drink, all the way down to the ice.

'Maybe she plays better than you.'

'Are you kidding?' he scoffed. 'My pop taught me; he was the best gin player in town; he had a cup he'd won, even. OK, she knows the rules, but she can't even shuffle the cards properly, for Christ's sake; she shuffles them like a kid, messing them all up together. It drives me crazy. But I know her, see, and I know she's up to something, and when I figure out what it is I'll kill her.'

'Yeah,' I said. 'You sound really mad. You'll probably smother her to death with kisses.'

He grinned, finished off his beer, and went and got us refills over my admittedly weak objections.

'Well, I don't know a hell of a lot about cards,' I said when he'd returned. 'I can't even win at Old Maid. But I know someone who does; I'll call him later, then I'll call you, so with any luck you might even be able to start smothering Linda tonight.'

He went over to the beanpole behind the bar, borrowed a pen from him, although I could have lent him one, and came back with his phone number written on a cocktail napkin. I didn't want to tarry too long as I had a date with my own little cheat later, so after just one more I took my leave and made my way back to my side of town, this time luckily against the main flow of traffic, diverting myself by wondering how much to charge Don's boss.

On the one hand, he was an extremely nice man. On the same hand was that wink from the cute lady sealing bottles; who knows what free samples that might lead to? On the other hand was the free sample I already had; could that not be interpreted as a slur on my manhood? Also, business was business, there was my time, several hours of it, plus my expertise, and how do you put a value on that. I'll tell you how. You multiply my hourly rate by the number of hours I'd put in and deduct the total from the fee I'd decided on, $500. That is how. I wonder how much Starsky gets an hour. Enough to keep him in blond rinses. Unless Hutch is the blond. Who cares.

After I'd gotten home and showered and powdered and shaved and aftershaved and deodorized and changed into my second-favorite Hawaiian shirt and clean cords and gotten myself a drink and turned the TV on to the all-news channel, I gave my magician pal Louis a call. Louis was really more of a pal of Benny's than mine; he lived in the next apartment to him, but I'd met him half a dozen times and had even seen him perform in clubs a couple of times. Louis worked under the name Lou Le Fou, which might give you some idea of his act. Then again, it might not.

As luck would have it, Louis was out, but his machine told me he was doing two weeks at the Magic Castle and be sure not to miss him. It even gave the times of his nightly appearances. Ah, show biz, I thought. I also thought Evonne would no doubt be displeased when I squired her to a magic show that night instead of letting her take me up into the last row of the top balcony of some seedy fleapit to eat popcorn and exchange salty kisses, but a gal can't be allowed to always have her own way.

I wasn't a member of the Magic Castle, which costs significant money if you aren't a professional, but mentioning I was a personal guest of Lou Le Fou's got me a table reservation for two at eight thirty with no trouble at all. Then I had to rummage around for a tie that went with my shirt because I remembered you needed one to get in, then I had to change my shirt because I couldn't find a tie that blended all that smoothly with purple, green and lilac. Then I checked with Evonne to see if the change of plan met with her approval; it did.

I picked her up at her place about eight; she was not only ready but raring to go in something short, backless, shoulderless and white that showed off her tan. Actually, she loved magicians. Her father had a whole repertoire he used to go through for his four daughters when they were little, she had told me more than once. My pop had never done any tricks that I could recall for his two boys; in fact, I can't remember ever seeing a pack of cards around the house. He did teach me to tie a bow tie once, but that was about it. Don't get me wrong, I'm not bitter, I'm a big boy now as I keep reminding myself, and anyway, I'm sure a steady supply of Four Roses with beer chasers and a just as steady supply of Irish music coming from the jukebox down at his local were a lot better company than two small, noisy kids. Sure.

'Teach, you look gorgeous,' I said before we drove away. 'You are gorgeous. Give us a smooch, heavy on the lipstick.'

She obliged. The lipstick was strawberry-flavored, my third favorite. A long, satisfying moment passed. Then she patted my cheek and said, 'For a country boy, you're sure some kisser.'

'Got it all from a book,' I said. 'Then I used to go into the woodshed and practice on a picture of June Haver, who looked a lot like you.'

The Magic Castle is, or was, if it's not there anymore, on a hill above Fountain. We got there on time, let the valet take the car, and went in. An interesting place, the Magic Castle, if you like that sort of thing, and why not. There's a skull that talks back to you and a piano without a pianist that plays requests, and you can eat and drink and wear a tie and watch some of the world's best magic, especially close-up magic. So we ate and drank, and a young chap whose name I've forgotten came to our table and did a four-ace trick and then a coin-through-table routine that even had me guessing.

After supper we went into the showroom, had a liquor and watched Lou Le Fou, who was first on the bill that eve. Lou had a drunk act and worked in a beret and a blue French workingman's smock, and his act that night was a version of the Chinese Linking Rings, only he didn't link the un-doubtedly solid, unbroken rings together; he accidentally linked everything else about his person and within reach on to one of the visibly and undoubtedly solid rings – his watch, his cuff, scissors, his keyring, a hacksaw, and so on. A smooth, funny and professional act, and he exited to well-deserved applause.

We tracked him down a while later talking with one of his fellow magicians at the bar, and I bought him a highly priced Coke and put to him Don's silly problem.

Lou Le Fou giggled. He was a rotund, bearded man with large, innocent blue eyes that blinked a lot, whether involun-tarily or as part of some sort of misdirection I never found out. He was bowled over by Evonne's beauty, charm and legs, and quite rightly, too, and immediately on introduction produced a cigarette out of the air, put it into his mouth, produced a wooden match from the air, lit the match, which instantly changed into a flower, which he took with the other hand and offered to her with a gallant Gallic bow. How was it all done? Alas, I am sworn to secrecy about such matters.

'So there's no chance she's a mechanic,' Lou said, referring to Don's girlfriend Linda.

'None,' I said.

'What's a mechanic, aside from someone who doesn't fix your car?' Evonne asked him.

'A manipulator,' he said. 'Someone who holds the deck in his palm, thumb on top, three fingers on one side and the forefinger at the front.' He took a deck of Bicycles out of his pocket and demonstrated. 'Pull the top card back with your thumb and you can second-deal.' He demonstrated. 'Pull the bottom card back with your middle finger and you can deal the second off the bottom after flashing what the bottom card is so the guy won't think he's getting it off the bottom.' He demonstrated. 'Flip two cards up a bit with your thumb, then you can take two off as one.' He demonstrated. Evonne loved it.

'So what's she doing to Don?' I said finally.

'There's two easy ways to cheat at gin,' he said, 'and don't think they're not done all the time, right Ralph?'

His friend Ralph nodded his agreement.

'In a cabana this time,' he said, 'in Miami, playing dime-a-point Hollywood; I couldn't believe what they were getting away with.'

'What you do,' Lou said, 'is glimpse the bottom card before you deal – easy in a friendly game – and that's all, just knowing one card is out of play gives you a better edge than you might think. The other way, even easier, is to hold out one card, a key one like a nine or ten. You can leave it in the box when you're getting the cards out to start. If it's the right kind of table, you can put it on the floor underneath before you start, or you can drop it innocently on the floor during the game and keep your big foot on it so if anyone ever sees it they'll think it got there accidentally. Even easier for Don's girlfriend is to play with a deck that's a card short to begin with that only she knows about. And if he's the suspicious type who counts the cards before they start, all she's got to do is wait till he goes to the bathroom or whatever and then hide one anywhere she likes. Easy, my friend. Cheating is all too easy. Right, Ralph?'

'The things I've seen,' Ralph said morosely. 'I kid you not.'

'You wouldn't cheat me like that, would you, dear?' I said

to my darling later as she climbed back into bed, handing me one of the two glasses she was carrying which were full of freshly squeezed orange juice with just a soupçon of vodka and a half a scoop of vanilla ice cream added. Stirred, not shaken.

'Would you?'

'What a question,' she said. 'Shut up and deal.'

CHAPTER TEN

Friday morn, not too bright and early, say ten thirty or so, I started my workday by neatly typing up a bill for Bill (Jessop) which seemed appropriate somehow, then woke Don up with Lou Le Fou's revelations on how Linda was probably putting it to him. Then I obtained a cup of coffee from Mrs Morales and called Mr William Summers' answering machine one more time to leave a short but pithy message, viz., that if he was the owner of a navy Seville, license number so-and-so – as I well knew he was – his car had been observed the night before illegally leaving the scene of an accident and would he call Lieutenant Simon, at Hollywood West soonest, or else. Then I called Lieutenant Simon, 'Simple', he was known as with typical cop humor, although he was anything but, and after the usual exchange of insults, which is what passes for affection between men for some reason, I asked him if a William J. Summers phoned, would he kindly give him the run-around in a polite but scary fashion.

'Why?' Simple asked me.

'For a free meal in any Italian restaurant whose set menu is under five dollars ninety-five cents,' I said.

'No way, Vic,' Simple said adamantly, affecting to be deeply shocked. 'I can't play fast and loose with the law of our land, you know that. I am a lieutenant, after all.'

'Eight ninety-five,' I said.

'You got a deal, goombah,' he said. Would you believe he actually made me set a provisional date early the next week before he'd hang up?

I was applying myself to some overdue paperwork when I

received the phone call I was waiting or hoping for from Maryanne Forbes, news hound. Or in her case, bitch. I'd assumed she would be more than willing to discuss the subject matter of certain photographs with me, but she was not at all forthcoming.

'I'm only phoning because Connie, who is right here beside me eavesdropping shamelessly, nagged me into it,' said Miss Forbes. 'But I really don't think I've got anything to say to you but goodbye and thank you anyway.'

There were the sounds of a brief scuffle, then Miss C. Forbes said, 'She doesn't really mean it, Mr Whoever-you-are.' Another scuffle. 'I can't read your name because my dear sister just tore up the piece of paper I wrote it on.'

'She does too mean it,' said Miss M. Forbes.

'Now, now, you two,' I said. 'And the name is Daniel. V. Daniel. V. for Victor.'

'Not this time,' said Miss M. Forbes in her dulcet announcer's tones, hanging up on me. A few minutes later, when I was seriously considering writing out a check for $125 for a guy I knew called Slider, which sum I owed him for the use of his Dodge truck one weekend back in June when Benny and I were briefly but satisfactorily involved in the fruit business, Miss C. Forbes called back.

'Listen,' she said in a whisper, 'I, Connie Forbes, a person in my own right, co-rent-payer here, officially invite you over, and the sooner the better. Do you know where we are?'

I said I did, because the address was on Maryanne's invoice, and said I'd be there as soon as I could get there, which would be in about half an hour.

I left immediately and so, unfortunately, had to leave Slider's check for another day. It took me a few minutes over the half hour to get to the girls; they had a small, self-contained house on Grandview, a narrow, twisting road that was a continuation of Kirkwood, a road that ran downhill into Laurel Canyon, which ran from Sunset Boulevard north over the hills and then down into my Valley of Tears. I knew someone who lived on Kirkwood and gave him a honk as I drove by, but I didn't see any signs of life inside; he was probably out back in his studio, inhaling turpentine fumes or trimming brushes or whatever it is artists do all day.

The Forbes girls had done well for themselves. Their wooden A-frame house was set back from the road, surrounded by pines and laurels and the occasional giant cactus, the spiky, broad-leaved kind, not the kind that Mexicans traditionally doze under. The downstairs high wooden gate next to the two-car garage was locked; I buzzed, and after a minute Connie's voice said from somewhere behind the gate, 'Who is it, please?'

'Me,' I said.

'Me V. for Victor?'

'Right on,' I said. I opened my wallet and showed her my license over the top of the door. She unlocked, opened up, let me in, then locked up again with a padlock that looked brand new. She saw me notice it and said,

'Yeah, I know, the story of my life; too little, too late.'

I smiled down at her. It was a long way down, too; she couldn't have been five feet tall on stilts. Connie had dark hair cut extremely short in that style that looks good on someone as pretty as Mia Farrow and didn't look that bad on Connie, who had a tiny face that was prettier than interesting but not quite pretty enough to be pretty. She was barefoot and wearing a pair of bright green cut-offs and a halter top not much thicker than a Texan's string tie.

I followed her cut-offs up the winding wooden stairs, through a sliding glass door and into the house. No one else was in sight, not even a mouse.

'Where's your sister?' I asked Miss C. Forbes.

'In there, sulking,' she said, pointing to a closed door at

the far end of the front room. 'Don't worry, she'll put in an appearance sooner or later just to see what I'm up to, if for nothing else.'

'No animals?' I said, looking around.

'Too many,' she said. 'But no more pets, the coyotes got our last two cats. Or maybe it was the bloody raccoons. Or maybe our flea-infested squirrels itched them to death. It could even have been a wolf. Anyway, no more. Hey, listen, sorry, have a seat, you want a drink or something, you want to go up on the sun deck?'

'I'm fine here,' I said. 'But something non-alcoholic would be nice.'

She trotted off to the kitchen; I sat on a white canvas sofa and had a look around. The living room was large; on three sides sliding glass doors led out to a wooden balcony. As we were quite high up, the view was predictably striking, especially if you like seeing smog from above. There was an open fireplace, stacked with those kind of logs that are made from paper, midway between the arch that led to the kitchen and the door leading to the rest of the house, behind which Miss M. Forbes was sulking. The walls that weren't glass had been tongue-and-grooved and were hung with an assortment of artistic representations and souvenirs: a pencil drawing of a pair of gnarled hands; a ballet poster depicting the young Nijinski doing something highly unlikely, in Paris, long ago; an old pair of ballet shoes on a long, faded ribbon; an Indian blanket that was all geometric figures; a couple of amateurish oil paintings of what might have been Big Sur; and a menu from La Maison that someone had autographed in a scrawl across the bottom, but, from where I was, I couldn't make out who. The room also contained an expensive sound system, a huge TV, a VCR, and a collection of tapes, both musical and video.

Connie came back with two large, tinkling glasses, one of which she handed to me.

'Prune juice, Perrier, and a slice of lemon,' she said.

'Terrific,' I said. 'Just what I wanted. Now, Miss C. Forbes, tell me what happened here, and I'll tell you my end of it.'

'Look at this place,' she said, waving one hand around. 'The original little old lady from Dubuque could break in here with her eyes shut. Maybe it was her who broke in last week.'

'How'd she get in?'

She took me over to the sliding door we'd come in and showed me; there was a scratch on the aluminum jamb right opposite the penny-ante lock. The little old lady could have popped it with a medium-sized screwdriver and then just slid the door open.

'That's the problem with this kind of door,' I said. 'If you want to make it harder for her next time, you cut a length of dowel or a broom handle, if it'll fit, and lay it in the runner there on the ground where the door slides so that the door can't slide, and she has to break the whole door in. Of course, there's always one door you can't do that with or how do you get back in, but if you've got one real door, like at the back, use that one.'

'Tell me more,' said C. Forbes, looking up at me. 'Lay it on me, V. for Victor.'

'A large dog,' I said. 'Preferably one that can outfight its weight in coyotes, raccoons, squirrels, wolves, and little old ladies put together, unlike one sweetheart I used to know.'

'Don't think we haven't thought about it,' she said.

'Connie, if you say one word, I'll murder you!' her sister called from behind the closed door.

'Ignore her,' Connie whispered, waving one hand again frantically. 'Oops.' She adjusted her halter. I averted my eyes but took my time about it. 'She hates being ignored. She'll be out in a minute.'

'Do I detect a note of sibling rivalry?' I said.

'If that's what jealousy is, you sure do,' she said. 'Wait til you see her.'

'What, exactly, was taken,' I asked her, 'by the little old lady? You told me almost nothing on the phone.'

'What else can I say?' She sucked at a piece of ice for a bit. 'Maryanne thinks she might have lost some pictures and some jewelry and some loose change, but she's such a scatterbrain she's not even sure what day it is. Maybe the rest of the stuff like the TV and the hi-fi was too bulky to take.'

'You must be joking,' I said. 'If it was the old lady, all right, she could hardly have gone tottering out of here with a twenty-six-inch console TV, but we don't really think it was an old lady, do we? That is merely our little joke, and also it takes some of the scariness out of it. If it was your normal breaking-and-entering type, he could have stripped this place of everything, including the wallpaper, the rug and the kitchen cabinets, had it out in his half-ton and been long gone in about three minutes.'

'So why didn't he, smarty?' Connie said. 'Why didn't he mess the place up? What kept him, already? Come on, let's sit down, I'm getting a crick in my neck looking up all the time.'

I sat on the couch again; she perched on the armrest beside me. I manfully finished off the last of my prune juice.

'I can think of a couple of reasons,' I said. 'Say he didn't want stuff like the TV because he wasn't primarily after money or things easily converted to money in the first place. In the second place, say he was after something that he hoped wouldn't be noticed if it was taken, or even if it was, it was something of so little value that the cops wouldn't even bother trying to find out who did it. You said yourself the place wasn't even messed up, so what's in it for the cops? Not that they could have helped all that much even if you had lost a lot of stuff.'

'Why not?' Connie said, looking highly indignant. 'Surely

they'd at least try; I mean, they do occasionally catch crooks, don't they?'

'Miss Forbes,' I said, 'you get seventy, seventy-five thousand burglaries a year in this town, and that's not counting the thefts from cars or robbery or all the other crimes against property, just burglaries, and you also have, what, two or three hundred cops working burglary. You figure out what the odds are.'

'No, thank you,' she said.

'Also,' I said, 'if, say, five grand's worth of stuff is taken, they do make some effort, visit a couple of times, maybe a visit from a print man, maybe they'll circulate a description of the stolen property if any of it is unique or identifiable, but otherwise forget it. And that is what I think our perpetrator wants, for it all to be forgotten as soon as possible.'

'Connie, I warn you!' her sister called out from the other room.

'Oh stop being so stupid and get in here!' Connie called back. 'V. for Victor Daniel is not only gorgeous, he's just your size, and he's dying to meet you, he's had a crush on you for years! . . . Bet you that'll do it,' she whispered to me.

'I wouldn't say gorgeous,' I whispered back. 'I'd say rugged. Like the Marlboro man, but a snappier dresser.'

Connie giggled. Sure enough, Maryanne appeared almost immediately. Like her sister, she was wearing very little but skin, but as she had approximately twice as much of it, the effect was even more pleasantly disturbing. It's often been remarked that if you meet a movie or television performer in the flesh, so to speak, they always seem smaller than you expect. Maryanne was the exception to the rule; she was a big girl, five foot ten at least in her shapely bare feet. A few square inches of the rest of her shapely bareness was more or less covered by a pair of short white shorts and what looked like a man's handkerchief knotted behind her tanned back. I wondered if the knot needed retying by any chance; you know how girls are with knots. Her hair was silver blond and cut even shorter than her sister's.

Maryanne gave me a disdainful look from large, brown, bedroom eyes and then swept out to the kitchen; not so easy a task, sweeping, when you're almost naked.

'Her hair,' I whispered to Connie. 'It's supposed to look like Doris Day's.'

'That's when she's got her wig on, stupe,' Connie whispered back. I don't know if you've ever noticed, but it is quite pleasant, whispering back and forth to a pretty girl who isn't wearing very much. 'She always wears it in public except when she wants to pass unnoticed in the maddening crowd.' We listened to Maryanne make what seemed to be a lot of unnecessary noise out in the kitchen for a while, then Connie called to her, 'Maryanne, get your big butt in here, will you? Stop being a large pain.'

Maryanne came back in holding a glass of what looked like chocolate milk. She strode over to us, looked down at me contemptuously, and said in loud, clear tones, 'I refuse to answer anything on the grounds that it's none of your business.'

Did I mention Maryanne was a big girl? She was. She was also tanned, and she did not have a big butt. She was also gorgeously gorgeous. She had a sprinkle, the merest hint, of freckles across the bridge of her nose. She had a small scar showing up whitely against one brown knee. Is it possible for a girl to be wholesome and exotic at the same time? You better believe it. If you don't, visit Sweden sometime. Finland would do.

'It could be my business after all,' I said as matter of factly as I could manage. 'What happened to you happened to my friends. They are gentle, peaceable, animal-loving folks. Now they are frightened. Now they have locks on their locks. One of their dogs was beaten to death. Their tarantula Maria has stopped eating again; she hasn't been able to choke down even a medium-sized hamster for over a week now.'

Maryanne rolled her eyes scornfully.

'Aren't tarantulas vegetarians?'

'Well, a small banana, then,' I said. 'A peeled grape.'

Connie giggled again. Maryanne tightened her perfect mouth still further.

'And it's not true I've had a crush on you for years; my battered and worn old heart belongs to another.'

M. Forbes gave me what she thought was a withering look. I who have had withering looks from experts didn't even flinch one flinch.

'Please, Miss Forbes,' I said. 'Do I have to beg? Help me out, answer a few, simple questions. Anyway, Connie will tell me everything I want to know, won't you, ma'am?'

'And get it notarized,' Connie said. 'Both copies.'

'Oh, shut up,' her sister said. She turned slightly so I could get the full effect of her (perfect) profile, then she turned back to me, increased the wattage in her big brown orbs, and said earnestly,

'Don't you see, I'm not the only one involved?'

'No,' Connie muttered, 'there's also the chief of the jerks.'

'Shut up,' Maryanne said automatically. 'And he's not a jerk.'

'The way he treats you is jerklike,' her sister said. 'What does that make him?'

'All right, calm down, girls,' I said. I stood up to let Maryanne get a look at my profile; at full stretch, if I do say so myself, it is quite an impressive sight. How impressed she was I don't know, because all she said was, 'God, how could anyone afford to feed anything that big?' And anyway, being an actress, or sort of, she was obviously adept at hiding her true feelings.

'When did it happen, can you tell me that much?'

'The afternoon of Friday the thirteenth,' Connie said promptly. 'Wouldn't you know.' That was one day before the break-in out at Wade's.

'Obviously, you were both out.'

'Obviously,' Maryanne tossed in.

'Were you doing things you routinely do that time of day, like working or jogging or taking a class or health-clubbing, or were you just out by chance?'

'Is that important?' Maryanne wanted to know. She lifted one long leg, looked at it critically, then waggled it. If she was trying to distract me, she was doing a hell of a job. I looked her leg over just to be obliging but damned if I could see anything wrong with it.

'It could be,' I said, taking a stroll over to the fireplace. On the mantle, among various other photos and knick-knacks, was a picture of Maryanne, Connie and a third girl who looked like she was in the family, too. 'Another sister?'

'Yes,' Maryanne said shortly. 'If it's any of your business.'

'Ah, yes,' I said. 'Business. The reason I asked if you were out because you always were at that time was because it could mean your place was broken into by someone who knows you or at least by someone who lives around here and sees you leave every day.'

'Gee, maybe he really is a detective after all,' Maryanne said sarcastically to her sister. 'Why couldn't it have been someone who telephoned and got no answer so he knew there was no one home? Or a door-to-door salesman who didn't get an answer when he rang the doorbell?'

'I would have thought a door-to-door salesman would have taken more than a family snap or two and a little loose change,' I said mildly, 'seeing as how he certainly had a car. Anyway. Can you remind me again exactly what was taken?'

'No,' said Maryanne.

I was beginning to tire slightly of M. Forbes' obstructive

behavior, so I said to Connie, 'Miss Forbes, is there any way you can convince your sister this is not a remake of *Wuthering Heights*? I don't want to scare either of you, but I will if I have to.'

'It's not a remake of *The Thin Man* either,' Maryanne said unkindly. 'And you couldn't scare me if you tried.'

'Me you could scare,' said Connie. 'Except I'm already scared, which is why I called you over her dead body.'

'Try this,' I said. 'Someone's gone to considerable risk and trouble to break into two, count 'em, two, places so far, that we know, killing a wonderful pooch called Shusha while he was about it. Now, whoever did it either got what he wanted or he didn't. If he didn't, he may come back. My friends think they've already had a repeat call. You girls are sitting ducks up here; would you like another visit some dark night? Am I getting through to you, Miss Forbes the Larger?'

'You're through, you're through,' Connie said, reaching for a cigarette from the end table. Her sister pursed her (perfect) lips but didn't say anything.

'One other little matter,' I said. 'It seems clear that it all started here; someone broke in for a specific reason – to steal some photographs. Why, I don't know yet. Now, on the back of photographs there is commonly the name or the name and address or the company logo or whatever of the company that processed the film – a little free advertising, if you like. Wade always stamps his. So does a nature-study specialist I know. So we can assume without straining our brains too much that the perpetrator was thus led to Wade's, which by an unstartling noncoincidence was broken into the very next night. Now what I'm wondering, among other things, is there anyone else for our perpetrator to call on next? Is there someone else in any of the pictures that will have to be visited just in case you made up a few copies for them? How about Mummy? Dear old Aunt Charlotte?'

'Chief of the jerks?' said Connie.

'Oh, God,' said Maryanne. 'Anyone want a drink?'

'Me,' I said. 'Anything but prune.'

'Me, too,' Connie said.

'Dear sister,' Maryanne said sweetly, 'why don't you be an angel and get them for a change while this positively huge person and I get to dislike each other a little better?'

'For a change. I like that,' said Connie bitterly. 'I've only gotten them the last fifty hundred times.' She got up nonetheless and went out to the kitchen. After a moment I heard the blender whirring.

'Is that the problem?' I said to Maryanne. 'The someone else who is involved?'

Miss Forbes the Larger moved dangerously – for me, anyway – close to me. She smelled of lemon and vanilla. And some sort of tanning lotion.

'Mr Daniel,' she said. 'V. for Victor Daniel. I've thought about this. I've been doing nothing else but think about it since my dear sister told me you were on your way over here. And I do know how to think, I've been doing it quite successfully for years. I'm sorry for your friends and their dog, and I'm sorry for Connie, and I'm sorry for me, and I'm even a little sorry for you, as I believe you mean well, but I am not going to say one more word to you, nor is Connie. Nor will I ever see you again or talk to you again if I can help it, and believe me, I can. Period. End of story.'

'I'm sorry, too,' I said. 'I'm sorry I never met you back in Frobisher High School. The best-looking girl in my class was Becky Epstein, and she only came up to my knees. And the word was she wore a trainer bra until she was sixteen.'

I turned away and headed for the front door just as Connie came back in with three tall glasses on a tray.

'You're not leaving!' she said to me.

'Yeah,' I said. 'Your sister chucked me out. What am I missing?'

'Connie's V-6 special,' she said. 'Carrot juice, beet juice, celery juice, onion juice, tomato juice and black radish juice.'

'Darn!' I said.

CHAPTER ELEVEN

Was I getting anywhere, was the question I put to myself and the midday breezes as I maneuvered my way carefully down the hill, took a careful left on Laurel Canyon and headed carefully back to the Valley; behind the wheel, a Juan Manuel Fangio I wasn't. Was I getting anywhere except back to my office? The only answer I could come up with is best expressed by 'mayhap', meaning, 'You'll be lucky, pal,' an elegant, if slightly outmoded term I'd seen in a magazine somewhere, sometime, in an ad for some mayhap long-defunct ballroom which commenced, 'Date for dining? Mayhap the drama? Want to make a night of it before you call it a day?'

It was coming up to noon when I arrived back at my home away from home. The first thing I did after turning on the air conditioner was to give Lew Lewellen a call.

'He's at the office, sweetie,' Rose Lewellen told me. 'Want me to get him to call you when he gets back, which shouldn't be late, although with Lew you never know?'

'I would deeply appreciate it,' I said.

'Is it anything I could help you with?'

'Mayhap,' I said after a moment's reflection. 'Do you know The Chief?'

'Fairly well,' Mrs Lewellen said. 'He's worked on half a dozen pictures Lew was on.'

'He has a wife, does he not?'

'Does he ever,' said Mrs Lewellen. 'Gloria. An amazing woman. She's been in a wheelchair for years with something disastrous like multiple sclerosis, but you still see her all over town on this committee or that one.'

'Does he have a girlfriend?'

'Isn't it hot for this time of year?' Rose Lewellen said brightly.

'Scorching,' I said. 'Do you or Lew know him well enough to get him and me together somehow for a few minutes?'

There was a pause, then she said, 'I presume you want more from him than his autograph, because you'd better.'

'You presume correctly, ma'am,' I said. 'Very correctly.'

'Let me think,' she said. She thought. 'How about drinks by the pool this weekend, either Saturday or Sunday late afternoon? I know he's in town, and I know Lew can come up with some tall tale to get him over here even if he doesn't particularly want to come.'

'That would be swell,' I said. 'Thanks, Mrs Lew, you're an angel.'

'I wish I was a teenage angel like I was once,' she said. She sang a few lines of some song I didn't remember about being that very same thing. 'I'll get back to you when we finalize, all righty?'

'You said it,' I said. I thanked her again and hung up.

All righty. It is time to reveal that The Chief is not The Chief's real name. I'm not using his real name for two reasons: one good one, and one better one. The good one being that I promised I wouldn't, and the better one being I want to go on living for a while. I suppose there might be two or three people in the world deep in the Hindu Kush who have never seen a movie or read a newspaper or looked at the cover of a magazine, so they might not know who The Chief is, like they might not know that Mr Gable was 'King' and Mr Wayne 'Duke', but all the rest of you know him and know him well.

I was watching an early Western of his one night with Evonne, trying not to get onion-roll crumbs in her bed, when she observed, 'Do you know, he's the only major male movie star whose first name is longer than his last name?' I thought about Rock and John and Kirk and Burt and Frank and Omar and Cliff and then I told her to please pass me the whipped cream cheese. The Chief had a reputation as unblemished as Sandra Dee's cheeks, not an easy task in show biz, and owned more real estate than Roy Rogers, even, most of it in the Valley, my unbeloved, once-green Valley. Like Mr Rogers, he also owned (or owned most of) a TV station, the one that Maryanne Forbes worked for, a gold mine that spewed out a deathly mixture of ancient re-runs of Lucille Ball and *Leave It to Beaver* interspersed with pleas from TV evangelists for mucho dinero – otherwise known as the source of all evil. And I seemed to recall seeing The Chief's wife once on television, pitching for one of those white, middle-American religions like the Fifth Day Shakers or the United Church of Practically Everything.

There were, of course, several clues that led me to suspect The Chief and Miss Forbes the Larger were an item. One was Connie Forbes' repeated use of the phrase 'Chief of the jerks'. One was Rose Lewellen's abrupt change of subject when I asked her if The Chief had a girlfriend. And one was The Chief's autograph on a certain menu above a certain fireplace, which I'd noticed when I'd strolled over to said fireplace purportedly to have a look at the photo of the three Forbes sisters. So there. It also made sense, as it gave Maryanne reasons aplenty for keeping her (perfect) mouth shut. Unfortunately, there were the same good reasons for The Chief to do likewise, but you never know, it was possible he could tell me enough to help me without compromising either one of them. Maybe he was also a dog lover, like all correct-thinking, considerate and halfway intelligent people.

What he was or wasn't, I wouldn't be able to find out until we met, so I decided to apply myself to other business matters. Unluckily, I didn't have any other business on hand that

Friday, at least not until that evening. I did find a couple of items of interest in the mail which I took the liberty of filling in with Mr William J. Summers' name and address; one was a request for a salesman to call some evening to discuss the advantages of owning the new, twenty-volume *Encyclopedia of Knowledge* – No Home With Inquiring Children Should Be Without It – and the other was an application for a second mortgage on his home. Then I sat around for a while waiting for the phone to ring or for some wounded gunsel to stagger in through my front door and then expire on my almost-new carpet after uttering some cryptic phrases about the Fat Man and a fortune in diamonds.

Neither of these two possibilities occurred. I called Evonne, just for something to do, but she was out. I tried Mrs Summers, but she was out. I called Jim at the Two-Two-Two, and he'd disappeared somewhere after opening up, Lotus told me, and she didn't know when he'd be back. I called Mom, but she was sleeping, Gaye said.

What the hell, a guy can always eat, so I went for a late lunch at the Nus' Vietnamese take-away next door. They weren't really equipped to serve customers on the premises, but there was one table at the back for the family, and I was almost family, so Mrs Nu installed me there and fed me her best, which was not terrific as Vietnamese food goes, but which was good enough for the likes of me, the kind of gourmet who puts a mixture of hot sauce and soy sauce in everything, including the tea.

Then I went for a long walk around the neighborhood, something I often did when I had nothing else to do, which was often enough. True, a stroll around my neighborhood was perhaps not as picturesque as the quays of the Seine nor as exciting as the Casablanca casbah or the Kowloon market, but you've got to go with what you've got, so the neighborhood it was. And my 'turf', as the Limeys put it, was not completely devoid of interest. Mart 'n' Merry's health-food store had a whole window devoted to yeast. Mr Papanikolas, at the Arrow Liquor Mart, had a special on a brand of scotch called King William IV, which I'd never heard of, and probably no one in bonny Scotland had either. I took a long, lingering look at some airedale puppies in the window of Patty's Pets up on Victory and noticed that at the Swedenberg Cafeteria next door their lunchtime special was goulash with noodles.

I noticed that at the adult cinema in the next block they were holding over *The Devil in Miss Jones* (Plus!! *Choice Sophie*) for another week. I drooled in front of Clark's Classic Cars, which had three blue Bugattis lined up in a row in the showroom. I waved at Mr Lubinski, family jeweler, through his barred window, bought some staples from Mrs Martel across the street, passed a derelict going through the garbage pails in the alley beside the Corner Bar, heard a lot of sirens and then saw a fire being put out in the second story of an office building, saw some kids being hassled by a cop in a patrol car, watched some other kids hassling a bag-lady, saw a guy walking along talking to his handkerchief, and made an instinctive grab at a kid in a windbreaker who came tearing by me, eyes wild. I missed him. A minute later an out-of-breath, middle-aged man in a suit puffed his way up the sidewalk toward me, swearing.

'I missed him' I said. 'What did he swipe?'

'Thanks for fuck all,' the man said, giving me a look of hatred.

At the corner of Victory and Splendido an elderly lady was being lifted into an ambulance. It looked like she'd been hit crossing the street, as there was an old Chevy slewed sideways against the traffic, and a cop was talking to a frightened fat man who must have been the driver.

A dead cat was lying in the gutter at the corner of Splendido and Mason. There were still half a dozen abandoned vehicles in the block between Mason and Lexington. A dog barked at me on 17th. I barked back. He barked again. The going-out-of-business sale at Lou's Household 'n' Hardware was now going into its eleventh month, I estimated. A young, pretty, but completely spaced-out girl walking with a tall black man wanted to know if there was anything at all she could do for me. No, thank you, I said. A child in pigtails, far too young to be out on her own, was waiting to be taken across the street back on Victory.

'Cross me, mister?' she said. I obliged.

'Thank you,' she said.

'Any time, darling,' I said. I watched her till she turned into Fresh Foods.

On the way back to the office I dropped into Seconds, a combination junk/antique/second-hand furniture/used-book store, where I exchanged idle pleasantries with Len, whose establishment it was, bought two Regency romances for Mom, half a dozen mysteries for myself, and an ashtray shaped like a pair of lips for Evonne.

'Use your phone?' I said to Len after forking over a grand total of three dollars and fifty cents for my purchases.

'Why not?' he said. 'No one else is.'

This time Mrs Summers was in. I told her of my latest moves in the harass-hubby campaign, to which she responded with hoots of laughter. Hoots, not ripples, and unladylike ones at that. She told me she planned to leave her place around eight that evening, or maybe earlier if the babysitter got there early; I said please make it eight precisely and let us synchronize our watches, which we did. I also told her not to worry if she didn't spot me, I'd be around somewhere and wouldn't be late.

In fact, it was just after seven when I drove past her drive-way for the first time. By then I'd been back to the office to pick up the car, driven home, bathed the body battered, had a word with Mom, exchanged lovey-dovies over the phone with the apple of my eye, attired myself suitably, snacked on a baloney and cheese sandwich, quenched my thirst with two weak brandy and gingers, picked up an item or two from my bedroom closet, and driven over the hills to festive West Hollywood and Sylvia Summers' unbugged apartment. Given my unfortunate experience the last time I'd been in those parts, I strove not to look suspicious. I wondered how whoever it was who was keeping an eye on Mrs Summers had gotten away without being tabbed by the neighborhood watch.

When, on my second circuit, I finally did spot the snoop, all became clear. First of all, he wasn't parked on Mrs Summers' street, which was one-way; he'd tucked himself around the next corner which if she was driving she had to pass – and who in L A didn't drive? I figured he figured there wasn't much risk in not being able to keep an eye on the apartment itself, given that it was tiny and she had a daughter living with her, and given the present state of affairs or lack of them between her and her hubby, she wasn't likely to entertain men at home in the first place.

He would have no trouble spotting her if she passed by in someone else's car, he would think, because she wouldn't be hidden, as the snoop was sure he hadn't been spotted, which was true as far as it went. Also, he was innocently parked along with several other cars in front of a small neighborhood grocery; no doubt he'd come to some suitable arrangement with the owner, which explained why the local watch had left him alone, along with the fact that both he and his car, a dark-colored Ford a couple of years old, looked equally nondescript, although admittedly I only had a quick glimpse as I drove by. I did notice that he had both front windows open, not surprisingly, the temperature still being well up in the seventies.

I took one more circuit past Mrs Summers' and the grocery some half hour later and then decided to leave it at that; he was watching the traffic after all, and my car was far from being nondescript, as (1) it was a Nash Metropolitan, (2) it was a convertible, and (3) it was painted pink and blue. My Metropolitan, or Metro, or Met, the brainchild of one George Mason, has been unkindly compared to a host of things, including a pinball machine, a bathtub and a bumper car. I knew it had been repainted at one time because the 100,000 or so that were made and sold between 1954 and something like 1962 were all either black-, red-, yellow-, or turquoise-and-white. Anyway.

After my second circuit I parked up the street out of sight, let another quarter of an hour go by, then strolled down to the grocery. The snoop was still there. I idled away a few minutes inside, picked up some pepperoni sticks and a six-pack of Corona I could always use, then left and strolled back up the hill to my car. The snoop didn't even turn his head to check me out; he was opening a stick of gum and looking bored. I noticed that his car was backed up against a low cinderblock wall that was nonetheless too high to back over, so he would be easy to hem in with my car, but I didn't think I'd bother as I only had to keep him occupied for a minute or so when Mrs Summers came past, and also he might dent my fender, or worse, trying to get out. I might not have mentioned it, but Nash Metropolitans which sold for $1400 originally now frequently cost over ten grand.

I deposited my shopping in the trunk, then timed my return so it was eight o'clock exactly when I got back to Cal's Corner Groceries; I estimated Mrs Summers would be tootling past in about two minutes unless the babysitter was late, or unless Mrs Summers went back in to remind her not to let Deborah have more than four slices of pizza for supper or to stay up after nine-thirty, or to spray her hair again. I unzipped my lightweight jacket so the shoulder holster was just visible, walked up to the snoop, took out a real-this-time sheriff's deputy badge in its leatherette case that I borrowed once from a chap when he wasn't looking, gave the snoop a good look at it through the open car window on his, the driver's side, then said politely,

'Sheriff's Department. Would you get out for a minute, please sir?'

'What's it all about, Officer?' said the nondescript snoop.

'If you'll just hand me the car keys and step out a minute, sir,' I said.

He handed me the keys and got out, not at all worried, because what did he have to be worried about?

'Driver's license, please,' I said. He dug it out and passed it over. I took my time looking at it. It told me the nondescript snoop's name was Amos Arnstein, that he was born in 1940, and that his weight was 156 pounds. I already knew he was about five foot five, had brown hair and wore glasses.

'Look, what's going on?' said Amos the snoop, taking a quick look at the intersection behind him.

'Do you own this car, sir?'

'No, my company does.'

'Have you the ownership papers with you, by any chance?'

'Jesus, I don't know,' he said. 'Maybe they're in the glove compartment.'

At that moment, Mrs Summers drove up to the intersection behind us and stopped, as required, at the four-way stop sign; we both spotted her at the same moment. Amos was pretty good, but it was obvious to a trained observer like myself that inwardly he was jumping out of his nondescript cotton anklets.

'Perhaps you'd have a look for me,' I said.

'Listen, Officer,' he said, 'I think they're back at the office, all right? Now can I go? I'm late as it is.' He held his hand out for the keys and gave me his idea of a warm smile. I pretended to think it over.

'It's like this,' I said after a moment. 'The local neighborhood watch has reported you for suspicious behavior over a number of days, and I got the call to investigate, but I must say I haven't seen any suspicious behavior on your part, Mr Arnstein, maybe it was just some old lady imagining things; you know what they're like.'

'Yeah, yeah,' he said bitterly as he watched Mrs Summers disappear up the street.

'Is it true you've been parking here every night keeping track of who goes in and out of that apartment right across the street?'

'Shit,' said Amos. He got out his State of California investigator's license, which unsurprisingly looked a lot like mine, and thrust it at me.

'Ah,' I said. 'And who do you work for, Mr Arnstein?'

'Lindquist and Baily,' he said. 'Anything else?'

'Gee,' I said, 'I've never met a private eye before. On a case?'

'I was,' he said.

'Wow,' I said. 'Anything interesting?'

'Fascinating,' he said. Maybe I'd overdone the innocent act a trifle, because he gave me a suspicious look then asked if he could see my shield again.

'Of course,' I said, getting it out again. 'Gruber. Working out of South.'

'Guess you know a Lieutenant Pally down there?'

'Sure,' I said. 'Known him for years.'

'And Captain Marshall, head of Vice?'

'Are you kidding?' I said.

'Say hello from me, Amos Arnstein, when you see them, will you?'

'Sure will,' I said. It was dollars to jelly donuts that if I ever did run into Messrs Pally and Marshall it wouldn't be down at South Station, if they existed at all, because what Amos was being was clever, he was proving to his satisfaction with his trick questions that whoever or whatever I was I certainly didn't work out of South, but he wasn't being as clever as me, because that's what I wanted him to figure out. He would report to the guy who actually ran Lindquist and Baily, one Rex Tolly, whom I'd seen at a distance once but had never met, and Tolly would report to William Summers that someone had rousted one of his men, and it wouldn't take long for William J. to deduce that the masked harasser had struck again.

After another moment or two of unamiable backchat I let Amos go on his way, and I went on mine; I had a late-evening date with Evonne, a roast ham and a Scrabble board over at her place. She looked so pretty in her nightie and with her blond hair up that I let her get away with using the word sanguine, which everyone knows isn't a real word. Greater love.

CHAPTER TWELVE

The following morning I was back home cleaning up the apartment, as I had Mom to pick up the next day, when I received a welcome telephone call from Mrs Lew. It was on for that afternoon, she said, anytime after four would be fine.

'Should I bring my trunks?' I asked her. 'I've got a nifty new pair I picked up in Mexico recently. Flew down and back, you know.'

'You can if you want, sweetie,' she said, 'but we've got a cabin full of them here.'

I said I'd see her anon and went back to the cleaning. We'd talked Feeb into putting in new wall-to-wall carpets almost a year ago but the Goddamn things were still shedding, and high on the list of things my mother didn't care for were balls of shedded carpet. Me, I could take them or leave them, like the dirty venetian blinds in the kitchen, but I cleaned them too, like a good boy, including the high-up bits that Mom couldn't even see. Then I thought seriously about defrosting and cleaning the fridge, especially the vegetable bin; I didn't do it but I thought seriously. I did squirt some blue stuff in the toilet, then went shopping and did this and that and then betook myself over to the Two-Two-Two for some well-earned refreshment.

When I went in, Jim waved a hand in greeting, then gestured disgustedly with his head toward a gaggle of gays who had taken over one of the large sofas at the back. He had a fair crowd in but nothing that Lotus couldn't handle on her capable own, so after a healthy luncheon – two Coronas and a package of those fake bacon rind things – I said to him, 'James, get your hat.'

'Never wear one,' he said. He was pinning up the three winners of last week's 'How many words can you find?' competition.

'That illiterate meat-chopper, Bill, won again,' he said, referring to Bill the master butcher from over at Ralph's supermarket. 'At least he's one of us.'

'Well, get your hat symbolically,' I said, 'cause I'm taking you for a ride.'

'Should I make my will first?' he said. 'Or do you really mean a drive?'

'O K, drive,' I said. 'Let's go.'

'Lotus,' he called out. 'I'm off somewhere with Vic. If I'm not back in, what?'

'Hour, hour and a half,' I said.

'Two hours,' he said, 'call the Feds.'

And it was all of two hours, as the drive over the hills to the hospice took forty minutes because of the Saturday traffic, which was the same as the Friday and Thursday traffic, to say nothing of Wednesdays' – a crawling log jam of citizenry enjoying its right to go nowhere necessary slowly in expensive machinery. Then I left Jim inside for a good half hour while I waited in the car like the chicken I was, and then we had the drive back. There was plenty of chatter on the way but, as it had been with Richard, hardly a word on the return trip. At one stage I did say something redundant to Jim on the lines of 'Enjoy the literature?' but that was about all.

When I dropped him off at the Two-Two-Two, he did say, 'Now what, Brains?'

'Courage, mon ami,' I said. 'I'm working on it.'

When I left him he was standing in front of his estaminet looking up at the neon sign. He told me once the original owner had told him the middle 'Two' in the name was a mistake, it was supposed to have been 'To', as in Two (o'clock) to Two (o'clock). Two to Two, the hours of business. Then again he told me once the original owner had told him the name stood for the three twos he'd held once in a poker game that had helped him to buy the place. I always thought the first explanation the most likely to succeed as the only time I remembered holding three twos in a poker game I'd been beaten by everyone else in the room, plus a couple of guys out in the hall.

However it was, I left the shaken James to his thoughts, returned home, started one of my new books, the hero of which was a muscle-bound jogging freak running a one-man detective agency in Bean Town, of all unlikely places, looked critically at my Mexican swimwear, decided against it, then dressed in a manner I believed appropriate for a poolside party at the Lewellens' – almost spotless tan cords, white loafers, dark blue sleeveless shirt, white summerweight jacket, and shades. No gun. No sheriff's badge. No fedora. A splash of Eau Sauvage Extreme (Eau de Toilette Concentrée) just in case. Then, off went the Hulk to face The Chief.

I had to stop by the office briefly to pick up a letter I'd forgotten to bring home with me the day before; it was tucked away in the safe somewhere, or at least I hoped it was still there. I hadn't seen it for over two years or used it for almost three. But it was there all right.

I arrived at the Lewellens' a fashionable three quarters of an hour late, identified myself over the intercom at the barred front gates, as before, drove up and parked, as before, only this time between a silver-gray Porsche and a Merc 220, the little one with the wooden fascia, and was let in the door by the same pretty Mexican girl.

'Qué tal?' I said to her casually, showing off my command of LA's second most widely used language and probably soon to be the first, the way things were going. That's leaving out movie-ese, of course, a language all of its own.

'Muy bien,' she said, giving me a nice smile. She led me

through the house to the open french windows that overlooked the pool area. 'Están todos allá,' she said. 'Que pase una
buena tarde.'

'Grácias,' I said and stepped out from the cool of the house
into the July heat and headed down the flagstoned path towards the inviting-looking pool. I wasn't the first to show, I
was pleased to see; there were people sitting at two of the
garden tables at poolside and a couple more already in the
water. I couldn't see the host, but Mrs Lewellen, in a one-
piece swimsuit and beach robe, was talking to a second pretty
Mexican señorita behind the portable bar who was mixing
up a blenderful of something, so I wandered over to her.

'What's cooking?' I said.

'Oh, hello, you. Some more of Conchita's wonderful margaritas,' Mrs Lew said. 'Want one?'

'Maybe later,' I said. 'I wouldn't say no to a beer, just to
have something to do with my hands.'

Conchita got me a bottle of Heineken from the ice tub,
opened it up and poured it out for me in a tall, green glass.

'Is he here?' I asked Mrs Lew as we turned away from the
bar.

'He's here,' she said, taking a sip of her margarita. 'God,
that's good sometimes. But he's inside with Lew, and they'll
be a while. Come on, I'll introduce you to the rest of the
gang.'

I followed her back toward the tables where without any
fuss she did introduce me to the rest of the gang. Some gang.
At the first table was Mr James Coburn, who gave me a wide
smile and said, 'Hi, pal. Hope you play pool. I've been waiting
for a little action.'

'I've ripped a few felts in my time,' I said as casually as I
could. After Mr Coburn came Miss Tuesday Weld, who gave
me a little smile and said almost shyly,

'Hello.'

'Isn't it,' I riposted foolishly. Well, what would you say if you ever came face to face with one of your dream girls, how clever would you be if Sandra Dee knocked at your back door and asked if she could please borrow a cup of sugar? Oh, yes, it's easy to practice your bon mots and witty repartee in the dirty mirror, but you try it on a July afternoon by the Lewellens' pool. Then Mrs Lew introduced me to the third person at the table, an ordinary-looking fellow in a pair of faded old cut-offs whose name I didn't catch, but as Mrs Lew introduced him as a failed scribbler who was just there for the free booze, I assumed he'd won a couple of Oscars at least.

We moved on to the next table where Mork of *Mork and Mindy* looked up at me, did a take at my size, did another one, popped his eyes and asked me if I'd ever played line-backer for the Denver Broncos.

'Are you kidding?' I said incredulously. 'You ever been to Denver?'

'Once,' Mork said. 'But it was closed.'

The lady sitting beside him groaned. I looked at her, then I looked again, who wouldn't? Her dark glasses and picture hat didn't fool me, I knew Miss Joan Collins when I saw her, even in a silver lamé bikini. Then I met the Adonis sitting on the other side of Miss Collins, who offered me a 'How you doin'?' and an amiable wave, then I said hello to the Lewellens' boy Stephen who politely stood up to shake hands. His mother asked him to please take care of me for the nonce, show me where the swimming stuff was if I wanted it and lead me back to the bar from time to time in case I forgot where it was.

'Sure,' he said, grinning at his mom.

I sank into the empty seat beside him. I wished my gang, which consisted (and still does) mainly of bartenders, inside men, petermen, con artists, cops and ex-cops, waitresses with tired smiles and feet, shopkeepers, Vietnamese illegals and bowling alley operators, could see me hanging out there so coolly with the Lewellens' gang. I'd rarely met any really famous people, in fact, I'd only known one at all well, our lives didn't mesh, our routes didn't cross, as they tended to have a lot more money than I did, to put it mildly, so they seldom dropped in to joints like Moe's and Fred's Deli and the Corner Bar and Mrs Morales' Taco-Burger. And their haunts, where you give the valet parker what I pay for a whole meal, weren't exactly on my normal rounds.

But Stephen wasn't surprised to see me in that fancy company, he knew I babysat his pop occasionally and once had even mentioned to me that he approved highly of the whole idea. So we chatted and watched the swimmers, and I tried to think up something devastatingly perceptive and witty to say to Miss Weld with a conspicuous lack of success, so I decided to play hard to get and let her make the approaches. Instead it was Mr Coburn who came ambling over after a while. He bestowed on me another of his famous grins and said, 'If you're not getting wet, care to shoot some pool, Fast Eddie?'

'Gee,' I said, 'I'm not sure I can remember all the rules. However, if you show me how to hold that long wooden thing, whatever it's called, I'll try and give you a game.'

I asked Stephen to tell his mother I'd be in the poolroom getting hustled if she needed me, then followed Mr Coburn back up the path and into the house.

The poolroom was down the hall past Lew's den; Mr Coburn, or 'Jim' I might use now without trying to claim any false friendship, as that is what I was calling him by then at his insistence, Jim not only knew where it was but had no trouble finding where the overhead light switched on and where the chalk was. The table was a beauty, an old Brunswick with elaborately carved legs and wood surround. Jim seemed to know how to rack the balls, too, and he also managed to unzip his own personal cue's leather case without too many problems and also managed to screw the two halves of the cue together without pinching his fingers.

'Just happened to have it along,' he said, lying through his teeth, and then making a few practice shots in the air.

'If I'd only known,' I said, fighting back as best I could. 'Mine's back at the maker's getting an extra half-ounce of weight put in the butt.'

We dragged for break; I won, broke, ran a few, then he ran a few.

'Lew ever tell you about the time some one-armed cowboy tried to hustle him?' he said after a while.

'Forget about "tried",' I said, cutting the eight-ball neatly into the side pocket to take the first game. 'I was there. Lefty took him eight games in a row as I recall and without even using the rest.'

Jim shot a fair stick, and I shot a fair stick from time to time, and we were three games all when Stephen came in to say his father wouldn't mind a word with me in the den whenever I liked. I would liked more to have shot a few more games with Jim and mayhap to have been asked casually when we were done why not drop by his place, say Thursday, if I had nothing on, and we could shoot a few frames and tell a few lies and put away a couple of Dos Equis, and if it wasn't out of my way maybe I wouldn't mind picking up Tuesday and bringing her, she played nine-ball like you wouldn't believe.

Well, you don't always get what you want, someone said once all too truthfully. I think it was Wrong Way Corrigan. I never did get to drop by Jim's place, say Thursday, nor did I ever get to watch Miss Weld shoot nine-ball. Next time around, maybe. Instead, I thanked Jim for the action, suggested he work a little more on his follow-shots, and went up the hall and into the den.

The Chief was in Lew's chair behind the desk, his back to the room, a glass in one hand, and Lew was pacing up and down waving his arms. He stopped when I went in and said, 'Chief, this here is the guy I was telling you about, his name is Vic, and he's OK.'

The Chief didn't say anything, nor did he move.

'All right, I'll leave you to it,' Lew said, moving to the door. 'Holler if you need help.' He departed, closing the door behind him. I sat down in the director's chair opposite The Chief. After a minute he swiveled around, looked at me and said:

'Prove it.'

'Prove what?'

'What Lew said.'

I had to think for a minute. Then I got out my license and tossed it on the desk.

'This'll prove I'm Vic,' I said. Then I got out the envelope I'd taken from the safe earlier and tossed that over to him. 'And that'll prove I'm OK.'

He looked over the license, then opened up the envelope and read the letter inside. It was a letter of thanks from the one famous person I did know who I mentioned briefly earlier, an opera singer who was the ex-girlfriend of the ex-governor of one of the less-populated mid-west states, one of those people who are so famous they only have one name. I do not want to make myself redden up to my big ears by quoting the whole communiqué, but it did mention in passing that I had been brave, smart, discreet, the opposite of greedy, and altogether amazing, in case anyone ever wanted to know. But that's another story, as Pagliacci used to say.

'Further testimonials on request of same,' I said as he was reading. When he had finished, he put the letter back in the envelope, then passed it and my investigator's license back to me. He didn't seem greatly impressed, in fact, he didn't seem greatly anything; he didn't even look much like I thought The Chief should look. What he looked like was a smallish, slightly built, tired, middle-aged man with a lined face and thinning hair. Now 'Jim' Coburn, he looked exactly like what I thought he should look like. However, I did not doubt for one minute that as soon as somebody shouted 'Roll 'em!' there The Chief I was expecting would be, not only as big as life but bigger. That afternoon he was wearing a white polo shirt with an alligator on it. The belt of his white slacks had a gold buckle. His suede sneakers must have set him back a hundred bucks each, not counting the laces.

'Talk on, Vic,' he said.

I talked. I talked about Cissy, Wade, Willy, Shusha and the porno king of 4420 Davenport. I talked about Maryanne and Connie Forbes. I said Miss Forbes the Larger had only told me one thing – never to darken her sliding door again. I told him of the signed menu, Mrs Lew's change of subject, and Connie's bitchy hints.

'If I'm wrong, I'll say adiós,' I said. 'But if I am wrong, would you be here talking to me? Well, listening to me, anyway.'

'Talk on, Vic,' he said.

'How about a question?' I said. 'If you could help me without hurting anyone or risking anything, would you? By the way, do you like dogs?'

'Not much,' he said.

I waited for a moment. When he didn't contribute anything else, I said, 'Can you at least tell me this, were the pictures involved taken of you and Miss Forbes?'

'No,' he said after another long pause; it has to be said that The Chief wasn't exactly a chatterbox.

'No?' That shook me up a bit.

'No.'

'What the hell were they of, if I may ask?'

'Me,' he said.

'Just you?'

'Just me.'

'You in compromising situations?'

He almost smiled. 'No.'

'But if they weren't pictures of you in compromising situations, who would want them?'

'You tell me,' he said. 'You're the detective.'

'I'm beginning to wonder,' I said. I pondered briefly. 'They couldn't be accidentally compromising, I mean for example an innocent picture of you eating spaghetti all by yourself somewhere, only you were supposed to be somewhere else when the picture was taken?'

'No,' he said.

'Well, I'll be,' I said. 'There goes that theory, that someone wanted the pictures to try and blackmail you, and there goes my other theory, too, that you wanted them to try and prevent it.'

'There's no proof of nothing,' he said. 'Not in those pictures.'

'Not even enough to, say, threaten to talk to your wife about?'

'She knows,' he said. 'They always know.' He finished off his drink. 'And that's it, Vic.' He got up and walked to the door. 'I won't be seeing you around. I won't be talking to you on the phone, either. Nothing personal.'

'I hope not,' I said.

'Oh.' He reached into a back pocket and took out a small envelope. 'Here.' He tossed it in my general direction; it landed on the floor between us. By the time I'd picked it up, he was gone. I opened it just enough to see what was inside – correct, the photographs in question, four of them, extra copies Maryanne must have sent him. Or so I hoped; they could have been publicity shots from his latest epic.

CHAPTER THIRTEEN

To satisfy all you sensation-seekers and gossipmongers, did I stay and dally with Miss Weld in the shallow end of the pool?

I did not.

Did Miss Collins slip me her private telephone number hastily scrawled in a book of matches?

She did not.

Did Mork and I convulse the assembly by improvising a hysterically funny routine on the high board?

We did not.

Did the 'failed' scribbler take me aside and tell me he was in the middle of a script for 20th Century which was about this aging gumshoe and he was prepared to offer me a grand a week for a little help in getting the background and all the technical stuff right?

Need I answer?

I know when I'm out of my league, so after another beer I said a general goodbye, thanked my hosts, and departed. The pretty maid saw me to la puerta. She watched until I'd driven to the front gates, pressed something to make them open, then closed them behind me. I drove slowly back to the low-rent side of town, metaphorically clutching the packet of pictures to my swelling bosom.

As soon as I got home, I opened the envelope and spread the contents in front of me on the cocktail table. Four color snapshots. One was a long-distance candid snap of The Chief waving from the top of one of those movable staircases that us world travellers go up to get into airplanes. One was a middle-distance candid snap of The Chief getting into a stretch limo outside a hotel. The third was an underlit candid close-up of The Chief, in profile, taken while he was gazing out of a window. And the fourth was an overlit candid close-up of The Chief making a mildly funny face.

And that was it. There were no overlooked pictures still in the envelope. There was no writing on the back of any of them. As far as I could see, The Chief was dead right – the pictures were proof of absolutely nothing. But, hell, there had to be something, or else why all the fuss?

I got out of my party duds and into my thinking clothes. I manufactured a tall brandy and ginger, the thinking man's drink. I turned on the air conditioner, then I looked at all the pictures again, one at a time, thoroughly. I picked up a few details I hadn't noticed the first time around. For example, in the first picture the plane was Air-Cal, and the stewardess standing behind The Chief had blond hair. In the second one a few pedestrians could be made out goggling at the celebrity. In the third one it was dark in the room but bright sunshine outside. In the fourth one, I made out part of a picture on the wall behind The Chief's head. It was also possible he had had a drink or two. Big deal.

Now what, Watson? What did I actually know about the damn pictures anyway? I knew they had been taken by Mary-anne Forbes, news hound. I surmised the interiors were a hotel room somewhere because the backgrounds looked hotel-like, and also the picture on the wall, or what I could see of it, was typical hotel bad taste – an idealized desert scene that seemed to be silkscreened rather than painted. Maybe a blow-up would reveal if it was screwed to the wall, like they do in hotels with pictures and everything else.

Furthermore, I surmised Maryanne had taken the two ex-terior shots – the one of the limo and the one of the plane – disguised as just another tourist, passing wigless and unnoticed in the throng, snapping away like everyone else from a safe distance, amassing a few precious keepsakes and enjoying the private joke intensely.

Did all that help me? Not a lot. The only thing I could think of was what if The Chief had lied to me, what if some of these snaps *were* innocently compromising because The Chief was somewhere other than where he was supposed to be at a time when he was supposed to be somewhere else? And it was all very well for The Chief to say his wife already knew about his mad passion. Even if she did – and she probably did, for like he said, wives always do – who else knew his wife knew? So maybe blackmail was a possibility after all.

What I needed was another drink. I made myself another drink and opened up a can of smoked almonds. I wasn't thinking clearly. Someone broke into Maryanne's house because he knew she had taken the photos. Therefore, she must have been recognizable when she took them. Therefore, she hadn't been in disguise, if *not* wearing a disguise can be called being in one. Therefore, she was being her public, large, beautiful, bewigged, snippy self. Therefore, she was somewhere officially, or overtly, anyway. Could I find out where she and The Chief had been recently, at the same time, together but not together? Of course I could, I was a skilled investigator after all.

HIX NIX STIX PIX
WALL STREET TAKES A DIVE

If these two famous headlines mean little to you, they both came from the so-called bible of show biz, *Variety*. It had to have a West Coast bureau, so I checked in the phone book, and there it was. Half an hour later a helpful, bespectacled girl at *Variety*'s front desk directed me to a pile of copies that went back to the start of July and informed me that if I wanted to go further back, merely to whistle.

Variety, as everyone knows, contains partly business and

financial reports and partly reviews of movies, the theater, club acts, and so on, but it also includes its share of gossip and chit-chat, including the movements of luminaries from the entertainment business between LA, New York, and Vegas. It also includes a lot of ads for out-of-work performers and a lot of ads for performers actually in work for a blessed change saying, come and see me while you can.

I settled myself in a corner, started with the edition of five days ago and worked back. I found what I was looking for in the 28 June number. MAJESTIC REBOOKS CHIEF TO MC MS TELETHON, it said, MS being multiple sclerosis and the Majestic a hotel, Caesar's Palace's main rival in the appalling-taste stakes. In the same edition I found Maryanne's name in a list of minor celebrities due to be in Vegas at the same time for the opening of a new local TV station.

And did all that help me?

Not a lot.

I replaced the copies neatly, thanked the girl, left, and made my way to Wade's, stopping for some gas and to have the oil checked at a Shell station en route.

'Nice wheels,' the attendant said as he was shifting the dirt around on my windshield, hoping no doubt to sweet talk me into tipping him. 'One of your classics, I guess.' I sidestepped his transparent ploy by paying with a credit card.

At Wade's, he and Suze were the only ones home apart from the animal life; they were in the garage doing something that seemed to involve a lot of giggling and not much working. I hung around while he made up two 8 × 10 enlargements of each of the four photos, then I sat down at his glass-topped table, turned on the overhead lamp, borrowed his collapsible magnifying gadget, and looked at them all again, thoroughly.

And did that help me?

Wade had brought out all the detail he could without the

use of a whole computerized set-up; I could see that the desert scene on the wall was indeed screwed on with little brass things top and bottom, so it was a hotel room somewhere, almost certainly somewhere in Las Vegas. That was sure pinning it down. A few of the faces in the background of the airport scene and the street scene were more or less recognizable if you knew who the people were. Or cared. I couldn't make out the license number on the limo, not that it would help if I could. It was obvious I was missing something, probably a few more working brain cells, because I wasn't getting anywhere with what I had, so I said, 'So long, keep your powder dry,' to the kids, wrestled briefly on the floor with Rags, shooed one of the felines off the top of my car, and wended my way back to my part of town and the Corner Bar, where for some mystical reason I've done much of my most productive thinking.

I was ensconced at the back by the pinball machine – a Gottlieb's Genesis – deep into my second brandy and ginger when I recalled something the porno king of 4420 Davenport had asked me; viz, was I barking up the wrong nature trail? All right, let us suppose I had been barking up the wrong trail, not for the first time, I am human despite considerable evidence to the contrary. Let us suppose the whole affair had nothing at all directly to do with The Chief and Maryanne. Let us suppose The Chief was where he was supposed to be when he was supposed to be. That made sense, because if he was where he wasn't supposed to be, what was he doing openly waving from plane doors and hopping publicly into stretch limos? Answer me that if you can. So at least one of the photos must be damaging to someone else, call him X, call him Ahab, call him what you will.

Of the four pictures, the two interiors I excluded, as they didn't show anyone else but my talkative pal The Chief. That left the limo and the plane. I got the pictures out again and moved over to the bar where there was marginally more light. Taking the two photos together, there were ten recognizable people, not counting The Chief but including the stewardess, why not? Always include stewardesses is my motto, or one of them anyway.

Working assumption – one of those ten was X. One of those ten was either sufficiently violent himself (or herself, although it was unlikely) to break and enter (twice) and to slaughter doggies (once), or to sublet the job. This X was also sufficiently worried to have done, or to have had done for him, the above. So X = male, worried and violent. Rule out the pretty blond stewie and the three other women in the photos. That left six males. Rule out the male halfway up the airplane steps, as he looked about eight. Rule out the driver of the cab right behind the limo, because although he was a cabby and thus worried and violent by definition, a cabby is only a cabby after all.

That left four.

Rule out the male at the bottom of the steps, as he was waving vigorously at the camera, was wearing Bermuda shorts and a baseball cap, had a camera dangling from his neck and a large stuffed animal under one arm. In other words, he wasn't exactly hiding from the limelight.

That left three possibles.

I was going to bet myself a drink that it was the guy whose face could just be seen looking back over the stewie's shoulder but then I remembered that particular snap was a long shot taken from above, probably from some kind of observation roof, and was it likely anyone could recognize Maryanne Forbes from such a distance? No, it was not. So I bet myself a drink it was one of the other two types, either the pedestrian with his face partly averted whose upper half could be seen behind the limo, or the passenger whose face could clearly be seen looking out of the cab's rear window. Neither one would have had any trouble recognizing the gorgeous photographer, who couldn't have been more than ten feet away at the time.

And did all that help? Mayhap it would.

It was Saturday afternoon, not a day on which I usually worked unless it was something pressing, but I didn't want to get a load on that early, because what would that leave me to do later on. Evonne had her once-every-two-weeks bridge party, get-together and gossip-mart with some girlfriends that evening, and I would be on my own. And, besides, my brother wouldn't be downtown at Records that afternoon because he never worked weekends, so I wouldn't have to run into him and either tell him a lot of lies or drag him into it or listen to him moaning about the cost of braces for his kids' teeth.

Thus I polished off my drink and downtown via the Golden State Freeway I went, blithe in spirit despite the murderous traffic — I was making progress at last. For once I found a place to park right in front of the old graystone mausoleum that housed Records, among other departments, went in, identified myself and finally got grudging permission to go downstairs to the basement. There, in a quiet, modernized, clean, smokeless room I found Sneezy, aka Sid Meyers, hard at it at his computer terminal. Sid was my brother's boss, although officially they were of the same rank — a miserable, put-upon little geezer who always worked weekends for the overtime as he was afflicted with one of the world's most addictive and expensive habits: women. He was also a genius at his job and had a phenomenal memory for everything but alimony payments and whose round it was.

'Sneezy,' I said, 'I got one for you.'

'Go away,' he said without looking up. 'I'm busy.'

'Oh, come on,' I said. 'I got one of those gadgets too. I bet you're playing Pac-Man or something.'

'I'm writing a Goddamned program,' he said crossly. 'Or at least I was until you came along uninvited, unasked, and illegally.'

'Sneezy,' I said, holding the photo of the limo in front of his screen and pointing to the pedestrian, 'is that anybody?'

He gave it a quick glance.

'Joe Blow,' he said. 'Like I wish you would.'

'How about the guy in the cab?'

'Joe Blow the Second,' he said.

'You sure?'

He gave me a frosty look. 'Does Ronald Reagan use "Miss Clairol"?'

'Shit,' I said. 'Well, thanks anyhow.'

'Don't forget to close the door behind you,' he said. 'It sticks sometimes.'

I was at the door when he said, 'That cabby.'

'Yeah?'

'Give us another look.' I went back and gave him one.

'It could be,' he said after a minute. 'Those shades he's wearing don't help. But if it is, what the hell's he doing driving a cab?'

'It could be who, Sneezy?'

He sighed. 'Don't you ever watch television? If it's who I think it is, there was a big stink a while back – he was caught having a party with six girls, none of them over twelve. Then just the other day, some Amazon had a microphone in his face and was asking him what the first thing he was going to do now that he was out. Know what he said?'

'No, but I know what I'd do the first thing,' I said.

'"Buy my dear mother some flowers" is what he said.' Sneezy got up, went over to the terminal on my brother's desk so he wouldn't have to interrupt the program he was working on, typed in the appropriate code, got the go-ahead, then entered a name. The green screen beeped once, then began filling with line after line of particulars. When it stopped, he switched on the printer, and that hummed away busily for a moment. Then he tore the printed matter off the roll along its little perforations, thrust it at me and started to go back to what he had been doing.

'No photo?' I said.

He gave me a look of loathing, went back to my brother's desk, did something, entered something, pressed something, and another minute later peeled a picture off a thick metal cylinder as soon as it had stopped turning, and thrust that at me.

I said, 'Thanks, Sneezy, I owe you one,' and headed smartly for the exit.

'You owe me about twenty,' he was muttering when I carefully closed the door behind me.

Upstairs there was a bench opposite the reception desk on which I sat and on which I perused the following:

'Marco Bellman, aka Marty, Mart, Mort. B. 16 Aug. 1944, Topeka, KA. M. June L. F. Matthew. PA 445 S. King St, Topeka, KA. LKA 18 Mirabelle Rd, Van Nuys, CA ... more ... Bus add: MultiCo, 188 Slauson Ave, LA.

'8 juvs (See Juv. Div., Code A-A ONLY). 16 Sept. 1964–23 Sep. 1966, Kan. Pen. Inst., 4 cts car theft + 1 assault. 4 Jan. 1969–5 Sept. 1970, Kan. Pen. Inst., arson. Topeka Cr. Ct: 17 Nov. 1970: assault w dw – acq. Same: 11 Mar. 1972: same – acq. San Diego Cr. Ct: 29 Mar. 1979: same – acq. Same: 2 Nov. 1979: LS – acq. Same: 9 Apr. 1984: con. CM – 3–5 yrs. Fresno Fed. Pris. St: paroled custody LAParD, 24 Mar. 1986. KA: Donald O'Keefe (d). Ellen Marie, no KA. Jackson M. Pink, aka Pinky, Fresno Fed. MORE FBI/447/95/LL. Close.'

Translating roughly, one Marco Bellman, also known as this, that, and the other, born back East in the sticks somewhere, had eight convictions while a juvenile, for details of which one needed a special code, as juvenile records are kept under a separate file and are supposed to remain secret. When he got to be a big boy, Marco served two years for driving cars that didn't belong to him and for also assaulting some poor citizen who chanced along; then he did eight months for arson; then he was tried twice more for assault and once, after he'd moved out West, for loan sharking, but acquitted all three times; then Marco was convicted of corrupting minors – and I don't mean tin – obtaining parole after serving three years of his five-to-seven-year sentence. Finally, of his three known accomplices, one was dead, one was still in the pen, and the address of the third, Ellen, wasn't known. Oh – more information was on file with the FBI.

Hello! I think I must have said it out loud, because I received a suspicious look from the lady who was sitting at the far end of the bench from me, eating something vaguely cheesy from a paper bag. I gave the lady a bright smile and said it again.

'Hello!'

'Beat it, or I'll call a cop,' the lady said.

I beat it.

I don't know how well you are up on the finer details of the California parole system, or any other parole system for that matter. It is, of course, a system whereby the authorities release certain malefactors from prison before they have served all their time. This leaves badly needed cots in which to put other malefactors. Parole is also supposed to be a reward for good behavior while in prison, which might seem fair enough except that good behavior in the clink is no guarantee of good behavior the second the con gets out. So, to encourage good behavior afterwards, the parolee has several courses of action he must follow, and a great many more he mustn't. He must report regularly and punctually to his (or her) parole officer. He must endeavor to find and keep suitable – needless to say, honest – employment. He is not supposed to borrow money from a legal lending source of same. He is not supposed to hide the fact that he is a felon on legal forms, if asked – on passport applications and the like. He must not change his address without the knowledge and consent of his parole officer. He must not keep bad company. He must not be drunk in a public place. Obviously, he must not commit another crime while out on parole, not even a misdemeanor, or he goes back to the can to serve out the rest of his sentence, and in the case of Marco Bellman, this would mean two more long, long years. And years are long when you are inside somewhere smelly and noisy that you can't get out of, where girls are but a hazy dream or a *Playboy* center-fold, and friendly estaminets are but a distant memory as are seasons, more or less, and mothers and beaches and south winds and sailboats and neon signs that flash on and off saying 'Two-Two-Two' or 'Corner Bar' or 'The Three Jacks'. Or even simply 'Eats'.

There is, of course, one more thing that penal authorities do not like you doing if you are out on parole, and that is what Marco must have done – cross a state line, because Los Angeles and Las Vegas are in different states, one being in the State of California and the other in the State of Nevada.

Which tidbit of basic geography did look like being a big help to me. So, kids, don't goof off in school. You never know.

CHAPTER FOURTEEN

Las Vegas, Nevada, has to be seen to be disbelieved.

The flight from the airport in Burbank got me there just after nine that evening – look at me, flying again, and so soon after the last time. But I couldn't put it off because the afternoon of the following day, Sunday, I was due to pick up Mom from Gaye and Tony's and take her for my three-week turn. And I did not want to ask them to keep her another day or so because they'd already obliged me that way twice that year, and I felt it a bit pushy to ask again. So I had decided to take my leave from Dave's Corner Bar and get moving.

First, home. Change. Pack an overnight bag. Remember to put in my Canon and some film, plus a copy of the limo photo blow-up. Check the available flights. Call my darling.

'Which would you rather do tonight,' I asked her, 'spend an unforgettable night with me in the fun capital of the Western world, Las Vegas, in a first-class hotel, naturally – on me, naturally – have a flutter at the tables, take in a show, go dancing under starry skies, or go down in three-no-trumps while nibbling on diet Nabiscos, sipping low-cal iced tea and pretending to have a good time without men around?'

'You sure give a girl some pretty tough choices,' she said. 'Could you run it through again for me?'

I ran it through again – the luxurious hotel, the discriminating cuisine, the thrill of a big win at roulette, then dancing til dawn on a moonlit patio with old Tall, Dark, and Hands, as that twerp Sara had once put it – or the pallid alternative of a night in with the girls eating rabbit food and taking apart all their other girlfriends who weren't there.

'First,' said my darling sweetly, perhaps a touch over-sweetly, 'we don't nibble rabbit food, we eat our asses off. Second, we drink our asses off, too. Third, hard as it may be for you to believe, we usually have more fun without men than with them. Fourth, you're a terrible dancer.'

'And fifth, you're not coming,' I said. 'I get the picture. I wonder where I went wrong.'

'Oh, I'm coming all right,' she said. 'But just watch it next time.'

'Yes, dear,' I said. 'Meet you at the Burbank airport at seven thirty. Bring your pretties. I'll be the guy next to the ticket counter with his large foot in his big mouth.'

We had no trouble getting seats despite the fact that it was a Saturday evening; it seems airlines are only full during the week when all the business types are flying hither and yon, trying to impress the unimpressible stewardesses by drinking a lot and adding up meaningless sums on their pocket cal-culators.

When we had taken off, and I had unclutched my fingers from the armrests and had forced my eyes open again, I gave Evonne a cocky smile and said, 'Funny how some people hate the takeoffs most.'

'Whereas you hate the takeoffs, the landings and the middle bits all equally,' she said, giving my arm a pat. 'But I am proud of you, dear. I wonder if they serve low-cal iced tea on this flight – I could use a drink.' Evonne was not without a certain sense of humor, albeit often vindictive. She settled for a vodka and tonic, and I settled for two quick brandy and Canada Dry ginger ales and began to relax a whit, or part of one anyway.

After a few minutes of looking out the window at a lot of nothing but air, she turned back to me, gave me a peck on the cheek, and said, 'OK, Daddy, what are we going to Vegas for? And don't start that line about dancing till dawn again, or I'll upchuck in your lap.'

So I told her what I'd been working on. She already knew the general outline, but I filled her in on the rest although, as usual, I had second thoughts about discussing the cases I was on with anyone but my pal Benny. This was partly because of a client's right to confidentiality and partly wanting to spare the listener the more gruesome details. There were probably other less flattering reasons as well, such as fear of being laughed at and the fear of revealing yourself as the balding, bumbling, incompetent clown you no doubt were. How much does a nurse tell her layman husband or a vice cop his wife? It was the old problem: the need to unburden and to share against the desire to protect the ones you love. If you unloaded too much on a wife, say, might not she become overloaded herself, possibly overloaded with worry for you? Some brave people, mainly women, would rather be told all as, one, they have the capacity for it, and two, they figure the truth in all its gory realism can't be nearly as bad as some feared or imagined truth.

Where the right and the wrong of all this is I do not know, but I do know I never bothered even considering such arcane matters until the blessed event of Miss Evonne Beverly Shirley, and I also knew if I didn't spill all or almost all to Miss Evonne Beverly Shirley, she'd let me have it but good. Rather, she wouldn't let me have it, and I don't only mean her long-legged, sweet-smelling body and raspberry-lipsticked lips, but I mean all the rest of her, too, her warmth, her brain, and her alarming intuition. When piqued, she froze into a kind of impersonal, banal small talk that drove me nuts.

I once said to her, 'You never tell me all the details of what you do all day.' And she said, 'Why should I? You'd be asleep in two minutes; all I do is type and compute and make lists and meet the same people in the same places over and over, but you're actually out there in the sick new world, drinking too much and getting stabbed and being hit on the head and even solving murders, for God's sake, so who should be telling who bedtime stories?'

Put like that, who could respond with silence? Still, I found it difficult at times, so I compromised by not telling her everything and making up part of what I did tell her, which was a workable situation until the shit hit the fan, as it no doubt would someday, given my imperfect memory and her intelligence.

Anyway, that day I spilled all the beans to my love, my sweetheart, 34,000 feet up, finishing with an account of the poolside party at the Lewellens'. I even mentioned that 'Jim' Coburn had taken three games off me at pool.

'I hear she's a complete and utter and ruthless bitch,' she said after I'd run down.

'Who?'

'Grandma Collins,' she said.

'Miss Joan Collins? She was perfectly polite to me,' I said a little stiffly. 'As well as being ravishingly beautiful, may I add, and in a bikini, too, may I also add, not easy to anyone who isn't still a teenager, except you, of course, my precious.'

'Uh-huh,' she said meaningfully. Exactly what her meaning was I can't pretend to know, but not being a complete idiot, I thought it expedient to change the subject. So I told Evonne I unfortunately had a chore or two to do in Las Vegas but they wouldn't take me away from her for long; I could probably do them while she was freshening up or perhaps getting her lovely hair teased at Vidal's, cost no object.

'What chores, "Mr" Daniel?' she inquired. She pointed down. 'Look.'

I looked. 'Ah,' I said. 'I believe that's called sand. Isn't there a lot of it? And don't forget, you're only seeing the top. Well. What chores? How do I prove Marco Bellman was in Vegas ten days ago? I could ask him, but he'll probably say no, then kill me. If The Chief or Maryanne Forbes would swear that the photo with him in it was indeed taken ten days ago, that might do it, but neither one of them will ever talk to me again ever. So then what?'

'You try and find the same hotel, which is probably the Majestic, that The Chief had just come out of and take a picture of it from the same distance as what's-her-name did, and I will witness it, and as the two pictures will be identical except for the limo and the taxi, that will show that what's-his-name sure was in Las Vegas,' she said. 'That is what you do.'

The steward or – pardon me ever so – inflight entertainment director, who was not a stewardess, blond or otherwise, but a short redheaded guy with a silly mustache, passed right then, so I asked him if he would kindly ask the attractive lady sitting next to me if she would care for another drink, as I was deeply impressed with her sagacity as well as with her vibrant beauty. He obliged, although not precisely in those words.

I don't mind a little bad taste – in fact, I rather like it – but Las Vegas is ridiculous; it's like Joan Rivers or Liberace expressed architecturally. It's been used as the locale for so many movies and second-rate TV series that luckily for all concerned I don't have to describe it in detail. Still, you almost have to admire someone's nerve, if nothing else, for even thinking of building that neon nightmare, that Disneyland with greed, in the middle of the desert. I'd been there once or twice before, briefly, I may add, on business, I may also add, but this was Evonne's first visit, and I was curious to see what her reaction to the town would be. If she expressed any admiration at all I was planning on filing for an immediate separation order, but as it turned out, she didn't exactly rave about the place, but it didn't bother her either. She was almost indifferent to the foolish pretentiousness of dumps like Caesar's Palace, which the cab driver pointed out to us proudly on the way to our hotel, and not at all bothered by the Saturday-night fun-lovers who spilled out into the streets, drinks in hands, comical hats on heads, lots of them waving large plastic cups full of coins won at the slots.

'After nine years in a high school,' she told me, 'have I or have I not seen it all?'

Before we left I'd booked us a room by phone at the Empire, one of the first hotel-casinos to have been built. It still enjoyed a modest reputation but was suffering slightly from age. Who wasn't? Don't think I chose the old Empire just to save a few bucks; none of the hotels in town, not even the newest and splashiest, were that expensive – room rates were kept reasonable as come-ons because that's not where their money came from, and ditto with their restaurants and bars. The reason was I had a pal who worked at the Empire, or at least he used to.

Our abode was right on the main stem, in hotel row, or one of them, and a doorman wearing a uniform out of *The Student Prince* ran down the steps, opened the cab door for us, and when he found out we had reservations, said reception was on the first-floor mezzanine, our bags would be waiting for us up in our room, and I was Mister . . .?

'Daniel,' I said. 'With an "e".'

I paid off the cabby, tipped him, then casually slipped the doorman a suitable sum. Well, suitable enough; although he did give me the merest flicker of a glance he didn't tear the dollar bill up into little pieces right there before my eyes. I had a look at the front of the hotel before going in, on the off chance; it didn't look much like the one in the limo photo, but without the photo in front of me I couldn't be completely sure, and, anyway, things look different in the daytime, as the black choirboy said to the vicar; so my business would have to wait till then.

Hotels in Vegas aren't laid out as they are anywhere else in the world, except perhaps for Reno and Atlantic City and suchlike; to get to the reception area you normally have to wend your way through a cunning labyrinth of slots, black-jack and crap tables, where hot-shots in sleeveless shirts and plaid, washable trousers shout potent incantations like 'Baby needs new shoes' and 'Little eighter from Decatur' and 'Little Dick the hard way!' The reasons for this are obvious, I believe. However, with great strength of purpose Evonne and I man-aged to make it up to the mezzanine not only with our fortunes intact but seventy-five cents up – Evonne hit two cherries on a quarter slot machine.

We booked in, took the elevator up six floors to our room where we found our luggage waiting for us as promised, then after a brief and amicable discussion I called room service and asked them to send up some nachos to munch on and perhaps a spot of liquid refreshment to wash them down with. Then, while Madame changed into her gladrags, I rang down to reception and asked if my pal Joel was working. After a minute I was told no, he was on eight to four that week, meaning eight in the morning to four in the afternoon, so I tried his home number and there he was.

'Vic? *The* Victor Daniel? Where are you?'

'Six floors above where you work,' I said. 'Where are you?'

'About two miles east, out 403,' he said. '– Honey, guess who! – After the turn-off south to Nipton, which you don't take, there's a billboard pushing the MGM and just after that a road which you do take. I'm the only house on it, you can't miss it. And step on it, you old fart, I'm just lighting the barbecue.'

I started to say, 'Hold it, Joel, I've got a partner to consult first,' but he had already hung up.

'Who was that?' Evonne asked. She was stripped down to her bra and panties and was holding a pale green gownless evening strap and looking at it critically.

'Just an old friend,' I said. 'Joel. Eh, dear, why don't you come over here for a sec, I want to whisper something into your shell-like ear.'

'Oh, no,' she said. 'No quickies. We're going out on the town, remember? Discriminating cuisine, remember? Take in a show, perhaps? Somewhere there's a moonlit patio in this town with our name on it.'

'Well, that's sort of what I wanted to whisper to you about,' I said.

One of the (many) nice things about Evonne is she doesn't hold a grudge – after twenty minutes she actually spoke to me. We were in a cab, a different one, tootling through the desert; she had changed back into the trouser suit she'd travelled in and was trying to smooth the creases out of the front of the jacket while I kept one eye on the meter and the other on the road.

'Joel who?' she said.

'Joel, known as "Lefty", Hunt,' I said. 'I'm glad you're not mad at me anymore.'

'I'm still mad,' she said. 'It's perfectly possible to be mad and talk at the same time.'

'Yes, dear.'

'Why Lefty?'

'Because he's only got one arm,' I said. 'It's called male humor.'

'I don't think it's so screamingly funny,' the cabby observed.

'Me neither,' said Evonne. 'How did he lose his other one?'

'A mortar, I think he said,' I said. 'In Vietnam.'

'My brother was in Nam,' the cabby said. 'Guess what he lost.'

'There,' I said, spotting the billboard. 'Left, if you please.'

Some nights you remember and some you don't, as the leader

153

of the SS *Titanic*'s orchestra was once heard to say to the pretty girl singer. That night at the Hunts' was one of the former. Not that anything dramatic happened. Joel, red-faced and energetic as ever, barbecued gigantic steaks out back of his house while his adopted daughter Kim, a little Vietnamese girl who was a new addition to the family since I'd last seen him and Monica, hung on to his leg and pestered him until he told her in no uncertain terms to hang on to his other leg for a while or else the Dreaded Death of a Thousand Kisses. During this Monica saw to the drinks and kept seeing to them and tossed the salad and then she and Evonne looked at the stars and listened to the desert while I looked at Evonne and Monica, who was a gorgeous, leggy, titian-tressed ex-dancer, ex-showgirl, and listened to the ice tinkle in my glass.

After the apple pie, Evonne delighted Monica by asking to be shown around the house, so Joel and I had a chance to compare notes about our respective jobs. He turned the outside lights on just long enough to take a look at the enlargement of Marco Bellman but not long enough to attract any more insect life; he said he didn't recognize him, not that I'd really expected him to. He did make a mild quip about the taxi, saying the word around town was all the cabs were not only radio-controlled but mob (controlled). Then he mentioned something of decided interest to me. He said there had been some kind of major meet earlier in the month outside of town somewhere of all the West Coast families; for a week they'd drifted into town in ones and twos – hell, there must have been forty or fifty, easy, the talk was – then afterwards they drifted away again, all keeping a low profile, none of them going near the tables or even near a nickle slot. The talk was, he said, some kind of ass-kissing, or rather, ring-kissing, ceremony went on, one of those pledging loyalty things that happens when a new capo takes over, or is reputed to, anyway. Remember show and tell in school? he said. Those guys had their own version: don't show and die. Anyway, that was the talk, he said, he didn't know nothin' for sure, nor did he want to, he liked his job and wanted to keep it, and that went for his house and family as well.

Not that his job was exciting, he said. What he did was sit in a room above the casino watching television screens, working around the three eights – midnight to eight, eight to four in the afternoon, then four to midnight – changing every three weeks like factory workers used to do.

'So you never close?'

'Midnight, New Year's Eve,' he said, 'for one minute. Otherwise, never. Not even for Al Capone's birthday. Would you close a money-making machine if you didn't have to?'

He told me the problems came mostly from the croupiers, occasionally from the drunks, less occasionally from a drunken lady, and once in a while from a loser, drunk or not. He said where he worked there were twenty-four television screens and thus twenty-four cameras covering the entire casino area; each camera was movable, so it could be trained on any one of, say, eight blackjack tables or cover a whole row of slots. Of course, the lenses of the cameras were hidden behind one-way glass, so a croupier couldn't tell if he was being watched at any given moment, and the movements of the cameras were randomly changed at random intervals unless overriden by guys like him. He said the croupiers were under surveillance not only from the cameras but by floormen who were connected by radio, using tiny earphones like those on hearing aids, with the security guys overhead. He said one $100 chip a night is all a croupier needs to lift to make an extra twenty-four grand a year, and a chip is small (I knew that), it can be palmed (I knew that, too), it can be slipped to an associate, it can be stuck on things like the back of a silver dollar, it can be slipped under the tongue or into a cigarette pack or swallowed. You can't keep an overall check on chips table by table, either, he said, as bettors walk away with them to other tables or come in with them or take one home as a good-luck piece.

'Sounds more interesting than it is,' he said, 'cause what it is is a fairly well-paid bore. But what the hell, Mehitabel, toujours gai, you can't have everything.'

'You're telling me,' I said. 'You can't even get a drink around here.'

'Excuuuuse me!' Joel said. 'Blush, blush.' We'd both switched to beer by then so he got us cold ones from the little fridge outside the back door, holding one in his left hand and the other against his chest with what was left of his other arm.

'Ever miss the old days, Lefty?' I asked him when he'd settled down again in the faded old deckchair next to mine.

'Sometimes,' he said, 'when the moon is in the seventh house. Sure miss taking your money at poker, I got to work for it now.'

When I first moved out to the LA area to help Tony take care of Mom I got a job with Brinks to get myself set up, and Joel had already been there a couple of years; he'd moved up from making money runs in those armored vehicles they use to a desk, organizing security patrols, among other things. One good thing about Brinks, they hired Vets, and they didn't care if you had no arms at all if you could cut the job. It was true I used to drop a few dollars to Joel at the poker table from time to time, but it was merely to keep on the good side of him, as he was my dispatcher, and there were hard patrols and easy ones. He used to come and visit me once in a while when I was working nights at an aircraft company out in Orange County, and once we actually caught three guys trying to break in – although why, God only knows, as the only things on the premises were a couple of hundred rebuilt Pratt & Whitney engines, and you try stealing one of those, let alone pawning it afterwards. Anyway, although Lefty was only about five foot seven, he took the biggest of the three, the one with the tire iron, and had him spitting teeth while I was still shouting after the other two, 'Halt, or I'll fire!' – a memory that still embarrasses me slightly as I didn't have anything to fire with at the time.

Evonne and Monica came back when we were still kicking around the so-called good old days; Kim had been tucked into bed and told a bedtime story. Then we had coffee and then, despite our objections, he drove us back into town. I knew he had to be up at six thirty or so to get to work by eight Sunday morning, but he claimed he never needed more than four or five hours of sleep anyway, so I let him convince me. Not only did he drop us off at the door, but he went in with us and up to reception, where he told the desk clerk to make a note that Mr Daniel's room, on his authority, was a C-Special, whatever that meant, but it couldn't be bad. Then we shook hands and he kissed Evonne and off he went back into the desert. Then, when we were going up in the elevator, I kissed Evonne.

'Sorry about all that,' I said. 'We could still go out if you want to. As you saw on the way in, the joint is still jumping.'

'Don't be silly,' she said. 'And the only place I want to go right now is to bed.'

The other couple who were sharing the elevator with us looked at each other knowingly. Evonne spotted it and added, 'Cause you're so generous, Daddy.'

Later, when we were in bed, all cuddled up, and I was almost sleeping the sleep of the deeply satisfied man, she said, 'That Monica is one amazing dame, did you know that?'

'Yes, dear,' I said.

'How would you like to be a showgirl and then get cancer guess where?'

'In Chicago?' I said.

'Right there,' she said, 'where your right hand is.'

'I wouldn't,' I said.

'How would you like to have three abortions before you're twenty?' she said.

'I wouldn't,' I said.

'How would you like to be in love with your husband and not be able to have any children?'

'I wouldn't,' I said.

'And how would you like to be six inches taller than your husband and never be able to wear high heels again?'

'That I wouldn't mind,' I said.

CHAPTER FIFTEEN

Evonne and I slept in late on Sunday, had breakfast in bed, shared the local paper, shared the shower, did what came naturally, shared the shower again, got dressed, and then went downstairs to attack the morn. I had my camera slung over one shoulder like any respectable tourist, the limo photo in a manila envelope under one arm and Evonne hanging on to the other.

'Hang on to that arm too long and you risk the Dreaded Death of a Thousand Kisses,' I remarked to her as we stepped out into the already blazing sun.

'Life without risk is a hot fudge sundae without the hot fudge,' she remarked to me as we turned left and headed up the main stem toward the Majestic. There were a lot of folks about and they didn't all look like churchgoers to me, in fact none of them did. I wondered vaguely if Las Vegas even had any churches, aside from those 'chapels' – of which there was one across the street from us – where you could get married in four minutes or divorced in three. If they did have a church, I decided it should be called the Church of Our Lady Luck.

The Majestic was only a ten-minute stroll away, and at first glance its frontage did look like the one in the photo. It looked like it at second glance, too, which I took with the photo held up right in front of me. So I posed my witness on the steps, which were right in the center of the original picture, and a pretty sight indeed she made with the breeze blowing her blond hair this way and that. I snapped off a whole roll from slightly different angles and varying focal lengths, overlooking the occasional wisecrack from the passers-by, then ascertained from the doorman that there had been no changes in the hotel façade during the past couple of weeks, and indeed, during the last couple of years. And that was that.

On the way back to the Empire I escorted my model across the street to the 'chapel' I'd noticed earlier – 'The Wee Kirk O' the Glen' – a small red-brick and wooden-shingled building surrounded by a low white picket fence. When I held the gate open for her, she fluttered her eyelashes at me coyly and said,

'Gee, that was a short engagement.'

'No such luck, babe,' I said. 'This call is strictly business.'

We went inside, directly into what looked like someone's living room, except there was a desk in one corner, a beautiful old rolltop. The combination of chintz drapes, muted organ Muzak and the plethora of pictures of happy couples adorning the walls scared the hell out of me.

Before the motherly looking lady sitting behind the desk could get any ideas, I said to her, 'Excuse me, is there a notary public in the house?' It had dawned on me that folks who perform civil weddings had to have some legal standing, and anyway, didn't weddings have to be notarized in the first place? I wasn't sure, but it was worth crossing the street to find out.

'You're looking at one,' the lady behind the desk said, reaching to a shelf beside her for a huge ledger. 'Four dollars per page.'

'That seems reasonable,' I said. 'Any chance of your throwing in a couple of sheets of paper?'

'All the chance in the world,' she said. So I wrote out a short statement saying that I, me, had taken said photos in front of the Majestic Hotel, Las Vegas, Nevada, at ten forty-three, 22 July, then wrote out a second one saying I, Evonne, had posed for said photos, etc. We signed them, so did the lady, then she put the official state seal on them and entered the details in her ledger. Marco Bellman, the noose is tightening. I paid up, thanked the lady, tore Evonne away from the wedding photos, and we headed for the door. On our way out, the lady said, 'Don't forget our weekend special, you two. Ninety-nine fifty, including organist and a gorgeous spray of orchids.'

'I'll get back to you on that,' I said.

'Now what?' Evonne wanted to know as we were walking back to our hotel.

'I dunno,' I said. 'We could have a swim, then some lunch, then go home. Or we could watch the ladies in shorts and curlers play the slots, then have a swim, then some lunch, and then go home.'

'Why don't we just go home?' she said, stepping out of the way of a merry band of conventioneers that was reeling down the sidewalk towards us.

We packed up and went back down to check out. I discovered Joel's C-Special meant our room was free, a courtesy hotels offer to big rollers, so to keep up the image I lavishly tipped everyone in sight, including the extra from *The Student Prince*, who got a fiver this time for whistling us up a cab. What the hell, you got it or you don't.

There were LA newspapers on the plane going back, and a quick perusal of the *Times* informed me that LA hadn't changed much in a day. A few new unneeded hotels had been built, also a new suburb or two, and a bank had failed, and 20,000 more sensation-seeking maniacs had moved to town seeking the good life, and the Dodgers had lost again, making more errors than they got hits, and all the hookers had been rousted from the Strip yet again to everyone's displeasure, and eleven houses had been carried away to oblivion by a mud slide in Malibu, and the fire north of Topanga was still raging out of control, and two deprived youths in East LA had shot and killed the owner of a hairdressing salon and taken the entire contents of the till – seven dollars. Plus ça change, someone once said. I'm not sure, but I think that means they took the change, too.

I parted from Sugar at the airport, and we went our separate ways, she to her garden and me to stretch out on the couch chez moi to watch the ball game on TV. I was just getting comfortable when someone rang my downstairs buzzer. I opened the window, looked down, and there she was, the original twerp, waving some sheets of paper at me.

'Yoo, hoo,' she said. 'Avon calling. Anyone home?'

'Oh, God,' I said. 'You might as well come up, seeing you're here.' I buzzed her in, opened the apartment door and watched her clump up the stairs. I wasn't positive the heavy work boots she was wearing went all that well with her shorts, halter top and Aunt Jemima kerchief, but it had been years since my subscription to *Vogue* had run out.

'Where you been, Pops?' she demanded as soon as she came in. 'I been trying to get'cha. How long you been living in this old folks' home?'

'Is there anything in particular you want, Sara?' I said. 'Because it is Sunday, and it is my day off, and I've had a long, tiring week, not counting the flying. If you just wanted to pester me, couldn't you have phoned it in?'

'Aw, come on, grumpy,' she said, stretching up to try and give me a peck on the cheek. 'I know you're glad to see me, why try 'n' hide it?'

'Who's trying?' I said.

'Here,' she said, giving me the papers she was holding. 'The latest brilliant report from agent S.S.' Then she made gagging sounds and pointed to her mouth with one dirty finger. 'Thirst,' she said. 'Must drink. Must drink cold beverage.'

'There's some nice, healthy buttermilk in the icebox,' I said. 'Help yourself.'

She went out to the kitchen, and I went back to the sofa, stretched out my weary limbs again and looked over her latest artistic endeavor.

21 July

Report No. 12

From Agent S.S. to V.D. (ha, ha)

'12 Fuji' – another dangerous and complicated mission for
   Undercover agent S.S. (*Sweet & Sexy*).

12 Fuji – real name Arnold M., address on request. Age
   twelve.

On the assumption that V.D.'s suggestion I pose as photog
   for *Punkopolitan*

Was but a weak attempt at humor and not a viable and/or
   constructive plan,

I, Sara the Great, after considerable thought, devised my own
   scheme,

Herein after known as the S.S.S. – Sara Silvetti Scheme.

(About then *Sweet & Sexy* herself emerged from the kitchen with my last bottle of Corona in one hand and some soda crackers in the other; with pretended nonchalance she perched on the arm of the sofa about a foot away from my head, and watched me surreptitiously while I skimmed through her rubbish.)

Thus, after locating and voyaging to the M. residence, I
   spied,

Then, I betook myself around the corner from same.

Thus, I located a phone that worked.

Thus, I phoned the M. residence, getting Mrs M.

Thus, I introduced myself to her as S.S., artistic consultant to
The School District that included Arnold's school.

Thus, I told her that the School District that included Arnold's
    school
Was planning to put out a yearly collection of the pupils' best
Artistic works – short stories, verse, humorous and other-
    wise;
Original artwork, photography, and design.
Thus, I told Mrs M., me or other members on the committee
    had
Written all the schools in question
Asking them to submit the names of their most promising
    pupils in each field.
Thus, I told Mrs M., I had been given Arnold's name,
Which is why I was calling.
'Really?' ejaculated the proud and startled lady of the house.
Thus, I said,
Could I pass by at some convenient hour and select some of
Arnold's work
For possible inclusion and
The sooner the better, please,
As we were pressed for time.
THE THINKING BEHIND: Do not allow Mrs M. time to
    boast to all
Her friends and neighbors and thus possibly discover no such
Collection was really planned.
So – I informed her that by coincidence I was at that moment
Nearby, and
Could be at her home in but a few moments.
'Come right over!' gushed Mrs M.
'Arnold's not in but I'm sure he'll be thrilled by it all.'
CONFESSION: I knew Arnold wasn't in because I knew he
    was out
(Rollerskating with one of his friends) because that's what I
    was
Waiting for

When, as I writ earlier, I spied – kids are almost as suspicious
As out-sized private investigators.
The upshot was, thus, at 11.45 I knocked on the door of the
    M. household,
Was immediately admitted by Mrs M. My outfit (disguise),
    one of
My mother's yecchy jumpsuits, plus half boots (suede) and a
    red
Beret, passed muster.
Thus, back to the back to Arnold's room. Room covered,
every
Square inch of, with his
Photographs, all neatly pinned up on dark brown corkboard.
    Arnold
Also had a record system in which he listed the details of all
His work – subject matter, time of day, exposure, type
    film,
Etc. etc. etc. Arnold also
Had a filing cabinet filled with his work.
Arnold was a serious boy.
'Sometimes,' Mrs M. wondered, 'I wonder if he's not a little
    too
Serious.'
'A true artist can never be too serious,' I responded.
Found the 12 Fujis.
Examined every exposure.
One was a roll of portraits of his father asleep in a chair out
Back o' house.
One was a roll of close-ups of a pair of hands.
One was a roll of close-ups of tree bark.
One was a roll of close-ups of a dead bird.
One was a roll of reflections in a pool of water. (More details
    on request.)
No people were shown in any of the rolls other than Daddy.

Thus I selected several photographs at random, saying we
   would
Write for the negatives when and if.
Thus, I retired gracefully, refusing Mrs M.'s offer of iced tea
Or perhaps something a touch stronger. She needed anoth-
   er touch
Of something stronger like you need an increased dose of
Nasty Pills.

Sez	Traveling expenses	– $3.00
Sara	Time & Trouble	– $12.00
XXXX	Beret	– $ 5.95
	Total	$20.95

'Well, Pops?' she said eagerly as soon as I had finished.

'There is no need for gratuitious insults, Sara,' I said, 'at
any time, let alone in an official report. Otherwise, a compe-
tent piece of work.' I didn't have the heart to tell her it had
all been a waste of time. 'And I hope you have a sales receipt
for that beret. And stop dropping cracker crumbs on the
floor, I just cleaned up the place.'

'You'd never know it,' she said. 'Where's your mom?'

'That's why I cleaned up,' I said. 'I'm picking her up later.'

'She any better?'

'No.'

'She any worse?'

I shrugged.

'Is it true what I read once that with what she's got you
lose your sense of smell first?'

'I don't know if it happens first,' I said. 'But it happens.'

'She-it,' said Sara. 'What a drag. Imagine not being able to
smell things like apple pies and flowers and perfume.'

'And Acapulco Gold,' I said.

She took a long noisy swig of beer, gave my hair a muss it

didn't need, then began wandering around looking at things. There wasn't a lot that was fascinating to look at; there was the living room with a small counter separating it from the kitchen area and two bedrooms and a bathroom out back. The furniture was serviceable but unexceptional, and there weren't a lot of knick-knacks or personal trinkets lying around.

'You need some pictures on the walls,' she said after a bit.

'I got some,' I said.

'Those are posters, not pictures,' she said.

'Sue me,' I said.

'So where were you when I tried to get you and you weren't here?' she said after another little while. 'Was it anything to do with twelve Fuji?'

'Indirectly,' I said. 'It sure had something to do with pictures. And it worked out pretty well, if I do say so myself.'

'Come on, Pops,' she said. 'Lay it on me. You're dying to tell someone how clever you were for once.' She pulled at her narrow halter top. 'God, this stupid thing is killing my boobs.'

'Don't take it off, whatever you do,' I said. 'My heart couldn't stand the excitement. But, OK, if you insist, I will show you how clever I was again, not for once.'

I bestirred myself, retrieved the limo photo and the other paperwork from my bedroom where I'd left them, and spread them out on the cocktail table in front of us. I told her the problem – for a certain reason – parole breaking – I wanted to place a certain hoodlum – Marco Bellman – in a certain town – Las Vegas – in a certain state – Nevada – at a certain time – the recent past, as in last week. For certain other reasons I could not depend on any witnesses, thus I needed definite photographic evidence. And I had it, if she would take my word that the undeveloped roll of film in front of her on the table did indeed contain shots of Evonne Beverly Shirley taken that very day on the steps in front of the Majestic Hotel in Las Vegas, Nevada.

Sara scrutinized the photo of Bellman, then the notarized statements from myself and Evonne, then turned her attention again to the shot of Marco in the cab and The Chief by the limo.

'Good work, Pops,' she said.

'Thank you,' I said.

'Of course, there is just one little thing.'

'And what is that, my child?' I asked almost fondly.

'What's to prove Marco was in Las Vegas when you say he was?'

'What do you mean, what's to prove?' I demanded. 'That picture of him you're waving around is to prove.'

'But why couldn't it have been taken last month sometime, or last year, or who knows, the year before that?'

'Because I know it wasn't, is why.'

'Yeah, but who's to say so? You got no witnesses. What's there in the picture to say when it was taken?'

'There's obviously something,' I said testily. 'Here, give me that thing.' I wasn't really worried yet, but I was getting there. 'It could be any one of a hundred things.'

'Name one,' she said, peering over my shoulder.

'And anyway, Miss Smarty,' I said, 'it couldn't have been taken last year because Marco was in the clink last year.'

'What about the year before that?' she said. 'When did they lock him up?'

I racked my memory and came up with April 1984.

'It's all incidental, anyway,' I said. 'There's got to be something in this bloody picture.'

'I don't see anything,' the twerp said. 'I don't see anyone holding up a newspaper with a headline that could be dated. I don't see any new-model cars, either. Nor do I see anyone attired in the latest fashions, fashions that just came in this year.'

'If you're finished,' I said. 'If you look closely at this photo, something you obviously haven't done yet, you will notice by the limousine – right there, see? – a certain someone you might recognize. I believe he's called The Chief. I also believe he's made a movie or two. And I happen to have unshakable evidence, i.e. the bible of show biz, *Variety*, that he was in Las Vegas, Nevada, ten days ago. I rest my case.'

'I did actually notice him,' she said. 'You don't have to be sarcastic, I'm only trying to help. I just hope for your sake he wasn't coming down those stairs a couple of years ago, because if he was, it's up shit creek for you, Pops.'

'Language,' I said automatically.

'Can you tell from a photograph how old it is? I guess you could if it was hundreds of years old, but is there any difference between a picture one year old or two years old?'

'Oh, shut up,' I said crossly. 'Who knows stuff like that.'

Newspaper headlines suddenly flashed through my mind: HIX NIX STIX PIX. WALL STREET TAKES A DIVE. MAJESTIC REBOOKS CHIEF TO MC MS TELETHON.

'Let me ask you something, Miss Know-It-All,' I said. 'What does "Majestic Rebooks Chief to MC MS Telethon" mean?'

'What's so hard about that?' she said. 'MC means master of ceremonies, MS means multiple sclerosis, rebooks means he was there before and the whole thing means you're up shit creek.'

'That's what I was afraid it meant,' I said. 'And I bet that bloody Chief's been doing that telethon for years, too, because his wife's got MS, and it's obviously her favorite charity. Goddamn it.'

'There, there,' Sara said, patting my shoulder.

'There, there, is right,' I said. 'Now that you've thoroughly ruined my day off, why don't you go somewhere, anywhere, and find someone else to point out things to they don't want to know and could have figured out for themselves anyway? On your way out, please leave your empties in the kitchen.'

'Since when is one bottle empties?' she said. 'And where's my money?'

'Who knows?' I said. 'I can't be bothered about a few measly dollars right now, stop by the office sometime, set a collection agency on me, do what you like, but do it somewhere else. Blow, will you?'

The airhead blew, but only after I'd come up with ten bucks on account. Kids today – their shiftless lives ruled by greed, drugs and hair dye.

I waited until both the weather and I had cooled off a bit, then drove over to my brother's place to pick up Mom. She was sitting in the front room, all packed up and ready to go, but was in one of her times of total withdrawal from the present. My mom would have been seventy-three back then; she was a small, still-pretty woman with curly gray hair and terrific legs of which she was justifiably vain.

When I bent down to kiss her, she shouted, 'You've been a bad boy again. I don't like you!' Then she slapped me as hard as she could right in the kisser. I was so surprised I didn't know what to do. Tony's wife Gaye came over and sat down beside her.

'Now, now, Mother,' she said. Mom pursed her lips and pushed Gaye's hand away. Tony beckoned me with his head, and I followed him out to the kitchen. Through the window I saw one of his kids, the boy, Martin, a Coke in one hand and a book in the other, sitting crossways in the hammock I'd brought back from Mazatlán and swinging idly back and forth.

'She's never done that before,' I said to my brother, rubbing my cheek. 'She packs a pretty good wallop for a lightweight.'

'Yeah, well she's been doing quite a lot of it the last couple of weeks,' Tony said. 'Never to me or Gaye or Martine, always to Martin there.'

'How does he take it?'

'Ah, he's a good kid,' Tony said. 'He shrugs it off.'

'What happens?'

'You saw,' he said. 'Suddenly she shouts something and then she clouts him. God knows what she's thinking about, maybe us when we were kids.'

'Maybe,' I said. 'Poor old Mom.'

'Yeah,' Tony said. He came to join me at the window. 'I don't know what the hell we're going to do.'

'Me neither,' I said. 'I'll call her doc tomorrow, but we know what he's going to say, he's going to say what he always says.' And what he always said was they had no way of arresting the disease at present but there were encouraging developments being made in the field, so there was hope. There was a new drug that showed promise. They thought they had identified at least one of the causes of Alzheimer's disease. 'Please remember that your mother suffers additionally as she is comparatively young and in her lucid moments is only too well aware of the problems she is causing her family.'

'I don't know what the hell we're going to do,' Tony had said. What to do wasn't the problem. We'd keep Mom with one of us for as long as we could, then the time would come when we'd have to put her in a home somewhere. Ain't life easy when you're logical. I'd just say when the day came, 'Sorry, Ma, but you need a full-time live-in nurse now, and I can't afford one, and even Tony and I together can't afford one, so it's off to Bide-A-Wee for you. You'll love it there, you'll have your own room and everything, and on Saturdays there's bingo and dancing.'

Lord love a duck, as my long-departed pop used to say.

CHAPTER SIXTEEN

Monday morning was one of those Monday mornings – you know the kind I mean. There were no coffee filters in the house, so I used a paper towel instead, but when the coffee wouldn't drip through, I tugged the edge of the paper towel to help the flow, which made a hole in the middle, so the first major choice of the day was whether to drink coffee that was all grounds, or none. I chose grounds, Mom chose none.

Then we couldn't find Mom's beeper, or rather, it was the opposite of a beeper – she pushed a little button, and it made a noise in a similar but larger electronic marvel downstairs in Feeb's living room in case of an emergency. Mom wasn't sure, but she thought she'd left it over at my brother's, but no one was in there, so I waited a bit, then had a word with Gaye when she got back from taking the kids to school, and she looked but couldn't find it at her house. I finally uncovered it in the kitchen cupboard behind the Rice Crispies, and don't ask me what it was doing there because all possible answers are upsetting, such as Mom was embarrassed to have to wear the thing at all or she was lonely and wanted me to hang around the place a while longer to keep her company or perhaps she just wanted some attention.

Anyway. We straightened that out, and then at the office, by canny deduction, I discovered that someone had tried to break in during the night, the canny deduction consisting of treading over broken glass by the back door where some would-be felon had smashed in the small window overlooking the alley but had been foiled by the interior bars. I got the mess cleaned up then got on the phone to a local glazier I'd used before who said as a special favor he might be able to drop by Friday afternoon, meaning Friday week, so I wound up replacing the glass myself, with all that involves, this time with the same sort of wire-reinforced safety glass that my front window was made of. I made a fairly neat job of it, all things considered, and only cut myself twice.

That took me up to noon. Then the mailman brought me the news that an estimate for a complicated security system for a complex of warehouses in La Crescenta I'd spent a lot of time, imagination and trouble on, had been rejected by the owners involved. The next letter I opened was even less fun, it was the announcement of the funeral of Robert Regis Brewer, in Walnut Creek, which is up near San Francisco somewhere. It took me a moment to place the name because when he'd worked at Brinks with me and Joel, the only name we all called him by was 'Stud', for the obvious reason. Jesus, he couldn't have been out of his thirties yet. The three of us, along with a skinny Vet who was all mustache and tattoos known among us as 'Mary', for some forgotten reason, perhaps from 'Hairy Mary', had run around a lot together in the old days, and whatever happened to Mary?

So I wrote a note extending my sympathies to the widow, an angry little blond woman whom I knew well. At one time, in fact, during one bleak period I'd obliged myself of the Brewers' couch for a week or so, that was when they were living out in Redondo Beach, right on the ocean, and we were all if not young and foolish, at least younger and foolish. Stud was the best-looking man I had ever seen, and as I had recently met 'Jim', to say nothing of The Chief, I mean he was handsome. He was so handsome for some reason his wife Belle was permanently angry at him. I do not believe anyone has been enraged at me for that reason, but that's just a guess.

I will skip over the rest of that blue Monday until that

evening, until nine o'clock that evening, when the council of war at Wade's out in thrilling suburban Burbank was well under way. Present in the kitchen were Maria of the hairy legs, also Cissy, Willy, Wade, Suze, Benny, Sara, and I, Victor Daniel, Supreme Commander. Occasional drop-ins were Rags and a feline named Minny. The kitchen table was, of course, laden with cakes, cookies, muffins and brownies as well as raw vegetables, fruit, and a bowl of assorted unshelled nuts, and everyone was drinking something or smoking something or both – me, Willy, Wade and Suze beer; Benny, ordinary tea with milk and sugar; and Cissy some awful-smelling herbal tea with lemon. Rags ate everything he could mooch, including cucumber peel.

We'd been at it a couple of hours by nine o'clock, including an hour in which I filled in the gang with all the details to date, and progress of a kind had been made, but mainly negatively.

For example, Suze had suggested that she phone up Marco saying she was calling from Las Vegas where she lived, and she was on the game, see, and a couple of weeks ago one of her Johns was drunk and shooting off his mouth about the Family get-together and how that crazy Marco not only broke parole but showed up driving a cab. So if Marco wanted to know the blabbermouth's name all he had to do was drop by her pad sometime and make it worth her while. Naturally, she wouldn't be anywhere near the address she'd give him, but one of us would be, and this time get a picture that could be dated. This we vetoed because we all thought it was unlikely Marco would risk another out-of-state trip, and what he would do, if he did anything, would be to send one of his heavies instead.

Benny had a similar idea: call up Marco in the guise of a small-time grifter. Tell him that he, Benny, had been in Vegas for a weekend not long ago and had been surprised to see Mr

Bellman, whom of course he knew by reputation as well as by sight, out of the state, given his circumstances and all. So he, Benny, was wondering if Mr Bellman wouldn't like to meet him somewhere without too many people around for a little chat, at which chat he, Benny, would be miked up, just in case, and would put the screws to Mr Bellman. Being the violent type, Mr Bellman would undoubtedly try and massacre him, Benny, or at least hurt him intensely, at which time the forewarned cop would jump out of the woodwork where he'd been hiding and nab him, Mr Bellman, for assault, if not assault with a deadly weapon.

This we vetoed as, again, we thought it likely Marco would send one of his boys instead of going himself, and also as being too potentially dangerous for Benny.

Wade, looking at the problem from the standpoint of a photographer, suggested planting something incriminating in the photo, a newspaper or whatever, that could be dated; technically, not much of a problem, he swore, and detectable only by another expert. This was vetoed when Benjamin pointed out that as Marco had a copy of the identical photo without, say, a newspaper in it, he would be rightly suspicious if one with, say, a newspaper in it suddenly showed up, and so would his lawyer. But what if he had already burned the picture he had, said Sara. And what if he remembered there hadn't been, say, a newspaper in it in the first place and called some other photographic expert, I said, to check out the retouched photo.

We all quite liked Cissy's idea, which was simply to say that she had taken the picture, she'd been in Las Vegas that weekend, and when The Chief suddenly appeared, she and every other tourist with a camera in the area began snapping away furiously. And who could deny she hadn't? Only The Chief and Maryanne Forbes and Marco. The first two of whom were no problem because of their adamant refusal to ever say another word about it all, and Marco was no problem because he'd deny it all anyway. This ingenious plan I had to veto, as it involved an amateur liar, Cissy, going up against professional liar detectors, i.e. the fuzz, also i.e. defense counsel, who would ask her a hundred questions she couldn't answer, like what was the weather like in Las Vegas that weekend, and where did she stay, and how did she get there, and where were her receipts, and then, if they had to, they'd slip in a few trick questions like was the Majestic's huge neon sign shut down for repairs that Saturday, or was it Sunday? The answer to which being either Saturday, Sunday, both, or neither, and how could she know?

We also all quite approved of the normally peaceable Willy's idea, which was simply to pay Marco Bellman a visit some dark evening, intercept him on his way home, hurt him a lot until he bled, and then have him arrested for littering the sidewalk. Cissy objected on the grounds that we had decided it more than likely wasn't Marco himself who had killed poor Shusha, so we'd be hurting the wrong man. Benny reminded her that if we were taking revenge, as we were, we would probably have to settle for Marco himself as it was unlikely we'd ever find out who else was involved. But aside from that, Benny (and I) felt Willy's plan lacked a certain imagination, there wasn't that feeling of absolute righteousness about it, of retributive justice at its best.

Wee Sara suggested working some variation of the badger game, i.e. getting Marco in flagrante delicto with some sweet little yummy and then putting the shaft to him. This I vetoed, as (one) I wanted to keep whatever we did in the family, and (two) to work, the yummy would have to be legally underage, and Cissy, Sara and Suze, although undeniably all yummy in their own ways, were no longer sweet fifteen. Anyway, it was too dangerous in the first place. Out.

With the unerring sense of timing which all good commanders seem born with, I then laid out my own scheme, or at least parts of it, for their delectation and admiration; I'd spent most of that afternoon and early evening thinking it up and then going over and over it for weak spots.

I needed a plan that would fulfill three conditions: Marco would have to get what was coming to him, and more; I wanted to use the people already involved – the ones in the kitchen; I wanted to utilize the existing talents and skills of Wade, Willy, Suze and Cissy and not involve them in areas outside their proven capabilities, such as trailing people, using violence, bearing false witness – for those we had me and my fellow pros Benny the Boy and Sara the Snoop.

Also, I'd decided to forget about using that damn limo picture, except obliquely; it had been nothing but trouble since the beginning. The original problem presented by the break-in at Wade's garage had been interesting, though, like that pooch of Arthur Conan Doyle's who didn't bark in the night – you had a burglar who not only didn't take anything, but what he was looking for in the first place didn't even exist. However.

What did our little revenge-minded band of adventurers have as talents I could draw on? There was roly-poly Willy, genius inventor and car mechanic. There was Wade, one hundred and thirty pounds of goateed photographic expert with a sideline in nature studies. There was the gentle Cissy, herbalist, astrologer, vegetarian and mad biker. Then there were Suze and Sara, the one built like a brick outhouse, the other a pipe cleaner with a lime-green top, to be used for communications, chauffeuring, rolling joints, and whatever else came up. Add to all that The Brain (me) and Benny the Boy, veteran of a hundred scams and man of a hundred faces, all of them innocent, well, poor old Marco didn't stand the chance of a one-legged man in an ass-kicking contest.

'Willy,' I said. 'Can you stop a car that is being driven by someone else within a hundred yards or so of a given point if you know in advance where that point is?'

Willy chewed on a bran muffin contemplatively for a moment.

'Does the speedometer work?'

'I don't know,' I said. 'But I can probably find out. They usually do, don't they, even in older cars?'

'Sure,' he said. 'What's to go wrong?'

'Another thing,' I said, 'the car that gets stopped has to be drivable again right afterwards, so whatever's wrong with it has to be fairly easily repairable by someone like you, but not by the driver.'

'Sure,' he said. 'No problem. I can think of three ways already, and I haven't started thinking yet. How long would I have with the car beforehand?'

'I don't know,' I said. 'That's something I'm worried about. Probably not long.'

'Leave it to Dr Willy,' he said.

'Wade,' I said. 'Let's talk nature studies.'

Wade had the grace to blush and look away, but he needn't have worried, I wasn't going to spill the beans.

'If I brought you some nature studies that weren't particularly offensive by legal standards, just your usual skin pix, then I brought you some other nature studies that weren't offensive at all, like, say, orang-utans frolicking and donkeys kicking up their heels in the greensward and friendly alsatians waiting for their supper and woolly lambs just standing around looking woolly, could you combine them somehow and produce some really offensive pictures, some highly illegal examples of bestiality at its worst?'

'No sweat, amigo,' said Wade, helping himself to another brownie. 'But like a guy with a cheap wig, the joins might show.'

'That won't matter,' I said. 'You still got illegal pictures, right?'

'Right,' said Sara.

'We'll need a lot of them,' I said.

'Like how many?' Suze asked.

'About four hundred should do it,' I said. 'And pass me those brownies, will you, while there's still some left.'

'Jesus,' said Wade. 'You better let me know exactly because I'm gonna have to get some supplies in. What size are we talking, are we talking color, what?'

'We're talking black and white,' I said, 'eight by tens, make it four hundred exactly; say, eight different shots, so fifty of each.'

'What do you think, Suze, it'll take us a day, day and a half?'

'At least,' Suze said. 'When do we get the originals?'

'As soon as I get them,' I said. 'Cissy.'

'Yes, dear,' said Cissy. 'Anyone want a sandwich or anything? How about grilled cheese and onion?'

'Do me a favor, will you Cissy, and take orders for the main courses later? Let's get on with it.'

'Ooh, I love it when he's dominating,' Sara said in a loud whisper to Suze, who giggled.

'Cissy,' I said sternly. 'Your motorcycle's not in a service station somewhere, is it, getting even more souped up? I didn't see it out front.'

'It's out back,' she said. 'Chained to a tree. I've been doing that every night since you-know-when. And don't worry, it works.'

'Good,' I said. 'Willy. How many cars you got that work?'

'One.'

'And I got wheels,' Suze said.

'Me, too,' said Benny.

'More than enough,' I said. 'Benny.'

'Yes, Uncle?'

'Think you are still capable of stealing a car by yourself, or would you need Doctor Willy's help?'

'I think I might manage it, Unk,' Benny said, looking modest. 'I've slowed up some, so it might take me somewhere between twenty seconds and three minutes, depending.'

'Depending on what?' Suze wanted to know.

'Old or new,' Benny said. 'Some new cars have security locks on the doors and are more likely to have some kind of alarm system or steering-wheel lock.'

Suze gave him an admiring look. 'Hmm. Where was you brung up?'

'Not too old, not too new,' I said. 'Just a car that works with nothing remarkable about it. And don't call me Uncle!'

'OK, OK,' said Benny, spreading some honey on a piece of Cissy's homemade banana-nut bread. 'No hay problema. Just tell me when you want it and where you want it.'

'You'll be the first to know,' I said. 'Now, did I leave anyone out?'

'Me, man,' said Suze.

'And me, Unk,' said Sara.

'You, I'll get to in a minute,' I told Sara. 'Suze. Acting on von Clausewitz's first principle, which is to secure your base, you will be required to secure our base. Also to be held in reserve for emergencies and possible counter-offensives. And most important, to man – or to woman – our entire communications network.'

'Meanin' I gotta stay here by the phone while all you guys is out there gettin' your rocks off,' Suze said disgustedly. 'I don't call that fair.'

'General Patton once observed that the skillful use of reserves has won more battles than everything except air cover,' I said.

'Oh, yeah?' Suze said, unmollified. 'And what did he say

about communications, be sure you always had a dime for the phone with you?'

'Now, Suze,' I said. 'This is no time for temperament. If our own private Mission Impossible is to succeed, we must all play our parts.'

'How about my part, Unk?' said Sara, finishing off the last of the umpteenth joint by swallowing the roach. 'What am I going to be doing, providing the air cover from a hang glider maybe?' She and Suze giggled again.

Ignoring them, I said, 'When I was down at LAPD Records on Saturday finding out about this guy Marco in the first place I had so much on my mind that I forgot to ask my pal Sneezy down there to check with the DMV for me to see if there were any vehicles registered in Marco's name, or maybe registered to his company. I do know he drives, as his rap sheet mentioned he once made his living stealing cars, which is not an occupation usually taken up by someone who has trouble finding reverse. Anyway, we have to find out what he drives and where he parks it. I don't want Benny anywhere near that guy or where he works or where he lives just in case he gets a lucky look at Benny, because Benny is going to meet Marco later and he better not be recognized, or else serious trouble.'

'That'll be the day a creep like that spots me when I don't want to be spotted,' Benny said.

'Yeah, I know,' I said. 'I know you're a man of a thousand disguises and all that, but why take a chance at all, even a long one? So I'm putting Sara and Willy on it because Sara is an experienced, intelligent and reliable agent when she's not being a total flake-out, and Willy because it might help if he got a look at the car he's going to rig before he has to rig it. I've got an address for Marco, also his business address. It's merely a suggestion, Sara, but if you telephoned Marco early, at his work number, before he gets in, being all polite and coy and girlish and saying it's personal, you might find out when he usually does get in to work and thus be lurking around outside somewhere nearby.'

'What if he's got to work already?' Sara asked.

'Do I have to think of everything?' I said. 'Be imaginative. Besides, whoever heard of a boss who got to work early? Then you'd stake out his house instead, whatever you like. You got a day or two. OK? Oh, I've even got a picture of Marco to help you out.'

'I don't see any problem,' said Willy, giving his beard a thorough scratch. 'Do you, partner?'

Sara snapped her fingers. 'A cinch.'

'All right,' I said. 'Now we're cooking. If there's nothing else, I think I'll take Sara home and then do likewise with myself. Wade, all being well, I'll see you sometime tomorrow with the nature studies, so you and Suze can get started. Willy, get thinking.'

'I don't have to,' he said. 'Like all intuitive geniuses, I simply allow the data to enter, then wait.'

Cissy wrapped up a couple of leftover muffins for Sara to take with her, we made our farewells, then I drove back to Studio City, dropped the twerp off, then dropped myself off at Dave's Corner Bar, where I was soon at the corner table with a large, refreshing drink, as, not being an intuitive genius, I had some thinking to do, and it's thirsty work, thinking.

CHAPTER SEVENTEEN

At ten thirty the following morning I was sipping a cup of the porno king of 4420 Davenport's excellent coffee, and she was doing likewise on her side of the desk. I was sipping from a proper cup, too, one that not only had a handle but a saucer as well, so I had my little finger well elevated in a genteel way. With the help of the porno king I'd concocted an elaborate ruse involving one of her girlfriends who worked one floor up to get me by that cheap crook downstairs at the front desk without him knowing I was going to visit said porno king, but wouldn't you know, he wasn't even there when I entered the building.

'And to what do I owe this unexpected pleasure?' the porno king, whose name turned out to be Mrs Ethel Frinks, asked me between ladylike sips.

'That's a nice way to put it, ma'am,' I said, 'instead of "You again." What I would like is a few more pictures, if you can spare them. Both kinds. We are going after the animal I told you about last time who killed my friends' dog. It's a little involved, but some pictures would help.'

'No sooner said,' she said. She reached behind her without looking, took a folder from a shelf and passed it to me. 'Animals. The four-legged kind.' Then she took a second folder out of a desk drawer and slid that over. 'Love's young dreams,' she said. 'Please help yourself.'

I helped myself.

'Do you mind me asking what exactly you intend doing with these?'

'Not at all,' I said. 'Wade and his faithful assistant Suze are going to cut them up and put a few collages together and come up with some results that will be not only highly unpleasant but also highly illegal.'

'Ugh,' Mrs Frinks said with a shudder. 'If there's anything I hate.'

'Me, too.'

'But why don't you buy them, they're not that hard to find.'

'No, but they would be expensive,' I said. 'And also this way it lets the kids contribute more to the cause. Of course, they'd want to anyway; it was their studio and partly, anyway, their dog.'

'Of course,' she said.

I selected a dozen of the animal studies, then managed to choose the same number of skin pix without losing my businesslike manner. Then I had a thought.

'I say. We might be able to kill two birds with one stone. Do you know anyone who does wholesale really filthy pictures?'

'Not personally,' Mrs Frinks said. 'Thank goodness. But the man I buy from once gave me the card of someone he said could provide anything at all in that line if I were ever interested; no doubt he was trying to promote a finder's fee for himself.'

'No doubt,' I said.

'I didn't keep the card, but in my efficient way I did make a note of the name and address.' She flipped rapidly through a rotary file that she took out of another drawer and stopped at the Ss. 'Ah-ha.' She wrote out on a piece of scratch paper: 'P(hotographic) P(leasures) C(ompany), (PPC), 12254 Entrada Road, Topanga Canyon. Tel. 445-9000.'

'Thank you,' I said. 'Why did you look under S?'

'Suppliers,' Mrs Frinks said.

I thanked the nice lady, collected my artwork and PPC's address and took my leave after promising to let her know how it all turned out. Then I dropped off the artwork at Wade's and told him to get busy; he and Suze had just gotten back from a supply house and they were busy changing the fluids in one of the developers. Willy had left the house about seven thirty that morning, Suze told me, to pick up Sara and see what they could see. He was due back any minute, but I didn't bother waiting; I had things to do myself.

The first thing, back at the office, was to look up the exact whereabouts of Entrada Road. According to my Rand McNally's map of Central Los Angeles & Vicinity, it was a small, winding road running off Topanga Canyon Boulevard not far north of Topanga Beach, which is on the mighty Pacific Ocean between Las Tunas State Beach and Will Rogers State Beach. It wasn't an area I knew well, although I did have one pal who lived out in those parts, but it looked perfect for our purposes as Topanga Canyon was mainly a hilly wilderness of scrub and conifers with a few houses dotted here and there, so there wouldn't be much late-night traffic. I needed a long, close look at the area, and I was just about to leave to do so when Mrs Sylvia Summers called.

'Truce!' she exclaimed gleefully. 'Truce has broken out between me and my dreaded spouse, that louse.'

'War breaks out,' I mused aloud. 'Convicts break out. Measles break out. Can a truce break out?'

'One just did,' she said. 'He's thrown in the towel. He threw in the whole linen closet. Were you really going to slap a paternity suit on him?'

'I was thinking of it,' I confessed. 'Among other things.'

'Tell you one thing,' she said. 'I hope you never get mad at me.'

'I never get mad at women as attractive as you, Mrs Summers,' I said, 'especially if they not only pour a mean drink but also have had the thoughtfulness to pay a hundred-dollar advance on their surprisingly moderate bill.'

'For you, Super Dick, anything,' she said. After she finally hung up I did make her out a bill that was, if not surprisingly moderate, at least reasonable, all things considered.

Then I put away and locked up and headed out of town toward Topanga Canyon, remembering to have the oil checked first. I drove past Marco Bellman's residence on the way because Willy had mentioned something about speedometers, and I wanted to check out the mileage from Marco's to Topanga and Entrada Road as closely as possible.

He turned out to live in a two-story apartment building that was shaped like a U around a pool in the middle, a common form of construction in Southern California. There was a garage for resident parking at one side that was firmly barred by one of those sliding gates that takes a special key to open, which wasn't the best of news. Anyway, from Marco's I picked up the Ventura Freeway again and headed west, in the slow lane, past Haskell, Balboa, White Oaks, Winnetka and the like, de-freewayed at Topanga and headed south, up into the canyon road and the hills – or rather the Santa Monica Mountains – that separated that section of my dearly beloved San Fernando Valley from the sea.

It was another hot July noon – what else is new? – and I had both windows open so my locks were being tossed hither and yon by the breeze. Some lady C & W singer on the radio claimed I had a cheatin' heart and that it would tell on me. I donned my shades, thought of Miss Tuesday Weld's enchanting smile, and decided that lady singer didn't know everything, some secrets will never be told.

Some twenty minutes of twisting canyon road later I topped the rise and began zig-zagging down the other side, passing the occasional inviting-looking tavern and the odd small cluster of houses. After a further twenty minutes or so I spotted the sign for Entrada Road on my left but continued on for another few miles until I came to a cluster of wooden buildings right out of some Western set – there was a country store, a saloon beside it, even a hitching rail and wooden sidewalks. There were lots of places to park both in front and in back, so I pulled in, pulled up, got out, stretched, said hello to two horses that were, suitably enough, hitched to the hitching rail, then ducked into the cool of the saloon for a hamburger in a basket and a couple of welcome beers.

When I asked the dazzling girl in leather shorts who served me about the bar's opening times, she dug a card out of her apron pocket and gave it to me. I rewarded her with my model of an enchanting smile and a sixty-five-cent tip.

'The Saloon,' the card read. '11.00 a.m. – Hot java. Breakfast in a Basket. 3.00 p.m. – Closed for siesta. 5.00 p.m. – 6.30 p.m. – Happy Hour. Hot Snax. Burgers 'n' Chicken 'n' Ribs in a Basket. 12.00 p.m. – You might as well be outa here, cos you ain't gonna get more beer.'

On my way out, I heard the bartender shouting into the bar phone, 'No, you can't!' Then he turned to the waitress and said to her through clenched teeth, 'Marge, if one more of your boyfriends makes one more personal call to you on the bar's business phone I will personally make it my business to strangle you!'

'Now, now, Frank,' Marge said reprovingly. 'Remember what your analyst told you.'

I never did find out what Frank's analyst told him, but I thought of a few likely possibilities as I got back into my car and started the drive home. On the way I'd seen at least a dozen locations suitable at first glance for my purposes; on the way back I pulled over twice and made detailed notes and even a couple of modest sketches of the two most promising spots. Both were stretches of road that had sharp turns leading into them, both were out of sight of all habitation, both had woods on both sides, and neither one had a side road anywhere near down which some unwelcome local might wander at the wrong time. I noted down as precisely as I could how far each one was in miles and tenths of miles from Marco's and in a sudden flight of fancy gave them both names – Marco's Misfortune and Catastrophe Corner. I always thought that one of the traits Evonne liked best about me was my ability to abruptly switch from being a man of action, two hundred-plus pounds of fighting fury, into a more contemplative, one might even say poetic, human being. Then again, I could be mistaken; lives there a male on this planet who has not occasionally been mistaken about women?

By three o'clock I was back at the office doing a few chores when the original space cadet sauntered in without knocking. She was dressed comparatively respectably, for her, in white shorts, T-shirt that didn't say anything, white anklets and almost clean white sneakers.

'Well, well,' I said. 'And to what do I owe this unexpected pleasure?'

'Just checking in, Unk,' she said aloofly, perching her skinny derriere on the corner of my desk after pushing some papers out of the way to make room for herself.

'Don't mess those up!' I said. 'I just spent an hour getting them in order.'

'Ever so humbly sorry and deeply contrite,' she said. 'You want to hear what we have been doing or not?'

I sighed and switched off the computer.

'I guess so.'

'I haven't had time to write it up yet, but if you want to wait, I'll go and do it now.'

'No, no,' I said hastily. 'Shoot. Agents have to learn how to deliver oral reports, too. Concise oral reports. Short, pithy ones.' Sara looked a little disappointed, so I said, I don't know why, call it a compassionate heart, call it sweetness of nature, 'Of course, I'll need a full written report at some time for my permanent files.'

She brightened. 'Do you really keep all my reports filed away? Cause I may need them someday for my memoirs, I didn't make copies of the first ones.'

'Of course, foolish child,' I said indulgently. Filed away in weeny shreds in the garbage is where they were filed.

'All right!' the earth's skinniest poetess said. 'Oh. Willy wants to see you when you've got time. He's got something to show you.'

'What?'

'You'll see,' she said. 'You know what curiosity killed.'

'Yeah,' I said. 'The cat, then you. Now will you get on with it?'

'OK, OK,' she said. 'Don't get your balls in an uproar. So this a.m., so early the birds weren't up yet, Willy picks me up, and off we go to the 7-Eleven around the corner so's he can have a coffee and I can phone that guy's office, cause I can't do it from home cause Mom's in the living room, and I don't have a phone in my own room, can you believe that? God, some parents are positively feudal, if you ask me. So, I do my number like you suggested, O Great One, and the secretary says Mr Bellman isn't usually in before nine thirty or ten and would I like to leave a number where he can reach me, and I said simperingly no thank you I'd call back later after I got back from having my nails done. Then me and Willy drive down to the guy's business address down on Slauson somewhere, more details on request . . .'

'How about less?' I said.

'. . . and we're sitting on a bench at a bus stop across the way from the guy's office building, which is like that one down on Davenport but half the size . . .'

I nodded to show her I was still with her.

'. . . so at nine forty-six precisely, up drives this car which Willy says is a last year's Ford-something. The guy in it honks the horn, and the doorman comes running out and shifts a couple of garbage cans he's got out in front to keep the parking space, and the guy parks and gets out, and it's Marco all right, both me and Willy recognize him from his picture.'

'Excellent,' I said. 'So now we know that he drives himself to, and, by inference, from work, also that he leaves his car all day where we might be able to get at it, unlike what he does with it at night, which is to put it in the security garage where he lives.'

'How do you know that?'

'I went and looked, didn't I? Anything else, my little sugar plum?'

'Willy says the guy didn't set any alarm or anything that he could see, he just climbed out and locked up. Then we waited till the doorman took the garbage cans around the corner and then came back and went inside, then we crossed the street and walked by the front door to see if the doorman guy's desk or booth or whatever he had overlooked where Marco's car was parked, but as we couldn't see it from the street, we figured it didn't. Then we split.' She dug out a grubby scrap of paper from her back pocket and passed it to me. 'Here, Pops. Expenses. Payment on demand this time.'

'I can't believe it,' I said. 'Here I am working for nothing, and with pleasure, it's the least I could do, because some of my oldest friends need help, because a wonderful, gentle pooch was savagely beaten to death, and all you can think of is a couple of lousy bucks of expense money.'

'Plus my wages,' the twerp said callously. 'Plus what you owe me from Sunday, which was ten dollars and ninety-five cents. It comes to twenty-six dollars and forty cents in all, and that's only charging five bucks an hour for my services, which is a joke, if you ask me; babysitters get more.'

'Oh, God,' I said wearily, getting out my wallet. 'Here's ten on account, now beat it, will you, I've got things to do.'

'You're not the only one with things to do,' she said, snatching the bill rudely from me. 'I got to practice.' She held the bill up to the light and looked at it suspiciously just to see if I'd get annoyed. When I of course didn't, she added, 'Don't forget Willy wants to see you,' waved bye-bye, and actually left.

I finished up my paperwork, then drove back out to Burbank. I called Willy first, but he said he couldn't show me what he had to show me on the phone, so there was no way of avoiding the drive.

When I got out there, I noticed the red warning light over the garage door was on, which told me the kids were inside printing. Willy and Cissy were around back working in the garden; she was carefully pinching off the dead blooms from a row of pansies or petunias or geraniums or whatever they were, and he was fussing with something down at the bottom of the garden near the compost heap. As he walked back towards me he looked pleased with himself. I handed him the piece of paper on which I'd listed all the mileages from Marco's apartment to the various spots out in Topanga, which I'd so carefully measured; he gave it a glance, then tore it into little pieces which he sprinkled over my head, saying, 'Happy New Year' as he did so.

'Cissy,' I called out. 'It's your husband. It's time to take him to the funny-farm again.'

'Watch,' Willy said to me. 'Watch carefully.' He rolled up the sleeves of his blue denim shirt with exaggerated precision. 'Nothing in the hands. Nothing up the sleeves. Be kind enough to direct your attention down past where Cis is working and off to the left and say when.'

I looked at Willy, then down past where Cissy was and couldn't see anything but two tin cans sitting upside down on the ground, a couple of feet apart. What the hell. I said, 'When.'

There was the sound of a sharp but muffled explosion, and both cans went flying ten feet in the air. Willy beamed at me.

'Very interesting, Doctor,' I said. 'Seems to have been a remotely controlled explosion of some kind. All in all, I'd suspect little Miss Innocent over there who is just pretending to talk to those pansies but really setting off bombs somehow.'

'Wrong,' Willy said with satisfaction. He took out of his shirt pocket a lump of something that looked like silly putty and tossed it to me; it was malleable like silly putty as well.

'Plastic?'

'Plastique,' he corrected me. He took out of his other shirt pocket what looked like a fuse for a car's electrical system, one of those little glass tubes a half-inch or so long and about as big around as a thermometer. 'Detonator.'

'And radio transmitter in your left-hand trouser pocket,' I said. 'I saw you sneak your hand down there. No problem switching an "on" button through a bit of material. Good work, Doctor. Where the hell did you get it all from?'

'Benny got me the plastique,' he said, leading me back around the house toward the kitchen door. 'Although where he got it from he didn't say.'

'Probably his top drawer, under his socks,' I said.

'And then we went and got the rest of it from that place you guys go to in Glendale, just off Brand?'

'I know it well,' I said. In the kitchen I said hello to Maria, then took a chair at the large, wood-topped table. Willy got us a pitcher of fresh orange juice from the fridge and poured out three tall glasses.

'I thought of using those things that look like kids' Jacks, only they're bigger and all the points are sharpened, that saboteurs use,' he said, 'but too many problems with them, not to mention the fact even Benny couldn't get any, and we don't have time to make enough of them. Running something off the speedometer or a counter of my own gets complicated and would need more access to the car than I thought we might get.'

'You thought right,' I said. 'It's locked in a garage where he lives, and at work, as you know, it's right out there in the open.'

'Also,' Willy said around a mouthful of juice, 'the problem was, what part of the car could be blown up and still be repaired in a few minutes? So I thought, what don't cars carry two of?' He brought down the cookie tin from the shelf.

I took an oatmeal one and said, 'I give up.' I could have easily figured out the answer, but why spoil the doc's big moment?

'Two spare tires,' he said. He took the micro-transmitter from his trouser pocket; it looked like a matt-black transistor radio, but without any station listings, which was pretty much what it was, although it sent a signal rather than received one. 'With this we can stop a car whenever we want and wherever we want, within a few yards.'

'If it doesn't go wrong,' I said.

'What's to go wrong? No moving parts, and anyway, we got a spare.'

'What's to go wrong,' I said, trying a piece of butterscotch fudge this time, 'is that the plastique, monsieur, which I suppose has been stuck to the inside of both rear tires, might fall off.'

'Using super-glue?' he said. 'Do me a favor, Vic; you know what that stuff's like.'

I didn't, actually, never having had an occasion to use it yet, but I nodded anyway.

'Amazing stuff. I suppose you already figured out how to do the sticking without being caught?'

'Sara figured it out,' he said, his mouth full of corn muffin. 'That's why she's at home practicing.'

Well, I remembered her muttering something about having to practice, but it hadn't even crossed my mind she was going to practice anything useful; I figured she was going to practice guitar chords or rolling joints with one hand.

'If I may be allowed to know,' I said, 'as I am El Supremo after all, what the hell is that twit practicing?'

'Rollerskating,' Willy said, taking another corn muffin.

CHAPTER EIGHTEEN

It was Wednesday, the calendar on my office wall informed me. The Timex on my wrist informed me it was two minutes before noon, and as I always kept it five minutes fast, that made it seven minutes. Kids, don't neglect your arithmetic, either. I did have a more expensive timepiece, a mouth-watering Patek Phillipe given to me by Mr Lubinski, family jeweler, for disentangling him from the attentions of some highly lethal ruffians, but I'd since seen a similar watch in the window of a jeweler's in Beverly Hills and now I was afraid to wear mine without an armed escort.

So far that morn things had continued apace with all the bits and pieces I was juggling. I'd taken a call from Bill Jessop of ginseng fame who first of all had asked me if it had started to work yet then had said that after some stern words with his dearly beloved brother-in-law Johnny-o, Johnny-o had taken some of the padding out of the new policy and also had agreed to waive his commission. He wouldn't lose, however, as he'd still be writing the policy, and so it would count in his yearly total. Thus, said Mr Jessop, he'd decided to go with the new company after all, as it would keep peace in the family, and under the new terms it wouldn't cost him but a pittance extra, so could I drop by sometime later that week and get started with the requisite hardware modifications?

I said I'd be delighted, how about Friday afternoon, latish, I'd be bringing an assistant, and please tell the sweetheart at the bottle-sealing machine her dreamboat was sailing back into her humdrum life. Then I got on to a whiz kid that Phil the Freak out at J & M Home Security Co. in Glendale had put me on to who worked for Phil sometimes and freelanced the rest of the time. He was free for Friday, he told me when I finally tracked him down.

Then I had a call from Richard, aka Miss Peggy. He bore, if you can bear over a telephone, the sad news that his friend had passed away in his sleep two days ago and had been laid to rest that morning. He said he'd decided to go on 'hold' for a while and to take himself down to Puerto Vallarta for a month or six to lie in the sun and do nothing and to hell with his complexion and that he'd get in touch with me when he got back and if I was lucky he might even send me a post-card.

'No pelicans,' I said, just for something to say. 'I hate postcards with pelicans on them.'

Then I strolled around to the Two-Two-Two; Jim wasn't open yet, but I knocked and he let me in, then went back to wiping down the bar. I could hear Lotus banging pots and pans around in the small kitchen out back. When he poured me out a Michelob, I held the glass up to the light and pretended to look at it critically.

'I had a dream,' I said. 'And in my dream a wonderful guy I know ran this estaminet for you and made you a lot of money so you, too, could have sunny vacations in México like me anytime you wanted to at the drop of a sombrero. And also, just to while away the lonely hours, you gave Dave a hand over at his place, although why he calls it the Corner Bar I do not know because it's in the middle of the block.'

'He told me it was supposed to be a joke,' Jim said. 'And if that glass is dirty, I'm Toots Shor.'

'You see, Toots,' I said, 'Dave tells me his girls are always quitting on him for one reason or another.'

'Correct,' Jim said. 'The reason being either Dave's left hand or his right one.'

'So there it was,' I said wistfully. 'In my dream. All wrapped up. No loose ends. Except the guy I know just had a death in the family, you might say, and he's taking off for a while.'

'Oh yes?' Jim said in some embarrassment, cleaning an already spotless ashtray. 'Perhaps it's just as well. His going away, I mean. I've been thinking. Maybe I'll just go on as I am for a while. What's a few nancies around the place, anyway?'

'Right,' I said.

'Maybe they'll brighten things up around here.'

'Right.'

'I get tired of seeing the same old lushes in here night after night.'

'Right. You took down your sign, I notice,' I said, referring to the anagram of 'faggots' that used to be above the bar.

'Must have been Lotus,' Jim said unconvincingly, looking around in case she was within earshot. 'Now are you going to drink that libation or just play with it?'

Just to please him, I polished it off and let him buy me a fresh one, then I strolled back to the office to answer the one item of mail that required an answer. It was a handwritten letter from a man down in Torrance wanting to know if I could help him find his mother-in-law. I suspected a joke, of course, and not a bad one either, but just in case I wrote him a note back suggesting he telephone me for an appointment sometime during the following week.

Afternoon found me working on timetables, lots of, and assignment sheets, also lots of. These I took with me when I made the short drive south through the Hollywood Hills to Rick's small house on Kirkwood; you may remember on the way to the sisters Forbes I mentioned an artist friend who lived just down the hill from them. Well, said friend was Rick. Rick was a Canadian version of the Mexican wetback, only in his case he skied across the border instead of swam. In all other respects he was the same, he had no papers –

except for Zig-Zags – he had a bizarre accent, and he spent most of his life singing sad songs to pretty girls. The rest of the time he painted them, in the nude, naturally. He told me he had succeeded more than once in convincing several of his scatterbrained models that to paint the female form with truth and proper reverence the artist had to be nude, too, but I took that as he took his favorite tipple, which was cheap tequila – with a grain of salt.

Feckless, reckless, womanizer, gigolo – call him what you will, he didn't mind, as long as he had a bottle, a brush and a couple of old Betty Page bondage magazines lying around for inspiration. Anyway, not only was he at home, he was more than delighted to dash off for me a proper map, taken from the feeble sketches I had made out in Topanga.

Rick and I had met 'cute', as they say out here in show-biz talk; I was parking in front of an English pub on Sunset when he got out of a cab in front of me and began weaving his way toward the door. Suddenly he froze, then he ran out into the street, waved after the disappearing cab, then jumped in beside me.

'Follow that cab!' he shouted. 'It's life or death!'

I took off, burning a little rubber.

'Who's in it?' I asked. 'Your wife?'

'My new Martin,' he yelled. 'Step on it, will you?'

We got back his Martin, which is, for you non-rock-and-rollers, a famous brand of guitar, and took things from there over a few pints of powerful Limey beer back at the pub.

After a tearful goodbye at Rick's I took the map, the time-tables and assignment sheets to the post office down on Fairfax, made copies, lots of, had a late lunch at Kantor's down the line, nodded to Alan Alda in the next booth, who affably nodded back, purchased some pickled tomatoes at the take-out counter, plus a loaf of their light rye, then went back over the hills to my side of town to get the rest of my act together.

Later that afternoon the whole gang gathered in my office for our second council of war, which was slightly selfish of me as four of them had to come in from Burbank and there was only one of me, but such are the perks of command. Everyone was on time but Sara, who else, who made her entrance twenty minutes late in full rollerskating gear complete with knee pads, elbow pads and thick gloves. I was surprised she wasn't wearing a crash helmet, too. I'd borrowed some extra chairs from the Nus next door, and when everyone was finally present and accounted for and sitting on something, I sternly called the meeting to order and looked over my troops.

Willy, in what looked like old army fatigues plus a pair of high-topped boots, slouched in one chair; beside him, Suze, in hotpants and skin-tight T-shirt, held hands with Wade who was beside her and just managing to stay awake. On my right, Benny, notebook in hand, occupied my own spare chair, looking, as usual, at complete peace with himself and the world and as inoffensive as a Cub Scout. Cissy sat primly beside him, a set of amber worry beads trickling through her fingers. Sara, of course, perched on the corner of my desk and immediately lit up one of her fake cigars she thought were so cool and with-it. I had the computer set up, mainly for effect, I admit, on the far side of the desk away from her, but that didn't stop her leaning across and trying to meddle with it, so I finally switched it off. Also on my desk, I might mention, was Cissy's replenished cookie tin, brought along for emergencies; Suze had already been over to Mrs Morales' for large, messy containers of liquid refreshments for everyone.

I cleared my throat.

'Photographic division. Report, please.'

Wade bestirred himself enough to say, 'We're getting there, man, we're getting there.'

'When will you arrive?' I inquired.

'Like tomorrow noon,' Suze said. 'If I have to drag him out of bed myself.'

'Obtain some brown paper,' I said. 'Do not leave your sticky prints all over it, and if you do, wipe them off. Wrap up the completed pictures in two packages, two hundred in each. Tie them securely. In the upper left corner please write, "From:" and under that, Marco's company's name and its address, which I will give you. In the middle, please write "To:" and under that, the address of one PPC, which stands for Photographic Pleasures Company, which I will also give you.'

'So give,' said Suze. I gave. I also gave them both a copy of their individual assignment sheets, which contained, among other things, the instructions just mentioned above.

'Peruse those sheets,' I told them. 'They contain the rest of your assignments. Transport. Willy?'

'We have my car,' he said. 'We have Suze's Volks, filled up and ready to go.'

'And we have my bike,' Cissy said. 'Ready to roll.'

'Marco's got Uniroyals on his,' Willy said. 'I've got a spare that'll fit; it's not new but it's good enough.'

'Better take along a second one,' I said, 'just in case Marco's dumb enough not to have a spare of his own or something's wrong with it.'

'Check,' said Willy, making a note on his pad.

'You don't have to make notes, Willy,' I said. 'I've got timetables and maps and assignment sheets for you all. Benny, my boy?'

'I checked out a supermarket over in Sepulveda,' he said, 'which has no security at all in the parking lot. You know, some of them have guys walking around with a piece of chalk on the end of a stick with which they mark the tires; what they're looking for are people who park there all day who aren't customers. This one is clean and not too far away but not too close, either, so there's no problem, you can have a nice, ordinary family car a couple of years old and with no identifying peculiarities anytime you want.'

'How about eight o'clock tomorrow night?' I passed Benny his own personal assignment sheet, along with a map and a timetable.

'Fine with me,' he said. 'I believe I'm free tomorrow.'

'Keys,' I said. 'How about them? Keys for Marco's car, keys for the nice, ordinary family car.'

He smiled at me pityingly.

'Plates,' I said.

'Plates I can obtain,' Benny said. 'I know a guy in that line of work. I know a couple, as a matter of fact.'

'One will do,' I said. 'Wade, you awake?'

'Sure, man,' Wade said. 'I'm just thinking.'

'On your assignment sheet,' I said, 'see what it says under "transport"?'

'I'm with you,' he said. 'No problem.'

'Sara. Explosive materials, detonating and delivery systems,' I said.

'In ze bag, Pops,' she said, swinging her skinny legs. 'We been rehearsing all afternoon out at Willy's.'

'It had better be,' I said. 'And stop banging those skate things against my desk.'

'Don't be hard on her, Unk,' said Benny. 'She is but a willful child, full of the unfocused energy of youth.'

'So was Squeaky Fromme,' I said. I handed around the assignment sheets and copies of the timetable and the map to those who didn't already have them.

The timetable looked like this:

1.   ?   a.m.   Sara phones Marco at office. (See Individual Assignments.)
2.   ?   a.m.   If 1. (above) successful, Sara & Willy plant plastique.
3.   ?   a.m.   If 2. successful, V.D. contacts police.
4.   ?   p.m.   Benny has borrowed car, delivered by 8.00 p.m.
5.   ?   p.m.   V.D. phones.
6.   8.00 p.m.   Plates. Equipment check.
7.   9.00–10:25:   En route.
8.   10.25:   Plates. Lights.
9.   10.30:   All in position and ready to go. (See Map.) Wade in Suze's car, Cissy on bike, Benny in borrowed car, in lot at Map Reference (MR) 1. Willy, MR 3. V.D. & fuzz, MR 6. Suze & Sara at base, MR 7.
10. 10.30 (approx): Cissy phones from MR 2.
11. 10.35 (approx): V.D. phones from MR 6.
12. 11.00 (approx): Action at Catastrophe Corner – MR 3.
13. 11.02 (approx): Willy at MR 3 contacts Wade at MR 1.
14. 11.05 (approx): Benny & Cissy en route from MR 1.
15. 11.15 (approx): Benny arrives at Catastrophe Corner – MR 3.
16. 11.15 (approx): Willy (MR 3) contacts Wade (MR 1).
17. 11.15 (approx): Wade en route to MR 3.
18. 11.25 (approx): Benny arrives at MR 5.
19. 11.30 (approx): Wade & Willy en route. Ultimate destination MR 7.
20. 11.30 (approx): Cissy to MR 6.
21. 11.32 (approx): Cissy en route.
22. 11.35 (approx): V.D. & fuzz en route

23. 11.45 (approx): Cissy to MR 5, then MR 1, then back to base (MR 7).
24. 11.45 (approx): V.D. & fuzz interception between MR 5 & MR 6.
25. 1.00 (approx): Festivities begin – MR 7.

My labors did not go unnoticed and unappreciated, I am pleased to report. After all, I was doing it for the kids, or mostly, anyway. If it had been just me involved I probably would have done something quick, simple and violent that might not have involved Mr Bellman breaking his parole but certainly would have involved him in the breaking of other things, as in parts of his body. However.

After another flying visit by Suze to Mrs Morales for more beverages, I ran over everyone's individual assignments with them so they could all see where their contributions to the Machiavellian Master Plan slotted in. Then we went our separate ways, not without a certain amount of back-slapping and 'It'll be all right on the night' and other such high jinks. Benny took Sara home, then went off to the Free Estonians Club for some undivulged reason. Although I knew little about Estonians, I knew a lot about Benny, and I thought it highly unlikely he was going there for either the food or the ethnic dancing. The rest of the bunch drove back to thrilling suburban Burbank to get down to some serious eating, and my landlady Feeb and I took Mom out for supper at a Swedish cafeteria that she liked but I didn't. Then we took in a movie, which for a reason that I won't bother to divulge turned out to be an embarrassing occasion for all concerned except Feeb, who didn't give a damn about anything except the LA Kings 'hockey' team and the San Diego Padres 'baseball' team. With those two to worry about, who had time for lesser embarrassments?

CHAPTER NINETEEN

The big day dawned early, as big days will do. Also small days, I've noticed. It also dawned hot, with the warning of a two-stage smog alert, meaning in LA lingo it was all right to go outside if you didn't inhale more than once every fifteen minutes, and then not too deeply. Mom made french toast for breakfast – I wonder why it's called that – then we lingered over coffee a while, I made sure she was beepered up, told her to be a good girl, and took off for my humble place of business.

I didn't have anything to do as far as the Marco Master Plan was concerned until the first of the troops phoned in, so I occupied myself with other things – reading the sports page – until ten forty-five or so when Willy called to tell me in a whisper that Sara had been on to Marco and it was all systems go. Then he said they were proceeding on to Stage Two: explosives and the planting thereof.

'For Christ's sake be careful, Doc,' I told him. 'Those things can be dangerous and so can Marco and his dog-loving pal. If there's any hitch at all, give it a miss, and we'll try something else. In fact, the more I think about that stupid plan the less I like it, there's too many things that can go wrong.'

'Not to worry,' he said. He sounded like he was enjoying himself. 'Leave it to me and Sara. She is something else, she is.'

'You're telling me,' I said.

He rang off. Twenty minutes later he called again.

'Stage Two completed,' he said, still in a whisper. 'Moving on to Stage Three. Over and out.'

'Roger,' I said. 'Or is it wilco?'

Then it was my turn to phone someone, i.e. the fuzz, and in particular, a Lieutenant Conyers, the LAPD's only serving midget. We were not exactly bosom buddies, the lieutenant and me, due to several factors, the main one being the crippling jealousy he suffered because I was almost three times his height. There were other reasons involved, such as the official law-enforcement agent's dislike of all those involved in my shady profession (jealousy again, no doubt), but my manly build was the main reason. Luckily, however, his pathological hatred of lawbreakers of all kinds including jaywalkers was even greater than his juvenile animosity towards me, so although he wasn't thrilled out of his skin to hear my voice, he didn't hang up right away.

'Shorty?' I said when we'd been connected by the switchboard. 'Guess who.'

'All right, all right,' he said. 'What is it this time, and kindly make it snappy. Unlike you I have a great deal of important work to do.'

'That sort of cheap gibe is beneath you, Lieutenant,' I said. 'If that's possible. Listen. Have you any connections in the Sheriff's Department?' I asked because Topanga Canyon didn't come under the jurisdiction of the Los Angeles Police Department but was part of the three thousand square miles or so the County Sheriff and his minions were responsible for.

'I might be able to come up with a name or two,' Lieutenant Conyers admitted reluctantly. 'If it were important enough, which I doubt.'

'Well, hear this,' I said. I sketched in enough of the background to get him interested, which didn't take all that much sketching because not only did he know who Marco Bellman was, he told me that when he was working out of Vice he had once busted him, or tried to, for indecent assault on a minor, but the case had never gone to court because someone had subsequently assaulted said minor so thoroughly that for a while it was questionable whether or not she could ever talk again, even if she wanted to.

The fact that Lieutenant Conyers did not have the fondest of memories re Marco Bellman helped. He finally agreed to get in touch with a sheriff's deputy he knew and to try and persuade him to drive them both out to hell and gone that night.

'But you, Daniel, you'd better deliver,' Shorty said just before hanging up, reverting to his usual nasty nature.

'Oh, ye of little faith,' I said, hanging up myself.

And little everything else, too, I was going to add. Don't get me wrong, I'm not against all short people per se. I suppose there are some well-adjusted, non-aggressive, contented, peaceable, sunny-minded shrimps in the world, it's just that I've never met any, and if I do say so myself, I have been around.

Then, with considerable strength of purpose, I went back to the tedious paperwork I'd been involved with before the spate of telephone calls. I was thumbing through my previously mentioned collection of headed stationery for something that might persuade one Samuel Beakins, owner of three small laundromats in the Studio City area, that he would be wise to pay his outstanding account with me, as I seemed to remember I had a couple of sheets somewhere that (purportedly) were from the State of California Water Authority, when the phone rang yet again. This time it was my favorite nerd, reporting that she and Willy were back home and everyone was busy but her, so did I have anything for her to do?

I checked my own assignment sheet and had a bright idea.

'Whatever Suze is doing,' I said, 'you take over and send her to that security outfit in Glendale, Willy knows where it is, and tell her to take some money and rent a couple of walkie-talkies. Tell her to tell Phil they're for me, and you'll probably get a deal on them. O K?'

'You got it, Pops.'

'Don't forget new batteries,' I said. 'And don't play with them until the batteries run out.'

'Perish the thought,' Sara said. She blew me a kiss and rang off.

I went back to work on the hapless Mr Beakins. When I'd polished him off, I phoned up Evonne and asked her if she wanted to ask me over to her place for lunch.

'Sure thing, Sugar,' she said. 'If you bring the lunch.'

So I stopped briefly at Fred's Deli on the way, loaded up and in no time at all was sprawled in a deckchair in Evonne's back garden looking at her long, tanned legs and nibbling delicately at a tongue and hot mustard sandwich on white while she destroyed her third helping of potato salad. Then, afterwards, when she was pouring us both some more iced tea, she ran her free hand over my ringlets and said, 'Feel up to a matinee, Big Boy?'

'Gee, I dunno,' I said. 'I don't usually go to the movies in the afternoon.'

'Very funny,' she said. She took her tea and headed back to the house. 'If you're not there in five minutes, I'll start without you.'

To show my independence, I held out for a good three minutes. Her lips tasted of mayonnaise and lemon. I don't know what mine tasted like to start with, but after a while they could only have tasted of her.

Talking of spates, as I did not long ago, late that afternoon back at the office I had another spate, this time a welcome rush of business and/or potential business. Large law firms, those employing, say, a dozen senior and junior partners plus all their associates, paralegals, clerks and whatnots, will often have their own investigator on the payroll, as they have more than enough work for him. Small firms must of necessity use independents like myself from time to time. I'd recently met in a social setting (a bar) a nice, laid-back type called Mel Evans who was a lawyer with a two-men-and-a-Girl-Friday outfit downtown just off MacArthur Park, which is not the MacArthur Park famed in song, which is, I believe, in San Francisco; L A's version is, alas, only famed for such things as number of winos per park bench and number of addicts per square foot of turf.

A few weeks ago Mel had called me up out of the blue and wanted to know if I could verify the alibi of one of his clients who otherwise could be in a lot of trouble, as in three-to-five for manslaughter. I said I'd have a go and finally did manage it after three tough days of interviewing people who didn't want to be interviewed and getting signed testimonies from people who were chary of signing their names to anything, including letters they'd written themselves. This time all Mel wanted was for me to escort politely but firmly, as he put it, what he dearly hoped was a friendly witness in an insurance case from the witness' home to the old courthouse downtown on the day of Tuesday 7 August at two p.m. I checked my diary and happily agreed.

Then he asked what I would charge to check through all available records – births, marriages, deaths, property owner-ship, vehicle registration, business affiliates and the like – for another of his clients who was thinking about contesting a will. I thought for a moment, came up with an hourly rate, and Mel said he'd get back to me on it next week but it looked like a go, so save him some time. I said I'd be delighted. Bits and pieces . . . the varied, multicolored bits and pieces that are the mosaic of the life of an investigator of all trades . . .

Mel had no sooner hung up than the twerp phoned again

to complain that she'd tried twice to get me earlier, but I'd been out and why didn't I get one of those answering machines, or better yet, a secretary, someone young and bright and of proven bravery and imagination and who could already type good enough. I told her it wasn't a bad idea and I'd keep my eye out for someone exactly like that. She said Suze was long back with the communication equipment in question, that I owed her, Suze, twenty-five green ones and that if I didn't return them within twenty-four hours I'd have to shell out another twenty-five.

'Roger, over and out,' I said.

Then I had a visit from a vivacious young miss whose face was almost hidden by a pair of huge, round, white-framed sunglasses and whose pink business card informed me that she was (Ms) M. Margaret Mehan. Ms Mehan was a space-seller for the local weekly rag and she was visiting all their regular and occasional clients to see if she could peddle them a few more column inches than they usually took. I was one of the paper's occasional clients – a few times a year I inserted a small but tasteful ad for myself which appeared in the 'Personals' under 'Miscellaneous Services', usually sandwiched between hopeful ads for trusses fitted in the privacy of your own home and '500-500-500 Stamps – 99c plus postage!' Then there was the occasional legal notice, and once in a while I'd taken a little box to offer a reward for any information leading to the recovery of certain stolen property – no questions asked – or sometimes a missing-persons announcement. That day I had nothing for Ms Mehan, I just didn't have any business. I told her all my advertising budget for the month had gone into TV, which elicited a wry chuckle from her, as the money required to buy thirty seconds on TV time at three in the morning could have bought her whole newspaper. She left, and I watched her walk past the picture window toward the Nus'. There was nothing at all wrong with her legs, but they weren't attached to Evonne Beverly Shirley.

Then, lo and behold, another call, this one from my friend Mr Lubinski, the Mr Lubinski who had presented me with the expensive wristwatch a while ago as a thank-you.

'Want to make some easy money, old friend?' he asked me.

'Is there such a thing?' I said. 'What do I have to do this time, clean up Dodge City?'

He laughed. 'Stand around stuffing your face.'

'Where?'

'At my niece Rebecca's wedding reception,' he said. 'She's my cousin Nate's eldest, and is he relieved. He even smiled once the other day. Not a big smile, but a smile. And when you see what that girl is going to get from wedding presents, you wouldn't believe.'

I asked him when; he told me. Then I told him apologetically there was of course a standard fee for such services.

'Which you just made up, you momser,' he said. 'How's this for standard, a hundred dollars and all the lox you can eat?'

'Settled,' I said. 'See you in a couple of weeks, then.'

'Don't forget to rent a suit,' he said.

'You mean a monkey suit?'

'Any suit,' he said. 'By the way, that timepiece still working?'

'Yeah, but it keeps gaining,' I said. 'It's gained almost a second this year.'

He laughed again and rang off. Lovely man, Mr Lubinski. I looked down at my appointment book with approval. It was filling up nicely. I used to keep all my appointments on the computer, but Evonne had given me something called The Sportsman's Diary and Desk Manager last Christmas in my stocking, so I started using it. After all, a guy never knows when he may need to find out when the trout season starts in Oregon or how to get a license to hunt moose. Also, that snoop Sara had once gotten a look at the screen when I was checking on my appointments and her unfeeling laughter when she saw such entries as 'Scalp treatment – 2 p.m.' and 'Call dentist to postpone appt' still rings in my ears.

Then Ma Bell made even more money, this time from Benny.

'Done,' he said. 'We are now the proud, if temporary, owners of a dark blue 84 Fairlane. Willy's out front now putting new plates on it.'

'Any problems?'

'Only one,' Benny said. 'A small, furry one.'

'How can you have a small, furry problem, Benny?'

'When it's a cat,' he said. 'It was in a basket in the back seat. Nice little thing. White. It's in the living room here playing with Rags and Cissy.'

'Well, don't lose the damn thing,' I said. 'We'll have to give it back.'

'Lose it?' said Benny. 'Are you kidding? It's having the time of its young life. By the way, its name is Sylvester.'

'How sweet,' I said. 'Anything else going on?'

'Cissy's making us stuffed eggplant for supper is all.'

'Glad I can't make it,' I said. 'OK, amigo, later.'

And later it was, ten fifteen to be precise. I was sitting across the table from Lieutenant Conyers in the saloon beside the general store in the wilds of Topanga Canyon. Through the window I could see the lieutenant's huge, black chum from the Sheriff's Department, Deputy Marvin Morrison, known to one and all, of course, as Marvelous Marv, who was lounging by the open door of his patrol car in which we had all driven out from town together. I held up my glass of Dos Equis in a friendly toast, but Marv's attention was elsewhere. Lieutenant Conyers scowled at me.

'Shouldn't do that, Shorty,' I said. 'It leaves lines.'

'Butt out,' he said.

'We are looking sharp tonight,' I said. 'What a natty ensemble.' Shorty fancied himself a clothes-horse; that eve he was sporting a pale yellow, lapel-less jacket worn over a wine-colored shirt and one of those pathetic string ties. Green slacks, yellow anklets and natural leather loafers. His narrow-brimmed, à la Italian brown fedora rested on the table between us. I wondered idly if there was a chain of stores the opposite of Mr Big, called Mr Tiny, where he went to shop, or did he just go to the boys' department? Anyway, he had it easier than I did; I've been in towns where I couldn't even get underwear my size.

The phone behind the bar rang. Frank the barman answered it, and having been prewarned by me, gave a wave in our direction. I excused myself politely and went over and picked it up. It was Suze, back at headquarters.

'Just heard from Cissy,' she said excitedly. (See Timetable.) 'Everyone's lined up and ready to go.'

'Roger,' I said. 'Wilco. Over and out.' I hung up, thanked Frank, and strolled back to the table.

'All systems go, Louie,' I said. 'Getting nervous? Want a downer to keep you cool?'

'No,' he said. 'I'll have another CC and Coke. And as you're buying, make it a double.'

I got him his drink and another beer for myself and then took a beer out for Marvelous Marv, and then we waited. And waited. Fortunately, some of us thrive on tension.

CHAPTER TWENTY

'For goodness' sake,' said the Special Invited Guest, 'will somebody please, please tell me what you've all been up to?'

'Certainly, my dear,' I said expansively. 'No sooner said than done, my sweeting. Sit back, relax, stretch out those slim limbs of yours and prepare your gasps of wonder and amazement.'

If you deduced from the above that (a) I was addressing my favorite blond, (b) in a certain living room in Burbank, and (c) I was feeling little, if any, pain at the time, your deductions were correct. All of my brave troops were there, with the addition of Rags and three felines, counting Sylvester, who was asleep in Cissy's ample lap. And were we not smoking, drinking, never thinking of tomorrow, and, in my case at least, nonchalant?

'Sara, my pet,' I said nonchalantly, 'from the top, if you please, if your brain is still working after all that home-grown.'

Sara finished off a glass of Hawaiian Punch and rum, just the thought of which would make any serious drinker shudder, and said, 'See, Evonne, there was this greaseball, and we wanted to fix the mother but good.'

'That much Mr Wonderful over there filled me in on the other day,' Evonne said with a loving glance in my direction.

'So this morning I phone the guy, Marco, from around the corner, like it says to do on my assignment sheet, which was all part of the master plan devised by Mr Wonderful over there.'

'Oh, just call me Wonderful,' I said.

'And I tell Marco politely: "Please sir, I hate to bother you, but you missed a copy of that photograph you were so worried about." There's a pause and he says: "Who're you?" And I say: "My name is Marge, it was my brother's darkroom you trashed, but please, sir, the last thing we want is any more trouble, you're way out of our league, sir, and we'd just like to give you the picture back because we sure don't want it, whatever it's about, but if you think it's fair, perhaps in exchange you could just help us out with a few dollars to get a new Polaroid and a few other things that got busted as we're small, and we're just starting out and believe me, sir, you'd never hear from us again. . . .'

'"Sounds fair," says the creep.

'"Only thing," I say, "and I hope it's not inconvenient, I left it where I work because my brother was too scared to keep it here."

'"So?" he says.

'"So," I say, "can you please come by tonight and get it where I work because there'll be lots of people around, and if you don't mind me saying so, sir, I'd just as soon not meet you alone in a dark alley somewhere after what happened to my dog."

'"What happened to your dog?" he says. So I tell him. He says it's the first he's heard of it and how sorry he is and he will have a stern word to say to someone about it, and I say: "Thank you, sir," not believing a word of his crap. So then I tell him where I work, which is at the saloon beside the general store in Topanga Canyon, and how to get there, and tell him eleven o'clock, please, and then I asked him to please, sir, come by yourself and not bring your friend because if I ever saw his friend I'd get so upset I didn't know how I'd react.

'"I'll be there," he says. "By the way," he then says casually, "how did you recognize me?"

'Not a bad question, I thought. A real shitter, I thought, because how did I?' And she looked at me accusingly.

'One of the secrets of my success,' I said to Suze in a confidential tone, 'is that I always leave scope for my troops to improvise on the spur of the moment; that way they are in a continual learning situation.'

'Sure, Vic, sure,' Suze scoffed, blowing air up into her bangs.

'So,' Sara went on. 'So I say, "Excuse me, sir, I'll tell you that tonight, it was an accident, like; my brother's screaming at me to get off the phone, you know how brothers are," and he says something like, "OK, then, later, and you better be there," and hangs up. Not bad eh?' She looked around the room for approval and was rewarded with a generous outbreak of applause, which, I freely admit, was not completely undeserved.

'Seems to me there's something else Mr Wonderful over there forgot,' Evonne said. 'What if Marco phoned up the saloon and found out there was no such person as Marge working there?'

'Ah, but there is,' I said smugly. 'I was out there, wasn't I?'

'OK, what if she goes to the phone and says, "Marco who? Never heard of you,"' Evonne said.

'Ah, but Frank the bartender won't let her take personal calls,' I said just as smugly.

'OK,' Evonne persisted, 'what if there was another bartender working who didn't care how many personal calls Marge got? Or what if Marge was off sick that night?'

'Ah,' I said. 'I'm glad you asked. If you will consult your copy of the timetable, you will notice by the number five it says, "V.D. phones." Guess where I was phoning.'

'The saloon,' said Evonne. 'OK, Mr Wonderful, I'll give you that one.'

'Then – stage the second,' said Willy around a mouthful of sliced salami.

'Emerging from the phone booth,' Sara said with an affected air, 'I revealed myself to be in full rollerskating regalia, complete with my second-favorite T-shirt, the one that says "Tits Aren't Everything" on it.'

'A thoughtful gift from some unknown admirer on your last birthday, I believe,' I said.

'So anyway,' she said, fluttering her eyelashes at me provocatively, she hoped, 'I make out like I'm just a beginner on wheels which is why all the pads and stuff I'm wearing – one of my brilliant ideas, thank you – and I skate round the corner and I happen to fall down guess where.'

'On your ass,' said Suze.

'Right behind creepo's car,' Sara said, 'as well as on my ass, Suze. My handbag, which is really a neat tin lunch pail thing, flies open and all the junk inside it falls out. A kindly passer-by comes to my aid, like the gentleman he is, unlike some I could name. Take a bow, Willy.'

Willy bowed deeply.

'Between helping me up and picking up my stuff, he sticks that Plasticine guck, which has already got the glue on it, where he wants it.'

'Out of sight on the inside of both back tires,' said Willy. 'Nothing to it. The doorman even helped pick up some of her stuff.'

'We rendezvous around the corner where we started from, called the mastermind over there, then split back here.'

'The doorman helped you?' Evonne said. 'Incredible. I presume that Plasticine guck you referred to wasn't the kind you roll on a table and make snakes from.'

'You presume correctly, as usual, my vision,' I said.

'Then what?' she said.

'Then item three on the timetable,' I said. 'I called an extremely short policeman I know.' I helped myself (by mistake) to a banana, bacon and marmalade sandwich. 'In fact, he is so short he has to wear heels to impersonate Toulouse-Lautrec.'

'Get on with it,' said the twerp unnecessarily. 'We ain't got all night to listen to old jokes.'

I ignored her and went on. '"If you want to arrest a malefactor," I said, "meet me in the saloon out in Topanga at ten o'clock precisely. Oh – and bring a friend, if you've got one, preferably one with jurisdiction out there." As it turned out, logistics demanded we all drive out together in the cop car. Over and out for now. Next?'

'Next was me, man, I guess,' said Suze, sucking the last hit out of her little silver hash pipe. Then she offered Rags a sliver of some uncooked vegetable which he took gingerly and then carried away. 'Me and Wade were just finishing up the last of the printing when Sara tells me to get my ass out to Glendale where some goofball rents me a couple of walkie-talkies. That reminds me, Vic . . .'

'Later,' I said hastily. 'We'll all settle up later.'

'Meanwhile, back at the ranch,' said Wade, 'me and Sara wrap up the photos like we're supposed to and address them like we're supposed to.'

From his recumbent position by the fireplace, Benny said sleepily, 'Item five. I happened by chance by the Ralph's supermarket out in Sepulveda later in the afternoon and there I noticed this 83 or maybe 84 dark blue Fairlane drive up and park, which pleased me mightily as it was one of the seven or eight models I chanced to have complete sets of keys for left over from the bad old days when I didn't know the difference between right and wrong.'

'Uh-huh,' said Suze. 'Nineteen eighty-four is sure the old days, all right.'

'By the way, Vic, the keys for Marco's car I had to lay out for, and they didn't come cheap.'

'Later, later,' I said.

'The rather attractive lady who got out of the Fairlane,' Benny continued, 'not only had a lengthy shopping list in one hand which meant she'd be in the store for a while, but she also said something to someone in the car before she locked up. So I strolled by and looked in the back window and there was Sylvester in a basket. Perfect, I thought.'

'Sylvester?' said Evonne.

'This is Sylvester,' said Cissy, stroking the bundle of white fur in her lap.

'Ah,' said my darling. 'Why was Sylvester perfect, Benny?'

'I will tell you,' said Benny, rolling over on his back. 'I liked the idea of the cat because Vic's master plan required not only a stolen car but one that had been reported as stolen, and as we didn't have a lot of time for all this to happen, it struck me that a car with someone's beloved kitty in it might get reported to the police that much faster than otherwise. A small point, admittedly. Then all that remained was to carefully drive the car, the cat and myself back here. Which I did. I thank you all for your kind attention.'

'And I had just returned here after purchasing a used automobile tire,' said Willy, this time around a mouthful of Ritz crackers spread with cream cheese and pimento, 'to go with the one I already had. Then I took the plates off the Fairlane and put them in the trunk of Suze's Volks along with the two spare tires. I checked out her jack while I was about it, it was fine. Then I put a different set of plates on the Fairlane, a set my friend Benny had kindly contributed.'

'Left over from the old days, too, eh?' said Suze. 'Like yesterday.'

'If you please,' said Benny. 'I borrowed them from a dear friend of mine.'

'Ah,' I said, holding up one finger. 'Evonne wants to know why bother to change the plates at all?'

'Do I?' said Evonne.

'Because,' said Willy in a professorial tone, 'it is chancy enough driving all the way out to Topanga in a stolen car anyway without taking the needless risk of leaving the original plates on because we didn't have the time or the proper equipment to repaint the car, which we didn't want to do anyway; how would you like not only to have your car borrowed but have it returned amateurishly repainted? I did hang some felt dice from the mirror and slapped bumper stickers on it front and back just to change its appearance slightly. Remember, all patrol cars are connected to the computer downtown at the DMV, and if you're stopped for any infraction, minor or otherwise, these days, while one cop is asking you for your license the other is running your plates through the system.'

'Moving right along,' I said, handing my peach blossom a copy of Rick's map, 'picture the scene. It is now ten thirty. Night has fallen. The stars are twinkling overhead. Suze and Sara are here at headquarters, getting smashed and holding down the fort. Me, Shorty, and a sheriff's deputy known as Marvelous Marv, are enjoying a cooling drink. Wade, in Suze's car, with one of the walkie-talkies, is parked in a small lot off the road not far from Catastrophe Corner. So is Cissy, on that killer bike of hers, with a spare crash helmet. And so is my old mate Benny, suitably attired and bespectacled as a harmless traveling salesman, in the Fairlane, in the front seat of which, please notice, are the neatly wrapped nature studies, two large packages of highly offensive and highly illegal studies in bestiality. By this time Benny has – number eight on the timetable – changed the plates back and broken one of the rear brake lights.

'Willy, in dark clothes, is lurking suspiciously in the underbrush beside Catastrophe Corner, his trusty radio transmitter in one hand, the second walkie-talkie in his other trembling hand, a spare transmitter in one pocket, and a flashlight and the set of keys for Marco's car in another pocket.'

'I need another drink,' said Evonne. 'I'm starting to lose my grip on reality.'

While Suze was doing the honors, I went on: 'It is ten thirty. Night has fallen. Cissy phones here from Tilly's Tavern saying all systems are go, meaning everyone is in place. Five minutes later Suze phones me at the saloon and relays the good news, numbers ten and eleven on your trusty timetable. We wait. Tension mounts.'

'I didn't feel any tension,' said Benny. 'Did you, Willy?'

'Absolutely none,' said Willy. 'I did go to the bathroom five times in fifteen minutes, but that was all.'

'I was cool, man,' said Wade, brushing some crumbs off his goatee. 'I was digging the stars.'

'All right, all right,' I said. 'So tension didn't mount. Anyway, then what happened, Willy?'

'Well, a little time goes by, and a car or two but not many, then, suddenly, there he is, our friend Marco, coming out of the bend. I press the button, and both tires blow like a dream with hardly any noise at all, just the normal sound a tire makes when it goes. Marco's driving so slowly because of the bend in the road he's got no problem keeping control, he just pulls over up the road. I get Wade on the walkie-talkie and tell him to get Benny moving.'

'Numbers twelve, thirteen and fourteen on your handy timetables,' I said.

'Which I do,' said Wade. 'I say, "Benny, move it, we don't want no other cars getting there first." '

'At which time, I moved it,' Benny said.

'I followed,' said Cissy. 'But not too close, and without lights. And when he stopped, I stopped.'

'I turned the corner and there was Marco standing beside his car looking most unhappy,' Benny said. 'Being a good

Samaritan, I pulled up behind him and inquired, "What seems to be the problem, friend?"

' "There's no seems about it," he said. "Two Goddamned tires at once, can you believe it?"

' "Jeez that's bad luck," I said. "I did notice a lot of glass on the road back there, maybe kids were breaking milk bottles or something. Listen, there's a phone just a mile or so up ahead at the general store place, I'm going right by it so jump in and you can call a garage from there, no sweat."

'Of course that's where he wanted to go anyway, so he looked at his watch, then took me up on my offer. He locked his car and came over to mine. "Just toss those samples on the back seat," I said, which he did, then he got in and off we went.'

'Followed by me,' said Cissy.

'At which point,' said Willy, 'I reported the good news to my bro, who showed up a couple of minutes later.'

'Numbers sixteen and seventeen,' I said.

'We can follow, Pops,' said Sara. 'You don't have to tell us the numbers every time.'

'Between me and Willy we have the old tires off and the new ones on in like five minutes,' Wade said. 'Then I follow him and we head back into town.'

'I had a little trouble with the door lock on Marco's car,' Willy said, 'the key wasn't quite right, but it finally opened and the ignition was no problem. I left Marco's car in front of his office as planned, then hopped in with Wade in the Volks and back home we came.'

'I'm still following Benny,' Cissy said. Sylvester got up, arched his back, turned around a few times, and then lay down again.

'And I am pulling over to the side of the road at Marco's Misfortune and apologizing to Marco that, Jeez, I just can't hold it any longer, you know what beer does to you. Leaving the motor running, I get out hastily, unzipping myself, and being a bit of a sissy and not wanting to go pee-pee in front of a complete stranger, slip behind a tree. Time goes by and I do not reappear. Instead I've snuck off a hundred yards or so up the road just in case he came looking for me. Then, all I had to do was wait for Cissy to come back.'

'As soon as Benny got out, I cruised by the car, still with no lights, then put them on and put my foot down, and it couldn't have taken me more than ten minutes to make it to the general store,' Cissy said, her eyes agleam. 'Do you know what a gas it is pushing it at night on a really winding road?'

'No, and I hope I never find out,' I said. 'Into the parking lot behind the saloon comes Mrs Evel Knievel here, giving it plenty of throttle to get my attention. The plan was, if all was well, and Cissy had either passed Marco while he was still waiting for Benny to return or passed Marco after he'd taken off by himself, she wouldn't approach me; that she would only do if something had gone wrong. I stood up, which was my signal to her, because why let Shorty know who else was involved, checked my watch, and said it was about that time.

'Ah,' I said with a pleasurable sigh. 'I wish you all could have been there to enjoy the next bit. Off we go, overhead light flashing, me in the back seat, Marvelous at the wheel, and Shorty almost invisible to me beside him. After a few minutes, my goodness, what do we see but the Fairlane approaching us. Shorty got on the battery-powered megaphone thing patrol cops use and asked Marco to pull over, please. He did, but I cannot believe he was too thrilled with this development. We stopped facing him, right in front of him. We all got out except for Marco. Marv and the lieutenant strolled casually but warily up to the Fairlane in the way cops have, and I could see that Marv was already starting to enjoy himself. I remained by the patrol car, also, may I say, enjoying myself.

' "Sorry to bother you, sir," Marv said unctuously, bending down to the car window. "But did you know your left rear brake light is broken?"

' "No, I didn't, officer," Marco said. "I'm sorry, it must have just happened. I'm surprised you spotted it, actually, being as you were coming towards me and the light is at the back."

' "I was blessed with wonderful night vision," Marv said. "Do you mind stepping out for a moment, I'll show it to you, and with any luck that'll be the end of that."

' "Not at all," said Marco graciously. He shut off his car lights, which gave me my first real look at him. There wasn't that much to write home about, frankly, he was a little guy with a narrow, tanned face, wearing rimless glasses, a short-sleeved shirt with his initials on the pocket, a pair of cream slacks and expensive loafers that might have been hiding an inch or so of lifts.

'While Marv and Shorty accompanied him around to the back of the car, I leaned in through the patrol-car window and fiddled with the radio, managing to produce some satisfactory squawks from it. When the three of them reappeared, Marv was checking Marco's driver's license. I went up to them.

' "Boys," I said, "give us a word alone with the gentleman for a moment, will you?"

' "Sure, amigo," Marv said. He handed Marco back his license. "Here, Mr Bellman, everything's in order, thanks. Oh, by the way, you've got a twenty-dollar bill tucked in there, careful you don't lose it."

'Marco tried to look sheepish. He followed me some ten yards or so up the road, out of the light.

' "What's it about, officer? I mean, it was only a tail light."

' "I'm not an officer, yet," I said. "Maybe someday. But, gee, Mr Bellman, I wish it only was that. Do you know you're driving a hot car? I just got it over the radio."

' "It can't be," Marco said. "I don't believe it."

' "You better," I said. "That computer doesn't lie. It doesn't always work, you know what computers are like, but when it does it doesn't make mistakes. But you don't look like no car hustler to me."

' "Oh, Jesus," he said. "This is all I need. Listen." He took me by one sleeve. "I was on my way in my own car to that general store up there, you know? Then I had two fucking tires blow. This guy came by, looking like a salesman or something, a nobody, he's giving me a lift to the nearest phone. Then he bails out to take a leak and that's the last I seen of him. He must be some kind of nut."

' "No kidding?" I said.

' "Why would I kid you? So I wait around for a while then I figure, shit, what's with him? Then I wait some more but still no show. So I figure, I'm a law-abiding citizen, maybe something's happened to him, I better make it to a phone and report it to the police. So that's what I was doing."

' "That makes sense, I guess," I said. "If the car was hot, maybe he tumbled you for a cop or something and got scared and took off."

' "Right, right," he said.

' "Still," I said dubiously, "you were in charge of a stolen vehicle when we stopped you, and with just cause, I mean facts are facts."

' "Hey, amigo," Marv called out to me then. "Guess what we found in the back seat? A little kitty-cat. It says on the basket his name is Sylvester."

' "Aw," I said. "Ain't that cute."

' "Listen," Bellman said. "OK, I admit it does sound fishy even if it is the truth, but I swear to God it happened. Can't we just forget about the whole thing? I promise I'll ditch the car up the road at the first phone, then you can report you found it, what's the difference? That way everyone gains something."

' "I see what you gain," I said, "you gain getting off the hook. What were you thinking I'd be gaining?"

'Marco pulled out his money clip, one of those silver ones with a silver dollar soldered to it, and started to peel off a couple of twenties. I saw there was some serious money underneath, as I expected, because what successful hood doesn't carry around a huge wad to make him feel even bigger, and also he'd been expecting to pay off Marge, so I took all there was in the clip and left him the two twenties. When he started to protest, I told him, "It's your choice, pal."

'He swallowed it, because what else could he do, went back to his car and was about to get in when Marv hit him with the next sucker punch.

' "Bellman. Bellman," he said. "Now where have I heard that name before?"

' "It's a pretty common one, Marv," I said. "Wasn't there a middleweight called that once?"

' "Tell you what," Marv said. "Lieutenant, why don't you ask the dispatcher to run Bellman, Marco through Records for me. Won't take a minute."

' "What about the wheels?" said Shorty. "Might as well run a check on them while I'm at it."

' "Come on, you guys," I said, "why waste time? He looks like a right guy to me, and, hell, it was only a rear light, give him a break."

'Marv appeared to think things over for a moment while Marco sweated the big drop. Then he said, "What the hell, might as well check. It's a quiet night, we got nothing else to do." I looked over at Marco and made a gesture of helplessness.'

'You big ham,' Sara said. 'Get on with it, will ya?'

'I'm just giving you the facts, ma'am,' I said, 'as they happened.' I took time out for a long swig of a fresh beer.

'So. Lieutenant Conyers came back after a minute or two,

taking his time about it, then he looked at Marco and shook his head disbelievingly. "Marv," he said, "you'll never guess what."

' "I reckon I wouldn't," said Marv.

' "Would you believe Mr Bellman here not only has a record as long as your arm but is at this very minute out on parole?"

' "No," said Marv. "I would find it hard to credit that."

' "And would you believe this nice Fairlane Mr Bellman was driving was reported stolen at five thirty-seven this afternoon by its owner?"

' "Someone's done me," Marco said. "And I'm going to find out who the fucker was."

' "Language!" I said. "Whom the fucker was!"

' "Old habits die hard, I guess," Lieutenant Conyers said, disillusion in his voice. "Would you believe Mr Bellman has already done time for stealing cars?"

' "No, I wouldn't credit that either," said Marvelous, shaking his head sadly. "What is the world coming to?"

' "All right, Stepin' Fetchit, have your laughs," Marco said. Marv gave him what looked like a playful slap on the side of the head but it sent Marco reeling back against the car. Then the lieutenant said, "Let us enumerate what we have already. We have a parolee driving a stolen car. We have a person in charge of a vehicle driving one with a serious equipment fault. We have the attempted bribery of a police officer . . ."

' "What do you mean, attempted?" said Marco bitterly, giving me a dirty look. "That crooked cop took every cent I had, practically."

' "Him?" said Marv. "Oh, he's not a cop. Did he claim he was?"

' "Actually, I denied it," I said virtuously. "It's a crime to pretend to be a law-enforcement officer."

' ". . . attempted bribery of a police officer by the age-old means of handing over his license with some folding money tucked inside. Dear me. Will it never end? And how about catnapping?" Lieutenant Conyers widened his eyes. "I wonder if that's a crime in this state?"

' "Sure is," said Marv. "It comes under 242-B. As does mistreatment of animals."

' "I never mistreated nothing," Marco said. "I never even knew the shithead was there."

' "So you callously ignored its piteous cries for food and attention?" said Marv. "Tsk, tsk." He opened the back door to the Fairlane and said to the cat, "There, there, you'll be home soon, little fellow." Then he said, referring of course to the packages of nature studies, "And what have we here?"

' "God only knows," Marco said despondently. "A fucking ton of coke, maybe."

' "Careful how you handle those," I said officiously. "With any luck, there may be prints on them, whatever they are." Marco, no doubt recalling he'd been the one to chuck them in the back seat, threw up his hands.

' "Phew," Shorty whistled after a bit. "Get a load of this, Marv." Marv had a look. "Now we can add to the steadily lengthening list the possession of illegal pornographic material and from the quantity, it is obviously meant for resale, not for his personal use, which makes it even worse."

' "Gee," I said, "I bet there's something like four hundred of those things in there. Oh, look, they're addressed to someone. Entrada Road, that's right near here. I'll bet that's where he was going."

' "I'll take 'em," Marv said, doing exactly that, with care, "and get 'em to Vice. With these they'll have no trouble getting a warrant for where they were going." He took them over to his own car and locked them in the trunk.

' "What were you doing in that cab, Marco?" I asked him while Marv was gone.

' "Keeping out of sight like I was told to," he said disgustedly. "Who looks at a cabby?"

' "Who was the passenger?"

' "My fucking cousin Lenny," he said. "It's his cab. I had some business at the Majestic I couldn't put off. And there she was, that stupid broad from TV who interviewed me, five feet away taking my picture, for God's sake." Then he said, "You. I figured it was you. Why?"

' "You wouldn't understand," I said. "But it was all because of de dawg." '

There was an ancient comedy record my pop loved so much he memorized it and when he was in a good mood he used to recite it for us kids. It was all about the owner of a southern plantation who went up north on business and when he returned he was met at the station by his faithful retainer.

'Well, Rastus,' said the plantation owner. 'Tell me all the news.'

'Ain't no news, boss,' said Rastus, 'except what killed de dawg.'

Well, it turned out that what killed de dawg was he ate sum burnt hoss flesh cos the stables burnt down cos a spark flew over frum de house when it burnt down and de house caught on fire frum one ob de candles around the coffin of his wife who died of shock at the death of her only child, so like I said, dere ain't no news but what killed de dawg. Or something like that.

Tony and I loved that story. I don't know about him, but I still do.

' "You'll get yours," Marco said. "I will see to it personally."

' "You'll have plenty of time to think about it where you're going," I said. "Which is not where I'm going, which is to the arms of a loving woman with a full liquor cabinet." '

'Not so full since you've been around,' my darling said.

'When Marv came back, I said, "Listen, you guys, I still think you're overreacting about all this. Mr Bellman here swears he left his car with two blown tires a mile or so up the road and just borrowed this one to get to a phone, which would make all the difference to him. Why would he lie about something so easily proved? Let's take a run back there and then sort it out."'

'Pops, sometimes I think you're a sadist at heart,' Sara said.

'Why sometimes?' said Evonne.

'Girls, please,' I said. 'Save the compliments. So Marco thinks he may still have a chance after all. When we were all getting into the patrol car to go and have a look, who comes by but the mad biker of Topanga.'

'Who is on her way to pick up Benny,' Cissy said.

'Who does get picked up, who does put the spare helmet on his head, and who does nestle up to Cissy's soft and welcoming body all the way back here,' said Benny.

'And that's about all she wrote,' I said. 'Of course Marco's car was not where he swore he left it, and what did that do to the rest of his story, because how could a locked car with two blown tires possibly get off that mountain? The boys dropped me back at the Fairlane, Marv called his dispatcher and got her to call up the owner of the car and tell her both it and her cat were safe and sound and both would be returned to her the next morning, which left me the car to drive back here in and which is why Sylvester gets to stay the night.'

'Little darling,' Cissy cooed to the kitty.

'The only thing I need now,' I said, 'aside from six more beers, is for someone to volunteer to return the car and cat tomorrow.'

'Why don't you take them home and do it tomorrow?' Evonne wanted to know.

'Ah,' I said. 'Because this way you get to drive me home, and I get to kiss you at all the red lights.'

To which she gave no answer.

'There's only one thing,' Willy said. 'My car.'

'What about it?'

'It's not what,' he said. 'It's where. You wanted an extra vehicle around for a back-up in case of emergency.'

'So I did,' I said. 'Sound military thinking. I got the idea from a book on Moshe Dayan.'

'Well, tell Moshe my car is at this moment in a parking lot in Topanga Canyon,' Willy said.

'Ooops,' I said.

The following day I shared out Marco's twenty-three-odd hundred dollars amongst us equitably, if not equally. After all, some lead, others follow.

Three days later Wade phoned to tell me the mysterious black dude with the small mustache had returned; Wade thought he was nuts at first because he kept asking him how was Mexico, but what it turned out the dude really wanted was to unload to private customers only any part of twenty thousand rolls of Super X at half the normal wholesale price. Whether or not Wade did business with the guy he neglected to mention.

Four days later there was a small story in the *LA Times* to the effect that one Marco Bellman had been apprehended while breaking parole and was not only back in the slammer completing his previous sentence but was shortly to stand trial on five additional charges.

The day after that I sent a copy of the clipping to The Chief, care of the Lewellens, one to Miss Forbes the Larger, and one to the porno king of 4420 Davenport, as I remembered I'd promised to tell her how it all came out. I never did hear from The Chief or the porno king, but a week or so after that I got a thank-you present from Maryanne. It was exactly what I wanted – a glossy 8 × 10 signed photo of her. On the bottom, in red felt-tip, a row of XXXXXXXs had been added. Enclosed was a note that read, 'Ha, ha. Be still, your heart. *I* added the kisses. XXXX (Signed) Connie.'

Merely one more example, if one were needed, of the cunning cruelty of the very short.

FOR THE BEST IN PAPERBACKS, LOOK FOR THE

In every corner of the world, on every subject under the sun, Penguin represents quality and variety – the very best in publishing today.

For complete information about books available from Penguin – including Pelicans, Puffins, Peregrines and Penguin Classics – and how to order them, write to us at the appropriate address below. Please note that for copyright reasons the selection of books varies from country to country.

In the United Kingdom: Please write to *Dept E.P., Penguin Books Ltd, Harmondsworth, Middlesex, UB7 0DA*

If you have any difficulty in obtaining a title, please send your order with the correct money, plus ten per cent for postage and packaging, to *PO Box No 11, West Drayton, Middlesex*

In the United States: Please write to *Dept BA, Penguin, 299 Murray Hill Parkway, East Rutherford, New Jersey 07073*

In Canada: Please write to *Penguin Books Canada Ltd, 2801 John Street, Markham, Ontario L3R 1B4*

In Australia: Please write to the *Marketing Department, Penguin Books Australia Ltd, P.O. Box 257, Ringwood, Victoria 3134*

In New Zealand: Please write to the *Marketing Department, Penguin Books (NZ) Ltd, Private Bag, Takapuna, Auckland 9*

In India: Please write to *Penguin Overseas Ltd, 706 Eros Apartments, 56 Nehru Place, New Delhi, 110019*

In Holland: Please write to *Penguin Books Nederland B.V., Postbus 195, NL–1380AD Weesp, Netherlands*

In Germany: Please write to *Penguin Books Ltd, Friedrichstrasse 10–12, D–6000 Frankfurt Main 1, Federal Republic of Germany*

In Spain: Please write to *Longman Penguin España, Calle San Nicolas 15, E–28013 Madrid, Spain*

In France: Please write to *Penguin Books Ltd, 39 Rue de Montmorency, F-75003, Paris, France*

In Japan: Please write to *Longman Penguin Japan Co Ltd, Yamaguchi Building, 2–12–9 Kanda Jimbocho, Chiyoda-Ku, Tokyo 101, Japan*

FOR THE BEST IN PAPERBACKS, LOOK FOR THE

CRIME AND MYSTERY IN PENGUINS

Call for the Dead   John Le Carré

The classic work of espionage which introduced the world to George Smiley. 'Brilliant . . . highly intelligent, realistic. Constant suspense. Excellent writing' – *Observer*

Swag   Elmore Leonard

From the bestselling author of *Stick* and *La Brava* comes this wallbanger of a book in which 100,000 dollars' worth of nicely spendable swag sets off a slick, fast-moving chain of events. 'Brilliant' – *The New York Times*

Beast in View   Margaret Millar

'On one level, *Beast in View* is a dazzling conjuring trick. On another it offers a glimpse of bright-eyed madness as disquieting as a shriek in the night. In the whole of Crime Fiction's distinguished sisterhood there is no one quite like Margaret Millar' – *Guardian*

The Julian Symons Omnibus

The Man Who Killed Himself, *The Man Whose Dreams Came True*, *The Man Who Lost His Wife:* three novels of cynical humour and cliff-hanging suspense from a master of his craft. 'Exciting and compulsively readable' – *Observer*

Love in Amsterdam   Nicolas Freeling

Inspector Van der Valk's first case involves him in an elaborate cat-and-mouse game with a very wily suspect. 'Has the sinister, spellbinding perfection of a cobra uncoiling. It is a masterpiece of the genre' – Stanley Ellis

Maigret's Pipe   Georges Simenon

Eighteen intriguing cases of mystery and murder to which the pipe-smoking Maigret applies his wit and intuition, his genius for detection and a certain *je ne sais quoi* . . .